The Last
Red August

The Last Red August

A RUSSIAN MYSTERY

Alexei Malashenko

Translated by Anthony Olcott

Charles Scribner's Sons
New York

Maxwell Macmillan Canada
Toronto

Maxwell Macmillan International
New York   Oxford   Singapore   Sydney

Charles Scribner's Sons
Macmillan Publishing Company
866 Third Avenue
New York, NY 10022

Maxwell Macmillan Canada, Inc.
1200 Eglinton Avenue East, Suite 200
Don Mills, Ontario M3C 3N1

Macmillan Publishing Company is part of the Maxwell Communication Group of Companies.

This is a work of fiction. Names, characters, places, and incidents either are the product of the author's imagination or are used fictitiously. Any resemblance to actual events or persons living or dead is entirely coincidental.

Library of Congress Cataloging-in-Publication Data
Malashenko, A. V. (Aleksei Vsevolodovich)
    The last red August: a Russian mystery / Alexei Malashenko: translated by Anthony Olcott.
        p. cm.
    Translated from Russian.
    ISBN 0-684-19571-2
    1. Soviet Union—History—Attempted coup, 1991—Fiction. I. Title.
PG3483.2.L338L38   1993
891.73′44—dc20   92-35181

10 9 8 7 6 5 4 3 2 1

Printed in the United States of America

The Last
Red August

1

Little Nadya

Nadya went into the empty office. The boss had left about ten minutes before and the head clerk had not yet made his traditional rounds, putting the chairs back in their proper places, testing the alarms, and generally tidying up.

She went over to the desk, with a habitual flick of her slender hand straightened the letters lying on top of it, then ran her finger across the pile of papers stacked directly in front of the boss's empty chair. She glanced out the window at the cupola of the church, which looked hunched and somehow dwarfed next to the bulk of the long, high Central Committee Building of the Communist Party of the Soviet Union where, for better or worse, Nadya worked.

Nadya let herself relax. She sat in the boss's chair, put her feet up on his desk. Pity the pig doesn't have a mirror in his office, she thought. It would have been interesting to see what her legs looked like in that pose. Nadya enjoyed being so pretty, enjoyed taking a brisk cold shower in the morning and then, admiring herself in the mirror, slowly pulling a long, long stocking onto her even longer leg (she refused to wear panty hose "on principle"), savoring her knowledge that half the men in Moscow would be more than willing to skip their buses and wait for the next if there was a faint chance that a stray breeze would lift her skirt a little bit higher than was generally accepted in Nadya's straitlaced homeland.

She laughed and slipped out of the chair.

What was it Oleg had asked her to do? To check what the boss had left on his desk? No problem there. As always, there was nothing. Her boss never left anything, because he never wrote anything. Nadya considered him a do-nothing and a skirt chaser. Not without reason; she had reached these "higher circles" precisely because of her feminine charms.

Her breakthrough had come at some youth conference or other where she had been working as a typist. They were writing speeches for the boss, and she typed them. After the last rewrite she took him the text in his hotel room; the conference was being held in some big provincial city. It was night, and he was drunk. Besides, she had been sent as something in the nature of a gift, a present. So instead of working on the speech, the boss had put his hand up her skirt. Nadya had poured him some coffee while he stroked her stomach and mauled her bared breasts. That was the real beginning of Nadya's career.

Nadya hated her boss, who had taken her with him from job to job, even when he became a member of the Politburo of the Central Committee of the Party. She loathed his fat, stupid wife, who knew that her husband would never leave her for some secretary. She despised all of them, all of those "comrades" who would put a chummy arm around her shoulder, but always with the clear hope of encountering some more interesting bit of her anatomy.

She knew that almost all of the bosses were impotent, able only to fondle and drool. She felt the same about their government and the system they had created, a system that offered Nadya only the role of first-class whore, a tempting morsel for the feeble but terribly lascivious leaders.

Now Nadya once again studied her boss's desk, the second drawer of which held three pornographic magazines he had bought in New York. One of the magazines was full of Japanese lesbians. For some time now the boss had been trying to convince her to try some lesbian loving. While he watched, of course. Nadya refused, though; even the thought of another woman touching her or putting a hand between her legs made her nauseous.

Today her boss had apparently been forced to work, or so suggested the pencil on the table, the upside-down telephone directory, and the wastebasket half full of wadded-up bits of paper. Nadya carefully flipped through the pages of her boss's desk calendar, which was printed in a pretty, ornate, and old-fashioned style. Meetings, more meetings, phone calls to make, phone calls expected. She had long ago grown used to the names that flitted through the boss's schedule book, names the entire country knew. To be on the safe side, though, she took notes on whom her boss intended to meet during the next few days.

She glanced at the door again, then bent over to fish a few of the uppermost sheets out of the half-full wastebasket. She smoothed them out. The first had been covered with figures of some sort, but the second one astonished her. It was an appeal, or more precisely, the rough draft of an appeal to the Soviet people. "Moved solely by the desire to save the Fatherland . . . the destructive forces that are destroying the nation, even though they call themselves democrats . . . because of his paralyzing illness, the president is no longer able to exercise his authority . . ."

Ho, ho! Nadya thought, imagining how stunned Oleg would be when she brought him these papers.

The door opened quietly and the cleaning woman Galya came in. Or materialized in the room, to be more precise. Galya was getting on in years, was very loyal, and was extremely quiet.

"Nadya, you're still here?" Galya's eyes suddenly narrowed, and Nadya understood perfectly clearly that she had been caught. Tomorrow morning her boss would be informed that his secretary had been seen going through his papers. Nadya straightened up.

"You can clean up here. I'm going."

"All right, all right, I'll just go get my broom."

Galya left, in no hurry.

Nadya hastily snatched up the papers she had read, thrust her hand into the wastebasket and pulled out a fistful more without looking at them, and then decisively stuck all the papers down inside her dress.

The door opened wide. Galya was on the threshold, holding her broom.

"I'm off," Nadya said.

She fiddled about a bit more and then left the office.

Galya was staring at her back, Nadya could feel it. Galya was going to inform on her. If she hadn't already informed on her. And that meant that tomorrow she would have to have a talk with the boss. Or even more likely, they would just fire her, toss her out. Especially since *they* for sure must know about her relationship with Oleg, whom they called a "rabid democrat," who didn't try to disguise his hatred for Communists, and who had already lambasted her boss in *Nezavisimaya Gazeta*.

But of course they wouldn't arrest her.

Would they?

She went to the end of the hall, looked around, and then ducked into the ladies', where she entered a cubicle. There, trying not to rustle the papers, she fished those dangerous sheets out from under her dress, folded them over twice, and then stuck them into one cup of her bra. Then she went to the mirror, washed her hands, redid her lips. Content with how she looked, she dashed away, down the carpet-covered stairs, flying past the two tall and rigidly erect guards with no more than a flash of her ID papers, and then she was out on the street.

She felt no fear. Rather, she felt like the secret agent Stirlitz, who was supposed to have penetrated the Nazi high command. Except she was female, of course. She wanted desperately to hear immediately what Oleg would say when he heard her latest, this incredible secret she was bringing to him, warm in her bra. As soon as she reached the metro stop on Nogin Square she phoned Oleg.

"Hi, it's me. I did what you asked, and even more. We have to meet. Besides, I miss you terribly."

"Great. There's news?"

"Bet your socks there's news! You're not going to believe what they're up to in there. You just wait till I show you what I've got. But don't worry, I'm calling from a box."

There was silence at the other end.

"What's the matter?" Nadya asked. "Can't you hear me?"

"I hear you, I hear you. All right, let's make it nine. Come over here. I guess I've got wine of some sort. Anyway, there's other things we should talk about, I suppose." His voice was distant and odd, lazy somehow, and a bit affected.

"You couldn't make it earlier? I miss you!" Nadya was a bit offended because she had thought her news would knock Oleg right off his feet. Instead, as if on purpose, he was almost stressing his indifference.

"Listen, be careful in the city. You know what things are like now, how bad the traffic is. So be careful. And I'm at your disposal from nine on. We can watch the Vremya news show together." There was a teasing note in his voice because it somehow happened that this was the television program that most often was on when they started their lovemaking.

"Whatever you say. Just don't regret your choices later on."

"All right, we'll make it nine then."

She hung up.

She went down into the metro, irritated and upset that Oleg had postponed their meeting. She had wanted Oleg to fish the papers out of her bra himself. That wouldn't have been a bad start to things, would it? And instead here he was worrying about her getting run over. "Be careful!" For crying out loud! As if she didn't know how to be careful without his telling her! Or maybe he was trying to hint at something? But why? Lord, if he only knew what a whorehouse the bosses were running up there! And they were fools, every last one of them! She'd been working in that office five years already, and the only thing anyone was interested in was what was under her skirt. Actually, that wasn't quite true. There were a handful who kept their eyes on other things. That Galya, for one. The cleaning woman. Remembering how stupidly she had been caught out, Nadya frowned. Oh, well, she thought, trying to cheer herself, as they say: Staying square with God doesn't feed the pigs!

The metro was crowded and airless. There was some swarthy Caucasian type crushed up against her breasts. He was brazenly eyeing her and trying to get an arm around her.

But Nadya suddenly felt in good spirits. She blew into his face, and the Caucasian glowed with awe. However, they were just coming up on the Prospekt Mira station, where Nadya, with a nimble little twist, wriggled her way out of the subway car.

She ran the rest of the way to her building, flung open the door, nodded at the frightened-looking concierge, and jumped into the elevator.

When the door opened at the eighth floor, she was grabbed by a man in a checkered shirt who neatly stoppered her mouth, choking her slightly. Nadya tried to jerk away, but someone else, behind her, grabbed her arms.

"Quiet, or things will be worse," she heard the someone behind her say. Then he flipped open the purse that dangled from her shoulder and dug out her door key. Not loosening his grip, he pushed her over to her own door and opened it.

They shoved Nadya into her apartment, which suddenly looked very alien to her; they let go of her and ordered her to sit on the couch.

Probably going to rape me, and maybe kill me, Nadya thought, instinctively squeezing her legs together, afraid to lift her eyes to look at the strangers.

"Where'd you hide the papers?"

She understood everything then. First she sighed with relief; these weren't rapists. They were almost her co-workers, in fact. She tried a little joke.

"What papers?"

Then she looked at them, and withered. These guys were capable of anything.

The younger of the two, about thirty, was wearing a light gray suit. He dumped the contents of her purse out on the table.

"Where are they?" Now it was the older one asking, and the disgust with which he studied her clenched knees made it clear that no mercy could be expected from either of this pair.

"Turn your backs at least," she asked. "Come on, please, turn around. . . ."

"What?" The older man raised his eyebrows. "Hey, Maksim!" he addressed the younger, "the lady wants us to shut our eyes. She's got the papers up there"—he nodded at her chest—"or maybe lower down. You want to shut your eyes?"

Maksim laughed, excited. "No, I'll search her myself instead."

"Well, all right, get on with it then, and I'll watch. It's been a long time since I've seen how it's done."

The young Maksim approached Nadya, smiling in a revolting way; savoring his unlimited superiority over her, and her complete defenselessness, he coarsely flipped up her skirt.

He admired her legs for a bit and then went higher, not bothered by her fear-frozen eyes or his partner's increasing drooling. He put his hand on the bare flesh above her stocking top.

"Not there!" Nadya shouted. "Not there!" She started unbuttoning her dress herself, which was what sealed her fate.

The older of the two, unable to endure any longer the sight of a half-naked woman's body, leaped up and stuck his hand into her bra. It was painful and terribly shaming. Nadya tried to cover her breasts with her hands, but then felt the young man reaching into her underpants.

The sheets of paper were already scattered over the floor, but both men were pawing her, in raptures. One of them was kneading away at her breasts, the other was fishing about between her legs.

Suddenly the one called Maksim tossed her away and sat down in the armchair.

"Hang on; we'll forget what we came for."

The older one also left Nadya and sat beside his friend, eyeing the woman they had stripped nearly naked and then tossed, legs shamelessly akimbo, onto a stool.

"Okay," the older man said, running a quick eye over the papers. "We've got all the documents, so we can say the search is over. So you can get dressed. And anyway, what kind of display is this? Sitting around naked in the presence of two government officials? Pull up your stockings at least, you whore!"

Automatically Nadya started to do as he had ordered. The phone rang. Maksim picked up the receiver immediately.

"Sure, everything's fine. We plugged the leak. What? Come on, how . . . But what?" He glanced at the sprawling Nadya. "All right," he said firmly.

"Things all right?" the older man asked.

"Yes." Then Maksim looked at Nadya. "But what are we going to do with you? Pity to let good material like you've got be wasted. . . ."

He walked toward her, staring into her eyes as he slowly undid his pants.

While Maksim was raping the girl, his partner watched their bodies move, enraptured.

"Your turn," Maksim said, getting up off Nadya. The older man didn't force himself to wait long.

Again Nadya had no choice about letting the shameless, sweaty-pawed man enter her, ogling every part of her body in his thrashing ecstasies, while she, weary of resisting, sprawled in dull indifference beneath him.

Finally Nadya sat up and stared out the window. She paid no attention to what the two chuckling men who had just abused her were saying to one another. She stood and, just as she was, naked, she stalked past them. She had already opened the door into the bathroom when she heard someone hurrying up behind her.

Once each wasn't enough for them? she wondered, sensing with the back of her head how close the man was. But Nadya had no time to turn around. A powerful blow knocked her forward, against the wall. Her body suddenly turned soft and very warm. She tried to take a step, but instead staggered clumsily and then suddenly crashed to the ground.

2
A Conversation
with Papa

Papa returned home drunk, contentious, and very happy.

Andrei liked that; it had been a long time since he had last seen his father in such a good mood. The last few months his father had been coming home wilted, snappish, and irritated with everybody. Not that there weren't plenty of reasons why the president of the Committee for Heavy Machine Building—a job considerably higher than that of any mere minister—would be dissatisfied. In general, though, all the reasons tended to amount to the same thing, that his father, Georgi Alekseevich, was angry with the Soviet government. To be absolutely precise, he was angry with Soviet government in its present form; in earlier days the Soviet government had given him a great share of the blessings of this world, and several that might have come from the next. Now the government was going to take those things away again.

Georgi Alekseevich had many blessings—a big, five-room apartment with a separate entrance that was guarded inside and out (very politely, but the guards still almost scared the pants off his son Andrei's visitors); a black Chaika limousine (which last month they had taken away, replacing it with a much more modest Volga); special stores that were almost as good as the ones foreigners got to shop in, except that Georgi Alekseevich's stores never had lines; yearly vacations wherever he wanted, and whenever; business trips abroad, which everybody had come to regard mostly as shopping excursions; special clinics and special hospitals; special places in the Bolshoi theater; special hunting trips, shooting at half-starved wild boars from special blinds constructed just the other side of the feeding troughs; special friends, too, solid people, well-known, even famous, but still somehow hopelessly dull. Even a special wife, sired by a Soviet marshal out of a voluptuous beauty, once just a simple nurse who had come to give the marshal an injection. Special children, too; his own, actually, but educated in special schools, which had been built in a special region, which was under the direct control of the Moscow party boss, Grishin, followed by matriculation at special prestigious institutions.

All this special life had gradually turned into nonsense for Georgi Alekseevich, had become a simple habit. It was ages since he had paid any attention to his special life, almost as though he had forgotten that people could live otherwise. What had become most important to him instead, what had become the central, most defining essence of his life, was having and exercising power.

Doubtless he could have survived without this huge apartment in the center of Moscow, and without the imported trousers, too; he could have gotten along without his wife and her precise, chilly hands. But he never would relinquish his power, his right to order people about, to speak offhandedly and condescendingly to them, to force them to report to him and to address their requests to him, to help them, to refuse them help, to reward them, to punish them.

He couldn't have survived even a day without his hot line, a telephone that had just four numbers and on which he could reach virtually every other phone in the Kremlin, to say nothing of the various ministers, many of whom considered it a great honor to tell people that Georgi Alekseevich was an acquaintance.

He relished his power; he loved it when his limousine barreled down Lenin Prospekt and his driver ran right through the red lights, scattering the poor simpletons who had to walk. He loved how great it felt to telephone some distant Siberian factory himself, asking with apparent sympathy, "Why are you letting the state plan down out there?" You could literally hear the heart of the terrified little local official who was unlucky enough to be on the other end of the line start to hammer.

He relished his power, too, when he went up the broad, gorgeously carpeted stairs into his office on the second floor, watching the people in his office freeze in awe as he passed. Solid people, too, influential people, who nevertheless were somewhere below him on the ladder of this life.

Georgi Alekseevich loved people who were weaker than he. He cherished every man who bowed respectfully as he spoke to him, every man who in the end was prepared to accept Georgi Alekseevich's authority and his right to that authority, every man who accepted his slightest word as absolute truth. What Georgi Alekseevich loved more than anything, though, was overpowering the independent-minded types; many years of observation had convinced him that once they were broken, these people made the most reliable agents of his desires.

That was also the basis of his relationship with his wife. She had tried for a long time to resist her husband, to demonstrate her independence, but in the end he had finally broken her. In the last few years, though, her obedient but eternally melancholy air had begun to irritate Georgi Alekseevich. He was no longer interested in this "kitchen warfare"; he was just sorry for his wife. No doubt that was why, when the whorehouse everyone was calling *perestroika* started, he had happily packed his wife off to Tomsk, to her mother. More exactly, he had put her "under the wing" of his old buddy— if he could be said to have buddies—who now held one of the top jobs in that vast Siberian region.

Today, back at home, Georgi Alekseevich studied his son triumphantly, then snickered and sat down.

"You want something to eat?" Andrei asked his father, also smiling. He was already enjoying the thought of the two of them at the table, sharing a drink, talking pleasantly about something—soccer, for instance. Andrei was weary of his father's daily harangues about "the whorehouse." He very much wanted to have just a plain, ordinary conversation with his father.

Georgi Alekseevich was silent a bit longer, then pronounced weightily, "I not only want to eat, I want to eat *now*."

Andrei nodded and went to the kitchen, but not before a decisive detour to the glass bookcase, where he opened one of the doors and pulled out a slim bottle of Moldavian cognac, flying cranes drawn on the pretty label. Andrei knew that his father preferred cognac to vodka when he was in a good mood.

In the kitchen, Andrei threw open the refrigerator, wondering what would go best with the cognac, and with his father's mood. Just as he was deciding on Moroccan sardines, which probably would have gone better with regular vodka anyway, he heard the phone ring out in the hall. Andrei banged the jars around in the refrigerator, so as not to eavesdrop. Which wasn't so hard, because his father did more listening than talking, and when he did talk, it was mostly in monosyllables.

"Early for congratulations yet. We're just starting," his father said to whoever had phoned.

"..."

"Possibilities of precipitation, as they say at the Weather Center. Yes, a cold spell coming. They're promising rain. Wind. Be ready."

"..."

"You're the general, Vitya. And not just a general, you're a major general. You watch, you'll be a marshal soon. I mean, what kind of a major general are you, eh, Vitya? ... Just don't celebrate too early."

That'll be Khokhriakov, Andrei thought. He always manages to call at the wrong time. Or drop in at the wrong time.

Andrei hated the man, whom his father called "a marshal,

minus two bricks." Andrei hated everything about Khokhriakov—
his loud, phony laugh; his long, slender fingers, better suited
to a professional musician, attached to his fat little palms;
his hairy nose; his incredibly wide, fat-lipped mouth, which
he smacked loudly as he ate. Andrei was always disgusted
when Uncle Vitya told his father about the nurses he had
boffed when he was a junior officer, and about the waitresses
whom he had also boffed, but as a general. Andrei's father
would sit and listen, smiling. During those conversations Andrei hated his father, too.

Uncle Vitya also loved talking about Stalin, whom he always referred to as "the Master." He would reminisce about
how the Master had stood on top of Lenin's tomb, and how
he, Uncle Vitya, had marched down below, celebrating May
1, or maybe November 7. Then Uncle Vitya would beam with
such pride that one might have thought it was he who had
stood on the tomb and Generalissimo Stalin who had paraded
down below.

Andrei could just picture the major general sitting in his
leather armchair next to the telephone, dressed in a T-shirt
and pajama bottoms with a stripe down the legs, his fat hands
wrapped around the telephone receiver.

"What? You understand correctly, but the celebrating comes
afterwards. For the time being just sit tight. Maybe you'll be
needed."

"..."

"How do I know for what? Right now we need every
bayonet."

Andrei's father hung up.

It was getting on toward twilight between the apartment
buildings. The rays of the setting sun flared on the big glass
panes of the building next door. It was quieting down, the
quiet of a summer evening coming on in the big city, with
no children shouting in the stone courtyards, none of the roar
of big trucks ramming their way across the city.

Georgi Alekseevich went over to the window, leaned on
the windowsill, and inhaled deeply.

"Papa, dinner is served." Andrei bowed theatrically, a towel draped waiterlike over his arm. He had set out two huge, hand-painted plates his father had brought back from some trip to Prague, heavy silver knives and forks to each side. He had also put out two crystal glasses that were engraved with birds of some kind, not quite grouse, not quite ptarmigan. There were two other plates, one with tomatoes, the other with the sardines.

"Papa! Dinner is served!" Andrei repeated, then sat down first.

His father came away from the window, glanced at this bachelors' dinner, smiled, and sat down.

That smile made Andrei suddenly angry. Good God, he thought. Have we really gotten so far apart now that even his smile bothers me? My God.

"All right, sonny boy, so let's eat. I'm bushed, rolling the damn rock up the hill all day long. And I really have rolled it to the top, you know. Now all I've got to do is let it roll back down onto those pals of yours, those damn democrats."

Andrei said nothing. He didn't want to respond. The hell with them all, all those Yeltsins and Yakovlevs, Lithuanians and farmers. Straight to bloody hell with all of them. Andrei loved his father and didn't want to quarrel with him because of the likes of them. They could burn up and rot in hell, the bunch of them. Today let it be like old times, "Glory to the CPSU!" and the Soviet anthem, "O Union Unsunderable!" and "Faithful to the Ideals of Socialism!" That was it, no more; he was tired. Andrei was tired and hungry and he wanted just to have a drink with his father, share some cognac and have a chat. About . . . about . . . well, even about cockroaches, if need be; about the cockroach he had squished in the bathroom yesterday. And let all that Supreme Soviet nonsense go stuff itself.

Georgi Alekseevich could guess what emotions were raging about in his son, but the chairman of his mighty committee also did not feel like talking politics, especially since these last three days he had talked about nothing but. He was tired of politics. He was content now simply to enjoy his thirty-year-old son, a half-wild intellectual, quarrelsome and punctilious, but whose articles on sociological subjects were already causing a healthy stir in scientific circles. Other circles as well, come to think of it.

Georgi Alekseevich's son had turned out well. Even if he hadn't gone into the old man's line of work, still he'd become a man who stood on his own two feet, a businesslike, consequential fellow. It was a good thing, too, that he didn't have one of those damn scraggly beards, like a lot of the kids seemed to have nowadays. He wasn't a drinker, either, and had contempt for that garbage everybody else called music. Andrei liked the Beatles. Georgi Alekseevich had come to like the English group pretty well himself in the last few years.

Georgi Alekseevich was only just beginning to sense that Andrei was growing away from him. Slowly, and not really wanting to, but growing away nonetheless. It wasn't so much that Georgi Alekseevich didn't understand why it was happening, but more like he didn't think it was happening for any good reason. All right, so they disagreed about politics. Andrei hated, absolutely loathed, Stalin, and in general he had no patience for Communists. And all right, so he loved Gorbachev, and now this new wise guy, this Yeltsin. So Andrei went to some of those foolish meetings, and now had gotten himself mixed up in that Democratic Russia bunch . . .

Georgi Alekseevich always thought of his son's actions as part of some kind of game. To tell the truth, he'd always figured even Gorbachev was simply larking about, like Khrushchev, with that damn silly corn.

And Yeltsin? No mystery there. They chucked his ass out of the Kremlin, so the man gets the wind up his tail; where's the surprise? And in general, why had they bothered to chuck him out over something so petty? But still, it was all a game. They'd all make their noises, do some shouting, and then everybody would wise up. And the people, bless their simple little hearts, they loved a firm hand. In general, Georgi Alekseevich always figured that all this *perestroika* business would eventually turn out all right.

That's why it had taken him such a long time to understand that it wasn't a game. It was only when Yeltsin was elected president of Russia that some inarticulate fear stirred in Georgi Alekseevich's heart, a fear for his well-being, his way of life, for his power. He suddenly sensed—*sensed* was the proper word, too, not *recognized* or *knew*—that his entire and eternal natural environment could actually collapse and disappear. He suddenly began to comprehend that when his son snapped out some phrase such as "when you types are all gone" it really had something to do with him, with Georgi Alekseevich. And if he was to just sit around and wait, doing nothing except smiling at everybody, like that Uzbek president, Rafik Nishanov, had, then they would make him disappear, too, once and for all, just as they had done to Nishanov.

So Georgi Alekseevich began to fight back in the ways that he knew, doing everything he could to save himself, his power, his system. His son.

There was already a certain anti-Gorbachev group, intelligent people working to save their system, save their power. One small part of that power belonged to Georgi Alekseevich.

And more and more often Georgi Alekseevich caught himself thinking of his son as an enemy.

The more clearly Georgi Alekseevich began to see the gulf that divided them, the more tenderly he loved his son. Still, it was hard, nearly impossible, to step across that gulf. It was strange; the more he wanted to be close to his son again, to find some common ground with him, the harder it became for both of them to compromise, to meet the other partway.

Like now, when the two of them were sitting here at one table, laboring unsuccessfully to find something they could talk about.

"So why did the general call? He still can't get used to the idea that they took away his dacha? I mean, he was the first one up there shouting about how the army officers don't have any living quarters. If he felt so strongly about it he could have given up that palace he calls a summer cottage."

"What are you starting up about him for? Tell me instead, did you phone your mother?"

"I did."

"So?"

"What so?"

"So how are things with her?"

"How could they be? You know yourself that she's getting fed better than anybody else in Tomsk, that she's living in a compound for *our* people. She said that in the town proper there's nothing to eat, the same as ever."

"Jesus Christ, why are you telling me all this like it's my fault? It's not because of me that there's no food in Tomsk."

"Ah, hell"—Andrei waved his hand in disgust—"like the important thing is 'guilty, not guilty.' "

"You staying home tonight?"

"I'm going over to Tatyana's."

"You coming home to sleep?"

"I don't know. We've got an article to finish. It's turning out not too bad, it looks like."

"What's it about?"

Andrei fidgeted. "A portrait of the average *nomenklatura* bureaucrat. That's the title of the article anyway."

"So why are you fidgeting? Upsets you to write about us, does it?"

"Not really. Doctors write about the plague, after all. It's interesting, you know. I was reading that there're even people who specialize in studying cockroaches."

"So, we're . . . now we're cockroaches, are we, sonny boy? Central Committee cockroaches, and NKVD types, and what else? Huh?" Georgi Alekseevich could feel his cheeks burning. "We're cockroaches, then, are we?"

"I didn't say that. But the way you're all hiding in the cracks now, just sitting and waiting, that's just like cockroaches."

"In the cracks, is it?" Georgi Alekseevich gulped down his

cognac, then poured himself another. "In the cracks?" he repeated, then downed that glass, and stood. "When we get through with that son of a bitch Misha of yours, that grade-A asshole ... We're going to make powder of that man, and then my pal Vitya will be a marshal. We're going to dig that man up by his roots, along with the rest of those damn Yid democrats!" Georgi Alekseevich pushed back his chair, shouting now. "He's down to his last three days now!" Then, suddenly, he grew calm.

Silently Andrei rose and went out into the corridor.

"So let him enjoy his last vacation in the Crimea!" Georgi Alekseevich shouted to his son's back.

The door slammed. Georgi Alekseevich immediately withered, and reached for the bottle of Moldavian cognac.

3
Andrei Thinks

Andrei hadn't meant to leave the house. Now he cursed himself, and felt sorry for his father. The man was sixty, for heaven's sake! Why start up with him? The whole argument had come up by accident. It was his fault, Andrei's fault. Here he preaches tolerance and patience to everybody, and then as soon as he's had a drink or two, he comes on breathing fire. Andrei was ashamed of himself. He tried to put the conversation out of his mind, but couldn't. He kept hearing his father's voice thundering in his ears. Jesus, what was Papa going on about this time? Cockroaches in cracks! Throw the bastards out! Grade-A asshole! And he was so nasty about it, so certain. Three days, he said.

Andrei stopped in his tracks. "He's down to his last three days," he had said. Meaning Gorbachev. Hold everything! Andrei had never heard anything like that before. Cursing Gorbachev, sure, but nothing about getting rid of the man. When you're mad, of course you'll say almost anything. But why three days, precisely, and not four? Today was what? August 15. A hot day, and no juice for sale anywhere. Goddamn it to hell, Gorbachev can't do anything right, not even get them selling juices on the street like he promised back in '85 when he stopped the alcohol. So, three days from now, was it? Three days made it Sunday.

His father said that Gorbachev was on vacation. And

Khrushchev had also been on vacation in '64. Ah, the hell with it, that's enough. No sense getting myself all twisted up, Andrei decided; better to go see Tatyana.

Except he didn't go to Tatyana's.

That August evening in Moscow was so pleasant that he even forgot about his fight with his father. Andrei walked the calm, somehow provincial back streets of the huge city, head raised to better admire the rococo touches on the old houses, many of which had retained so much of their charm and their self-esteem. He savored the clean evening Moscow air, finally purged of the terrible exhaust fumes that had stood over the city since early morning. He stopped from time to time to read the handwritten ads glued crookedly to the walls: "Military family offers large rent for suitable flat"; "Newlyweds seek flat, will pay hard currency"; "Graduate student needs room for one year. High rent guaranteed." Whenever Andrei read ads like these, he always thought how good it was that he had never had to rent a flat from anybody, that he had never had to promise to pay extra, that in general he had never had to write any ads. All of which was thanks to Papa. Whom once again he'd booted in the butt today.

Andrei came out on Prospekt Marx, then turned down Kuznetski Most, then headed left, toward Sretenka; the street was uninviting, half torn down, half fixed up, and most of all, irrelevant somehow. In the evening, when it was deserted and the store windows seemed emptier than ever, this narrow little street looked even more pointless than in the day.

If he had kept going along Sretenka, and then out onto Prospekt Mira, he eventually would have come to VDNKh, the Permanent Exhibition of Economic Achievment—a pompous and stupid park set with a number of huge stone pavilions that had been planned and built before the war, designed to impress foreigners and country bumpkins. Right or left off Sretenka, though, and he would have been back in old-fashioned Moscow, which by some miracle had survived the depredations of Soviet urban planners; he also would have been certain to meet at least one person he knew, since it was just

fourteen years before that Andrei had graduated from one of
the most prestigious and rarefied of Moscow's special schools,
right here in this neighborhood.

Andrei walked another block along the narrow, steeply descending back street, then stopped. Behind him he heard loud,
even footsteps; a man was approaching. Andrei waited, and
the man went past, not looking at him. Something made Andrei
keep watching, though, until the stranger went around the
corner. Andrei looked all around himself. What the hell? he
wondered. Why did this passing stranger, now vanished into
the maze of little streets, bother him? Andrei couldn't understand what it was about the man that kept him thinking
about how he had appeared, passed by, and then disappeared.

Then Andrei suddenly realized what it was. It was the precise calculation of the man's indifference as he went past.
Professional indifference. The man had walked past Andrei
as if he had attended classes in how not to pay attention to
whatever it was he was interested in. Andrei began to get
worried. He didn't try to talk himself out of his conviction,
to tell himself that he had simply imagined it. Andrei trusted
his intuition too much for that, and his intuition told him
that the man who had walked by him, for all his even, unhurried gait, was very much interested in Andrei. Which is why
he had not-noticed him.

Then Andrei realized that this man had walked with the
same unhurried, assured pace as the one used by the men
who guarded the building where he lived with his father. The
same thing could be seen in the neighborhoods where KGB
people had their apartments: calm, smiling people strolling ab-
sentmindedly along, thin business files tucked under their arms.

God, how Andrei wished he were wrong! The more he
thought about it, though, the more he was sure that his intuition wasn't playing him false. This passerby had been from
there. But why? Why had he not-noticed Andrei like that?
Why had he been walking here?

Come to think of it, why was he, Andrei, here? Why, in-

stead of going to Tatyana's, had he come down here? And
what connection did all this have to his recent spat with his
father?

No sooner had the questions formed than his brains, com-
puterlike, spat out the ready answer: Andrei was headed for
his friend Oleg's. He had meant to tell Oleg what his drunken
father had blurted out. Too cowardly to just go and tell Oleg,
Andrei berated himself, but you couldn't keep quiet either.
The fact is, maybe you didn't do it consciously, but you came
here to betray your father to Oleg. Oleg Viktorovich.

Oleg Viktorovich Bukin, Andrei's classmate, now hooked
up with the main Moscow evening paper, where he published
articles about popular psychology. He had floated to the surface of public attention about three years earlier, at first with
articles about the problems of the mentally disturbed, then
about human rights, and next about the psychology of aging.
Then, not even pausing for breath, Oleg took up political
psychology. It had been just a short step from there to the
Democratic Russia movement, where he had become an ac-
tivist (although so far just on a neighborhood scale). It was
this that had made Georgi Alekseevich declare Oleg Bukin
persona non grata in their house.

Did Andrei revere Oleg? Probably not. But he respected him
very highly. And not just because Oleg had gone into
Democratic Russia and become a somebody. Rather, Andrei
liked Oleg for the certain enthusiasm the man had, his easy
way of getting on with people, his internal independence, his
ability to express thoughts that were wholly his own, not just
some clever rehash of other people's ideas, the way most people do.

Andrei was also drawn to Bukin because Bukin knew how
to listen, knew how to say just the right thing in a conversation at just the right time. Over the past few months Bukin
had made his choices, had cast his lot. Andrei, on the other
hand, still ate in his father's house; just this morning he had
been stuffing down groceries delivered from a special store

just for ministers, and right now he was wearing a suede jacket that had come from a special supply. He was still unable to cast his own lot, to make his own choices.

Now, though, by heading for Oleg's house, it seemed he was making some kind of choice after all.

A red Zhiguli was parked across from Oleg's building. Andrei slowed down and glanced carefully inside. Two men, one of whom shifted position slightly. Andrei was pretty sure they were watching him in the rearview mirror. No, maybe not. . . .

Decisively he gripped the long iron handle of the outer door of Oleg's building, pulling it. The door squeaked, opened. The landing inside smelled damp. Suddenly the handle was jerked from his hand and the door slammed shut with a resounding bang. Andrei shuddered and instinctively looked around. The man on the driver's side of the Zhiguli smiled and then signaled with a finger that Andrei should come over.

Andrei leaned forward, still not understanding fully that this strange summons was meant for him. He resisted, knowing what they were going to say to him. He knew who these people were and what they wanted. Even so, though, he went over, obeying the bent finger.

"Excuse me, a word with you if I may?" The polite, self-deprecatory voice didn't match the imperious gesture. "Andrei Georgievich, please understand, your friend is really too busy to see you right now. No, no, everything is fine. Nothing untoward has happened. But I do ask you sincerely, please put off your visit. Pardon me for not introducing myself." The driver got out of the car and with a theatrical flourish presented his identification card, with photo.

Andrei stood rooted in his confusion.

"No, no," the driver went on, smiling softly and flexing his little fist, open, closed, open, "you could come see him tomorrow, for example. Believe me, that would be better for him, and for you, too."

Whenever anybody asked Andrei to do something in that tone of voice he was powerless to refuse. If this KGB man had yelled at him, or even just scowled, then Andrei would have gone upstairs just to spite him, on principle. But instead the man had *requested* he not go up, and had even explained why, very nicely. Andrei even knew that this was how they were being trained to do things now, that they got special lessons in talking politely, now that shouting didn't work with everyone the way it used to. Things worked better this way, everything nice and polite. Manners, manners . . .

Lord, I'm going to do what he wants, Andrei thought. I'm going to leave. Well, maybe it'd be better to go, but then phone from the street someplace. Or no . . . I'll just leave. The hell with them and their always trying to convince you to do something.

He stepped back, but then walked over toward the Zhiguli again; he was beginning to pace. That was enough for the pair in the car.

"Thank you," Andrei heard one of them say. "You did the honorable thing. That will help your friend."

Andrei muttered something back—"Thank you," more or less—and then, his shoulders hunched, he walked back toward Sretenka Street, headed toward the metro. At least that's what he told himself, that he was headed for the metro; in fact, he was just trying to hurry as far away as he could from this spot where he had just betrayed his friend. He knew that's what he had done—betrayed Oleg.

Andrei rode all the way to Dzerzhinsky Square before he remembered that he could still call Oleg.

But if they see me call, they'll know immediately who it is I'm calling. All right, so what? There was nothing in the agreement about not telephoning, was there? What am I talking about? What agreement? Who'd I agree anything with? he argued with himself.

He stepped into a phone booth and dug in his pockets, looking for a two-kopek coin. Finally he found one, stuck it in the slot, then dialed Oleg's number with deliberate care. The telephone rang. And rang. Five times. Six. Seven. Sighing with relief, Andrei hung up, thinking that that meant he wouldn't

have found Oleg at home, even if he had been brave enough
not to turn away. So, where would Oleg be, then?

Leaving the telephone box, Andrei immediately noticed the
man who was slouching around near the curb barrier. The
man was watching him entirely too attentively. Andrei
walked a few paces in one direction, then turned around
quickly. The man who had been watching him was already
in the telephone booth, energetically twisting the dial. It's
nerves, Andrei told himself. Just nerves.

An enormous red cat was staring at him from the sill of a
first-floor window, studying him with intense interest. Andrei
smiled broadly, shook his head, and loudly said, "Meow!"
The cat certainly heard him, because her long fluffy tail
twitched vigorously. Andrei meowed again, then cursed, without much passion. Then he broke eye contact with the cat,
muttering to himself, "One more call, just to keep my conscience clear."

He found another telephone booth, dialed Oleg's number.

Someone picked up on the fourth ring. Andrei didn't recognize the very pleasant voice, which said to him, "Andrei
Georgievich, I did ask you not to disturb our mutual friend
right now, didn't I?"

The stranger hung up.

4
Andrei Acts

Even before he was out of the telephone booth Andrei knew that something bad had happened to Oleg Bukin. What exactly, he didn't know, but he was certain that whatever Oleg's bad luck might be, very soon it would be bad luck for many, many people. For some reason Andrei's brain connected that calm, and even happy, voice on Oleg's telephone to his father's triumphant monologue of a few hours earlier. Well-trained in scientific observation, Andrei was able to isolate the most likely cause for his own sense of alarm.

My God, can it really be starting? he wondered.

Well, if it was, then what should he do? What *could* he do? He, the son of his father, the father who had cursed "spotted Misha"?

Wait a second! He had wanted to do something about it before! He had gone out to warn people. Maybe his warning might mean something to all those loudmouthed fools who called themselves democrats, who were so brave and so ineffectual next to his mighty father, or against the power of that polite, cultured voice on Oleg's phone?

Andrei hurried back the way he had just come, almost racing toward Oleg's. Twice he stopped sharply, then looked all around, figuring that anyone following him would also have had to dogtrot, which would have told Andrei whether or not he was being followed.

No, I'm not being followed, he decided. But Lord, who knows? Even Papa assumed his phone was bugged, just to be on the safe side. And Papa was one of the most reliable men there was. Why was? Always was, always would be! Yes, people have to be warned, he told himself. And the hell with whatever that costs you. All right, so they arrest you. But if they were going to arrest you, maybe they would have already? No, they wouldn't, because your father would have interceded. But then Andrei knew that was wrong; they *had* to arrest him. He was their enemy. He felt he had a duty, too. But to whom? *Them?* Well, what about his duty to his father, then? Andrei asked himself whether he had considered his father in all this; then he decided, yes, he had. Nothing would happen to his father. They trusted his father. But then he thought he was being an ass; who would trust a father who had a son like Andrei? What's that supposed to mean? he caught himself thinking; now he was turning himself into some kind of big hero? Who doesn't act out of fear for what would happen to his father? Ha! Andrei berated himself with the bitter truth: It's *you* you're afraid for, *yourself!* But, no, he was afraid for his father too. . . .

Even so, he thought, he still had to go alert everybody. But what everybody? Oleg Bukin is everybody?

Andrei was thoroughly muddled now, but still his legs carried him decisively forward. He was almost at Bukin's apartment building when he suddenly stopped. "Idiot!" he cursed himself out loud. If he really wanted to warn people, then why was he racing right back to where something horrible had already happened? What did he mean to do, talk to Oleg with *them* there? And why was he in such a hurry to get there anyway? To do something real and worthwhile, or just to ease his conscience a little? Then he wondered if maybe there was another way of doing this. . . .

His brain was functioning erratically, now frothing with ideas, now spinning dryly, as if deliberately refusing to think. When that happened Andrei himself slowed almost to a crawl, tangled in the logic of his thoughts, unable to decide

whether or not he was right in his calculations. Finally he
stopped completely. A man on the opposite side of the street
and a little ahead of him stopped, too. Andrei ran his hand
down his face. "No, no, that can't be it. I'm wrong. That's
wrong," he muttered, then turned on his heels and went rap-
idly back the way he had come. He stopped at the first cross
street, where he watched the other man, who was continuing
his unhurried stroll, but now also in the opposite direction.
Andrei ducked down an alley and then ran. He came to the
entry of a courtyard, dashed into it, ran through to the other
side, and came out on the next street. He cut across that,
found another courtyard, and at last came flying out onto
Tsvetnoi Boulevard.

He stopped there. He thought about what he must have
looked like, weaving through those dirty, littered courtyards,
and he laughed; if they had wanted to pick him up, or even
just follow him properly, all he would have done was amuse
them. So all they must have wanted was just to give him a
good scare.

But what should he do? Maybe it wouldn't hurt to ask
Tatyana's opinion? It was a good thought, and he wondered
why he hadn't had it earlier. He should tell her the whole
story. She knew how to handle these things a lot better than
he did. He didn't realize that as he was thinking he had
walked to the Tsvetnoi Boulevard metro stop. When he realized where he was, Andrei entered the high-ceilinged vestibule, which stank of fresh plaster. He stepped onto the
escalator. Out of old habit he studied the faces of the women
on the up escalator. At this time of day the women were
particularly pretty, their faces and postures bearing the stamp
of well-earned leisure. There was nowhere now that they had
to be hurrying; the stores were shut, and their families were
fed. In the murky light of the metro tunnel he caught a saucy,
bright-eyed glance, immediately broken off.

Andrei began to relax. Tatyana, his sweet, gentle Tanya,
would, of course, be able to tell him what to do. Even Andrei's
father said the woman had a clear, cool head.

Among the ascending passengers there was a face that seemed familiar.

Oleg!

First Andrei smiled, then he waved. Then, when he saw that he wasn't being noticed, he shouted, "Oleg!"

Oleg turned toward the sound.

"Meet me down there! Downstairs! I have a present for you!" Andrei shouted, with no better idea how to convince Oleg to meet him.

Oleg nodded.

Andrei jumped off the escalator at the bottom, then craned his head, aching to catch sight of his friend. It was a long, unpleasant moment until Oleg appeared, running down the steps of the escalator.

Andrei motioned him over to the platform, looked about, then said, "I have something for you. It's very important."

"So, what is it?" Oleg said.

A train rumbled out of the tunnel; both men waited for silence. When the train stopped and things grew a bit quieter, Andrei began a quick retelling of his conversation with his father.

A second train came, interrupting them again.

When that train pulled out, Andrei recounted what was going on at Oleg's apartment building.

"You should have started with that part," Oleg said irritably.

Another train appeared, disgorged passengers. Then, as the doors were just about to shut, Oleg suddenly leaped at it, forced the door nearest them open again, and jumped into the car, pulling Andrei after him.

Two minutes later they jumped out again, at Chekhov Station, crossed the platform, and caught a train headed in the opposite direction. They rode out to Timiriazev Station, then switched trains to Novoslobodskaya Station. They switched trains again and rode in to Presnia Station, where they got out and walked down toward the Moscow River. Opposite was the wall of the new American Embassy, and beyond was the white marble building that had once been the headquarters of COMECON and was now the headquarters of the Russian Federation. The air was thick with the exhaust of all the cars that thumped over the potholed road, thick with the muck and dust of Moscow. Oleg remained silent while Andrei told and retold the events of the evening.

"Do you understand any of this, Oleg? Do you believe what I'm saying?"

"Yes," Oleg said, then suddenly became excited. "Hang on a second, I have to make a phone call! Right now!"

But the closest public telephone was all the way up by Kutuzov Bridge. Nadya didn't answer her phone. Which meant that either she had already started for his place or had never gone home.

"What should I do, Oleg?" Andrei asked.

"So far you and I are the only ones who know about this, correct? I mean, there's another man who knows, too, of course, but . . . Which means the main thing is to spread the word. As well as check all this out, too. It seems awfully likely it's true, though. That's really what your father said, 'That'll be the end'?"

"That's what he said. But Oleg, listen, keep my father out of this, all right? Please."

"I'm not a judge; I don't make cases. Listen, thanks for this. Besides, it isn't hard to figure out why it'd be a tough thing to defend your father. Right now the main thing to do is to save us."

"That's what I'm doing, saving us." Andrei shrugged.

"You're not the first person to mention this to me today. I talked with a girl who . . . Well, she's a worldly type. Good-hearted and dumb. But now I understand that maybe she's already got the same sort of surprise that's waiting for me. She promised she had something incredible for me, and now she's disappeared. I'm worried about her. Say what you will"—Oleg shook his head—"but this sounds a lot like it's the real thing."

"Well, all right, my friend, I've told you what I had to tell you. Now you decide what to do with it. I've done my part. See you later. I'm off to Tanya's." Andrei sighed, then nodded good-bye before setting off across the bridge, headed for the Kiev train station, on the other side of the long span.

5
Bridges Burned

Georgi Alekseevich ran his hand over his face. He had not meant to, but he had fallen asleep right there in his chair, without even taking off his tie and jacket.

He hadn't slept for long, but he woke up refreshed and completely sober. His ability to shake off drink so quickly had always astonished his wife, as well as his bosses. He was pleased with himself that, for all his sixty years, he still hadn't lost this ability.

I've still got the stuff, he thought happily. Still got the stuff. A man's a man, whatever his age.

He got up to pace springily about the apartment. His spirits soared; not until he noticed the table, still set with their interrupted supper, did he even remember the quarrel with his son.

Hell, why'd I start up with Andrei like that? Georgi Alekseevich thought. He really wanted to talk, it seemed like. But I was so worked up and happy that . . . Except there's nothing to be happy about yet. All right, so some people got together, talked about this and that. But they did do more than talk, didn't they? Took a decision, more like. The thought made him shiver. He wondered what the thing should be called, since it was going to be there, in Moscow. A military coup? A junta? God, to see something like that happening here! he thought. A military coup of our own. In

Russia. God, we've never had anything like it. Except in 1917, of course. But that wasn't a coup. That was a revolution! The Glorious! Great! October! Socialist! And so on! Still, it was like the song says: "Moshie marched with Heimie, in three straight lines. . . ." And a devil of a mess those Yids made of their revolution!

Then he stopped, frowning at himself. That's bad, that I'm thinking like this. I'm a Communist, after all. A *Communist*. A party member.

He poured himself a leisurely glass of cognac. He drained it, thinking.

I shouldn't have insulted the boy like that. He's got a lot of living to do yet. Soon as Misha gets the boot, then the boy will be getting what's due him, too. Not on Day One, of course. Plus, I'll do what I can to keep them off him. But they'll still rub a little salt in his hide. Hell, they'll have to! But so what? He and his pals have had their fun carrying on, so now let them answer for it. I'll do what I can for young Andrei, of course, but it wouldn't hurt to let them teach him a lesson.

Then Georgi Alekseevich began to wonder what would happen if it was they who got arrested instead. For their plotting. Collar the whole damn emergency committee. That fool Khokhriakov had started flapping his tongue clear last January, boasting about how "we" were going to fix those Lithuanians, hang their leader by his nuts. Maybe the fool hung himself instead?

The telephone interrupted his thoughts.

"Georgi?" The caller's voice was hearty and false. "Georgi, I'm coming down to see you right now. I have to have a word or two with you." It was Khokhriakov, obviously nervous. The man hadn't even said good-bye, but instead just hung up. That meant he was in a hurry, which Georgi Alekseevich didn't like.

Vitya Khokhriakov—who was a Soviet general, hard as that was to imagine—showed up in the apartment about fifteen minutes later. Red-faced, round-nosed, and bright-eyed, he looked like a clown in a provincial circus company. The general was wearing a brand-new, custom-fitted uniform jacket, but in accordance with the new "democratic" fashion he wasn't wearing his dress ribbons. Khokhriakov was obviously pleased with himself; the jacket was well cut, and a lot of time had gone into making it flatter him, so that he would look like a real battlefield general, not the chunk of general staff deadwood he really was.

"Georgi, I have to talk to you a second. Your boy's out? That's good. Anyway, listen, Georgi, somebody's ratted on us already. Actually, they wanted to rat, but we caught them in time. It was this girl, Kulik's secretary. She swiped something off his desk or, I don't know, dug it out of his wastebasket, papers of some kind, Kulik's papers, that he was writing on. You know, the announcement. Or maybe the declaration of martial law or something. But it was something about what we were talking about, you know what I mean. . . ."

"So?"

"What so? They stomped the girl down in good time, thank God. When Kulik heard about it, he about shit his pants, but those boys from Dzerzhinsky, they're regular hammers. They did their job quick, and they did it quiet. But anyway, what I'm trying to say is, you should keep your tongue buttoned right now."

"You came all the way down here to tell me that?"

"Yes," Khokhriakov said, then hemmed and hawed a bit before adding, "Plus which, Kulik sent me. 'Georgi's got a son,' he says. 'A son who's talking. A pity,' he says."

"What's a pity?"

"Everything. Your son. You . . . Oh, well, I'm sorry, I've got to run."

Khokhriakov took Georgi Alekseevich's proffered hand, but then, discourteous, didn't shake it so much as just squeeze it. Then he unlocked the front door and left.

Georgi Alekseevich spit heartily at his back, as one might at a devil.

The general's visit put today's quarrel with Andrei at the

dinner table in a somewhat different light. Georgi Alekseevich had, in fact, said far more than he should have. Not that Andrei would run right out to tell everybody on the street what his father had said, but still, the quarrel left an unpleasant taste. Besides which, they might be following Andrei. Ah, the devil take them all. They'd gag Andrei, of course, just to be safe. And no, it wasn't pleasant. On the other hand, he'd cursed Gorbachev so many times that his son must have stopped even paying any attention to it. Although he wouldn't have minded knowing where Andrei had run off to. To that Tanya of his, probably.

And you had to like Kulik, didn't you? The genius throws his scrap papers into the wastebasket and never gives a thought to what happens to them after that. He must figure that as long as he's stuffing his secretary, she won't be giving it to anyone else. When, in fact, she's probably giving it out like cream puffs at a tea party, the silly cunt.

Oh, the hell with the whole thing. There's just a little more of this to endure; it won't be too long before we settle all our scores. If we win, of course.

He laughed.

And what if we lose?

No, Georgi Alekseevich didn't believe that could happen. But if it did, then the best thing was "a bullet in the brains and close the case." He opened the drawer of his desk to look at his ancient TT pistol, which he had been issued almost thirty years before, in 1963. He'd kept it in good shape, but he couldn't imagine ever having to use it. It was a rigged lottery, with no way of losing. The Soviet people were tired of all this *glasnost* and *perestroika* nonsense. Twisted out tight and dry by the whole thing. People were saying that there wasn't a blessed thing to eat anywhere, nothing but meetings and demonstrations. Fucking television had nothing on it but Yids. And Misha with the spots on his dome was starting to look like the worst kind of weak-kneed pussy. No, the Soviet people were entirely against the government now.

Except Yeltsin, of course. He was the one they should just string up.

Georgi Alekseevich shivered at his simple but basically logical thought. Yeltsin was the one whose wings they had to clip first.

Georgi Alekseevich had hated Yeltsin since the first time he met the man, just after Yeltsin was made First Secretary of the Moscow City Committee of the Communist Party. Georgi Alekseevich didn't know why he hated Yeltsin so much. Maybe it was that quality in the man of a yearling bull, so full of himself that he refuses to back off. Everything about Yeltsin bothered Georgi Alekseevich—how he looked at you, how he talked with you. His manner wasn't comradely, somehow. It was as if he thought he was better than Georgi Alekseevich. Plus, he had that silly, slanted smile. It made him look like he was always up to something. Well, now Yeltsin *was* up to something, wasn't he?

Those goddamn elections, that's what he was up to, for one thing! First the elections that had brought him to the Congress of People's Deputies, and now this latest one, which had made Yeltsin president of Russia, of all things. Jesus, the hordes of men he has behind him, and all those hysterical women screaming his name all over the streets. Not to mention his damn portrait everywhere. And how about the scum he surrounds himself with! Gdlian and Popov, the corruption investigators who see themselves as a couple of fucking Sherlock Holmeses, and that Stankevich, who acts like he's God's gift to government, plus that kike Bonner, Sakharov's widow . . . Not to mention that Yeltsin is tearing everything down, destroying it right down to the ground. Destroying what other people made, but he doesn't do a bloody thing himself. All he does is destroy. The strangest part of it is that the man is no dummy. The fact of the matter is, Yeltsin is really one of *us*, Georgi Alekseevich mused.

Which was why Georgi Alekseevich *really* hated Yeltsin. Because he had been one of *us*, one of the inner circle.

Well, it's a new day coming now, Georgi Alekseevich thought. Let's see how all these democrats scamper away when Spotted Misha steps down and they have to go up against Yeltsin. Not that that bunch hasn't managed to pretty well cover themselves in shit, too. And they're cowards. Oh, well, even if they're scared stiff, there's nothing else they can do now. Pretty interesting that that little scrap of wool, Kulik's secretary, was able to find us out like that. Lord, what incredible fools Kulik and the rest of them are! Slobs, the whole lot of them.

Georgi Alekseevich had to confess that he was a fairly pretty sight himself. Shooting his mouth off like that in front of Andrei. Who had since gone missing, by the by. So where in the hell could Andrei have got himself to? Where could he have gone?

Suddenly Georgi Alekseevich was engulfed by black rage—at the world, himself, his son, Khokhriakov, Kulik, even at Kulik's luscious little secretary. He recalled all those conversations "among friends" about how it was high time that somebody do something about all this, high time to remind the country who the real master was. He knew that all those "chats" had ended with everybody nodding vigorous agreement, everyone blathering about how things had been when the Master was alive, how there had been real order then. Georgi Alekseevich knew full well what kind of order there had been then. The kind of order that gave all of them great power, and what's even more important, unchecked power. They had had *power* then, which now, month by month, year by year, those others were taking away from them.

So they had complained, and stuck what sticks they could in Spotted Misha's wheels, and cursed Yeltsin, and belittled Yeltsin's team, but this was the first time they had begun to *act*. After they'd had that cursed Yeltsin presidency hung around their necks.

The rest of Georgi Alekseevich's circle thought Georgi was a pain in the rear, like some henpecked husband who wouldn't chase girls, instead always blithering about moral principles, staying faithful to an ugly wife for reasons none of them could understand. Georgi Alekseevich was like the guy who, when he and his colleagues were all out in the provinces on business and everybody else went to watch the local dancers to pick out a girl to spend the night with, instead went up to read reports in bed. They hadn't paid any attention to him three years before, when Georgi Alekseevich had started warning them about the danger they all faced. They had likewise ignored him when he suggested that they should let at least some of Gorbachev's reforms go through, which would salvage the situation a bit and at least delay the collapse a little longer.

Which made it all the stranger that they had finally listened yesterday, when he had insisted in his slow, ringing voice that the time had come to act. Immediately, right now. Tomorrow, Monday. Things just could not be put off any longer.

What a pity that Andrei wasn't on his side in this thing. And why? The kid had everything he could want in life, didn't he? Even today he had walked out. Had a spat with his father and just walked out. The whole thing was insulting. And frightening, too, somehow.

Suddenly the doorbell rang. Georgi Alekseevich opened the door without bothering to ask who was there. It was Khokhriakov again, as Georgi Alekseevich had half expected.

"Vitya, long time, no see," he said sarcastically.

Khokhriakov, though, was obviously beside himself, not capable of understanding sarcasm. Sparks seemed to fly from the general's eyes as he shook his head back and forth, apparently not knowing how even to start.

"Vitya, what's happened? Things are falling apart already?" Georgi Alekseevich joked heavily.

The general finally began to speak. "Jesus Christ, Georgi, Jesus Christ. What in the hell have you done, huh? What the fuck did you do? We always figured that you were the smartest one of the bunch, and here you—"

"Wait a second, Vitya, stop spitting all over me. What in the world are you talking about?"

"Just what did you say to that boy of yours? You tell me that, Georgi, just what in the bloody hell did you say to your boy?"

Georgi Alekseevich's gut turned to ice. He didn't know what to say to Khokhriakov; should he tell the truth, or was it better to lie, to do what he could to protect his son? He knew that whatever had happened, matters were probably past repair. Khokhriakov had never dared speak to him like this before.

"What happened?" Georgi Alekseevich said, forcing out the simplest sentence he could manage to get from brain to mouth.

"What's happened? I'll tell you what's happened. Not an hour ago, your son was seen in the metro, in the company of a certain . . ." The general stopped, getting more and more agitated as he tried to think of a fittingly ugly term; when he finally did, he relaxed a little. "In the company of a certain Yid-loving asshole. And your . . . your *boy* was obviously telling him something very interesting. Then they both jumped into the train and disappeared. Right now there's people looking high and low for them all over Moscow. Your boy will eventually turn up here, of course, and that Yid-lover—Bukin, his name is—him we're going to round up. But what are we going to do with your kid? Kulik said we should let *you* whip his hide."

"All right, I'll whip him." Georgi Alekseevich tried to turn the conversation into a joke.

"Tan his little butt," the general said, growing calmer. "But watch out that nobody else ends up needing his butt tanned, too, all right?"

Suddenly Georgi Alekseevich took the general's arm with unusual urgency. "Listen, just don't let anything happen to Andrei, all right? Look me in the eye and promise me that, Khokhriakov!"

The general met his stare. "Don't worry! We're all friends here! The main thing is, you should keep a better eye on your boy!"

Georgi Alekseevich said good-bye, shut the door, and then sat down where he was, on the richly patterned hall rug.

6
Tanya

By the time he reached Tanya's place Andrei was calmer, even a little bit happy. It was dark already; as always, it was hard to get used to the early dark of August, which seemed wrong somehow against still-vivid memories of the long, pearly-white June and July evenings. It was hard to see stars in the city; there was always something in the way. Besides, people would think you were crazy if you just flung back your head, right there on the heat-softened asphalt with the cars rattling and roaring all around you, to look for the Big Dipper, say, or Orion.

Even so, back in the dark canyons of Moscow's alleys, which still pulsed with the warmth of the day, you could find the North Star if you looked carefully. Of course, you also had to be very relaxed and thinking about something pleasant, or maybe not thinking at all. Andrei gave himself over fully to this pleasant inactivity, soothing his soul after the honorable discharge of his civic duty. He wished he could just gather Tanya up and fly away with her on a flying saucer or something. They would fly and fly.... But no, Tanya was a pragmatist. She wouldn't be interested in flying just to fly. She would have to have someplace definite that she was flying to. A destination.

Tanya had one gift that was extremely rare these days—she could listen. She didn't pretend to listen; she actually, really, listened. She enjoyed listening, found it interesting. It is a great rarity for a person to find another person interesting.

She lived on Vernadsky Prospekt in a tall, rectangular building. Her windows looked out on a cozy, almost old-fashioned Moscow courtyard. She lived quietly. She had been married, until her twenty-eighth year, to a very solid and very dull husband who talked incessantly about "order" and "doing the proper thing." Then Tanya found out that he had a lover in an apartment just two buildings over on the very same street. A big, fat woman, ten years older than Tanya. That same evening she threw her husband out of their apartment. Now she was in no hurry to marry again.

It was Oleg Bukin who had introduced Andrei and Tanya, which as far as Andrei's father was concerned was the only dark spot on Tanya's otherwise perfect biography. Andrei thought Tanya was the ideal woman; her single defect was that she was in no hurry to become his wife.

Tanya had been expecting him and was happy to see him. Even so, Andrei could feel a certain strain in his enthusiastic, lively voice. He smiled at himself; this was no doubt the effect of the tension of the last few hours. It made him see things that weren't there. He was convinced that he was always being followed. . . .

He settled down into the big armchair and closed his eyes. Tanya's entire apartment breathed peace and contentment, from the gay long-tailed birds hopping about the brownish wallpaper, to the old worn carpet, to the crystal chandelier with the upswept arms. Even her selection of books seemed elegant, the more so because Tanya even took the time to read them. Andrei was also charmed by her bouquet of withered, dried-up flowers in a china vase. The flowers varied with the season—narcissi, lilies-of-the-valley, sweet peas, violets, or marigolds—but whatever flowers she put in the vase seemed to wilt immediately. Andrei could never quite understand why, particularly since Tanya got tremendously upset every time he informed her that the vase was almost dry.

Tanya bustled out of the kitchen carrying a brass Turkish

coffee maker, its long handle like an elephant's trunk. She placed the pot on her little desk, ran her fingers through Andrei's hair, and then tried to slip into the kitchen again. Andrei grabbed her hand before she could get away, but she tugged free. Her bathrobe flared open for a second, but she was gone, and Andrei was once more alone.

He had the feeling that she was deliberately taking a long time with the cups and sugar bowl, even too long setting them out on the round, flower-painted tray. Andrei was seeing secret designs in everything today.

When she finally came in to him and was sitting across from him, studying his face with unfamiliar caution, Andrei at last understood that something had happened. Today it was she who had something to get off her chest, not he. Today it was he who would play the role of listener, not she.

Tanya pulled her chair closer, poured coffee for two.

"Listen, I hate to have to talk to you about this, but I have to. I wasn't even going to bring this up, but it's better that you know about it. Especially since they asked me to tell you."

"So, talk," Andrei said, although he already knew—or, more precisely, guessed—what she was going to say.

"The short of it is, I had a very polite phone call, somebody asking me to tell you that . . . that you should be more careful. That it's in your best interests that what you found out . . . Well, the idea is that you should keep your mouth shut. I understand, you're a man, you make choices, and you've made yours. You have principles and friends and all. But the man who called, he added . . . He said that I should also have an interest in keeping you quiet."

"He threatened you?"

"No, no. Do what you think you have to do. But still, I thought you ought to know."

"You recognize the voice?" Andrei asked, realizing as he did how stupid the question was. It looked as though the battle had already begun, and his opponent, what the newspapers called "the administrative command system," was being fronted by people who were far from feeble. Call these people whatever you liked—KGB, bloody executioners, spies, and informers—the fact remained that they were professionals. Unlike Oleg Bukin and his people, the other side did their jobs with quiet expertise.

Andrei's face had darkened, which Tanya noticed. She didn't want to see him being afraid, so she rose and went into the kitchen.

The frying pan began to hiss and Andrei smelled sausages cooking. "How many do you want?" Tanya yelled from the kitchen.

"A couple," Andrei replied. He didn't actually feel like eating anything after the coffee, but he knew from experience that if Tanya had suddenly dashed into the kitchen, that meant she was upset about something.

She fussed a long time in there, rattling plates, until at last she returned with sausages, tomatoes, cucumbers, and bread. Then a half liter of vodka and two tall crystal goblets appeared on the table; the glasses seemed better suited to champagne and a fancy holiday dinner than they did to a quick snack for two anxious people who did not fully understand what was happening to them.

Andrei didn't know what he should say to Tanya; ought he to reassure her, or do the opposite and confess that he, too, was afraid of this enemy who was invisible but very close? Should he tell her what his father had said? Or maybe that information wasn't so important to her? What about his having been followed on the street, though? And that strange meeting with Oleg?

They sat in silence, sipping from the idiotic goblets and chasing the vodka with sausages.

It was hot and stuffy. The lights of the building next door shone through Tanya's thin curtains, and periodically he glimpsed people walking back and forth past their windows. A television screen flickered in one apartment. The air, stale and used after the long summer day, seemed to pull the room's ceiling even lower. Andrei's fingers left smears on the polished tabletop. The overhead light made Tanya's forehead shine. She had gotten a little tipsy, but felt none of the giggly lightheartedness that inebriation usually brought.

Andrei was the first to finally break the silence.

"I actually think it's a done deal."

"What is?"

"See, the thing is, what I'm supposed to keep mum about, or what they are *ordering* me to hush up about, I've already told to . . . Well, I won't say who I told. You don't need to know that. I didn't know that I was maybe getting you mixed up in this when I told . . . who I told, but it's too late now, there's nothing to be done. I'll leave in the morning, and if they phone again, tell them that you don't know anything, that I didn't tell you anything. Even tell them that we don't talk much when we get together."

"You mean I should just let them think I'm this month's belly-bounce? In the first place, I'm pretty sure they are well informed about the state of our relationship, and in the second place, that's kind of insulting. I mean, you also come over here for conversation, correct?"

Andrei's words had offended her, made her feel distant from her Andrei, even made her feel that he didn't need her anymore. She felt like crying.

And those momentary tears on her eyelashes, and her thin arms resting on the arms of her chair, and her bathrobe, all this suddenly stabbed Andrei with a piercing tenderness for this creature, this woman who was so tied to him but who still valued her independence so highly. He forgot about his father, about Bukin; he even forgot why he had come to Tanya's. Instead he took her hand.

"Just be quiet. Do as I tell you. You don't know anything. Thank God. I came here . . . for advice. But now I understand that you shouldn't know anything about any of this. And I'm not going to tell you anything, either. Well, there is one thing you ought to know. It looks like I really have stumbled into the middle of something. How should I put it? I'm investigating something that could be as dangerous as a second

Chernobyl. But please, let's pretend that we're two people who don't mean much to each other and that my danger doesn't have to be your danger."

"If it's your danger, that means it's my danger, too."

"All right, all right. I'll stay with you today, but tomorrow we have to stop seeing each other. Try to understand that!"

He hadn't known that Tanya was so tied to him.

Tanya stood decisively.

"The hell with the phone calls, and the hell with your stupid secrets. But tonight you're staying here with me. And I don't give a damn who that bothers over *there*. The hell with *all* of them, and the hell with you, too. Today I'm going to be with you. Today . . ."

She laughed, then came over to him, kissed him on the lips.

She was good at kissing. And not just kissing.

When he woke up it was toward morning, not yet light but growing gray between the apartment buildings outside. They were covered by a thin sheet. Pink, with flowers. Tanya's glass of cold, sweet tea still stood on the table. Tanya loved to drink cold tea in the breaks between lovemaking, and every time Andrei came over she would make up a whole jar of the stuff, chilling it in her refrigerator.

Now Tanya was sleeping with her mouth slightly open, snoring softly. Snoring women usually disgusted Andrei, but when it was Tanya, even snoring seemed charming. Her chest rose and fell, her breasts covered. Her knees were peeking out from beneath the sheet.

Jesus, Andrei thought, why did my father have to tell me about *that*? Why couldn't he have just kept quiet? How can I be here in bed with a woman, with this woman, and think about . . . well, God knows what.

He stroked her forehead, and Tanya stirred. Andrei got up on one elbow, glanced at the coming day through the window, and then fell back asleep.

Morning came.

He fussed about aimlessly in the kitchen, trying to put together something for breakfast himself because he had sent Tanya downstairs to get her newspapers from her mailbox. But in the box there had been also a strange envelope—with "Andrei" written on it.

She handed the letter to its addressee in silence. Andrei shuddered, knowing that as soon as he opened it he would find something dreadful. He didn't want to open it in front of Tanya. He could tell that she was terrified, too.

"Let's have breakfast first," he said.

"No, better we should find out right now. Don't be afraid. It's too late to be afraid."

"I'm not afraid, but I hate this. And I'm scared for you," Andrei said.

"What's to be afraid of? Besides, I can open the thing myself and see what's in it."

"No. Pour the coffee instead."

Tanya understood at once. He didn't want her to read it when he did. He needed time, even if just a few seconds, in order to absorb the blow first.

When she left the room, Andrei slit the envelope open. It held three photos of a nude woman who had been beaten to death. There was also a single sheet of paper with "Silence!" scrawled across it.

7

Bukin

Oleg Bukin felt like a total idiot. Not for nothing, either. After his friend had told him of the "guests" at his apartment and the strange telephone conversations, he had gotten spooked, so spooked that he couldn't think clearly or intelligently about this news that someone was preparing to settle scores with Spotted Misha. Oleg wondered whether he ought to save himself first and then worry about the general cause. Or should he inform his people first and then go weep some tears onto *their* lapels? The stupidest part was that they might just laugh at him. Everybody was talking about a coup, but nobody believed one was possible. All sorts of thunderous articles were appearing in the papers, and everybody took great pleasure in telling everybody else: "When they crack down, they'll throw my ass in the gulag for sure!" Deep down, though, nobody believed it. The words *coup, conspiracy*—all that sounded too remote, too alien. Maybe nobody believed in the possibility of a conspiracy because they were certain that *they* could never manage a proper conspiracy. And people were right. *They* couldn't.

At first Oleg Bukin kept checking behind him as he walked, out of habit. At last he was sure; nobody was following him. Either *they* had lost him, or else he simply wasn't of any use to them. But if that was the case, then why was somebody tossing his entire apartment? Was Andrei simply making all this up? Imagining it? Or maybe it was some practical joke that his dim-witted friends were trying to play.

Still, there had been something in Andrei's words that forced Oleg to be cautious.

Plus, Nadya's telephone still was ringing unanswered. Three times Oleg had called her. She shouldn't have told me all that on a public phone, he thought. But hell, nowadays everybody says whatever they like on the public phones. And nobody would be bugging his phone, either; he was too small a fish for that. Then he laughed. "You said it yourself! You're too small a fish, in fact!"

But time was passing and he had not been able to come to any sort of decision. He wasn't even sure whom he ought to tell about all this. Should he look for somebody who would know how to get to the famous anticorruption investigator Telman Gdlian? Or maybe he should go try to get in to see Yeltsin himself? Or go over to the Democratic Russia offices? Hell, everybody would laugh at him! And they should! Those people were all busy doing important things. And him? What was he doing? It was only for Andrei that he was "the great democrat." In fact, Oleg was the smallest of small fry. Oleg Bukin was a minnow. A hatchling minnow.

Suddenly he had a thought. What if he were, in fact, to force his way in to see one of the "pillars of *perestroika*" and convey his astonishing news? That is, if something actually were to come of it ... if the warning actually meant something ... Well, it would give his career a boost up, wouldn't it? Even if God alone knew nowadays what was "up" for a career and what was "down."

Bukin dragged along the street like a tired soldier, mechanically looking from side to side, mechanically noting the exhausted, oppressed faces of the women around him, automatically noting their indifference to themselves, to their appearance. Suddenly he was hungry. He had no idea how he could feel hungry when a constant nervous tremor was winding its way through his body, but he did. Bukin was as astonished as any stranger would have been at his incredibly inappropriate hunger. No matter; his stomach was insistently demanding to be fed. Worse, his stomach's demands were clouding Bukin's brain, overriding his fears and insinuating themselves into his memories of Nadya.

The cracked glass doors of the café Oleg finally found looked like the gates to Paradise, for the moment at least. Laid out on the dingy café counter were some herring sprinkled with wilting slices of onion, next to some reddish, dried-out meat patties. Behind those were two rows of glasses filled with some yellowish liquid. There were about ten people in line ahead of him, men and women. The last, who was now in front of Bukin, stank of vodka and, beneath that, a lifetime of cheap cigarettes.

Bukin settled down to wait. Being a little closer to the food that his stomach was so worried about appeared to let his brain function better; he began to get pangs of worry, wondering why Nadya had disappeared. Now he was absolutely certain that her disappearance was connected to their conversation of earlier in the day, which meant that Nadya was in danger. Which meant that he was in danger himself, because whoever had been in his apartment today, it wasn't his pals playing a practical joke but something considerably much more serious. Looked at in that light, what Andrei had said about his father's careless, angry words also looked completely different to Bukin now. The danger seemed so obvious that Bukin shuddered.

"My God, what are you feeding us?" he heard a woman complain from the line. "Just look at this crap. Those cutlets actually *stink*!"

"You don't want 'em, go eat at home. I'm not the cook here, you know. Come on, take 'em or get out of here. You're holding everybody up," the woman behind the counter scolded in a tired, indifferent voice; she didn't even sound nasty somehow, but as if quarreling was simply an old habit.

"No, first you tell me how come you're trying to sell us kitchen slops! You think that there's no laws? I'm going to find—"

"Go find whoever you want, just get out of here! Next!"
The woman at the counter was obviously in no mood for a
shouting match.

The mumbling drunk in front of Bukin suddenly began to
shout in an unnatural, hysterical voice. "It used to be that
there was a law for people like you! It used to be that we had
everything we needed! But now we've got all you parasites
hanging 'round our necks! God damn black marketers!" He
began stomping around in front of Bukin, trying to get the
counter lady's attention. "We'll find the collar to fit 'round
your sort; we'll find one for all of you! Put you up against
the goddamn wall, bitch like you!" He choked back his drool.
"No, sir. No, sir, we need some order, that's what we need!
Kill all those goddamned bastards."

"You're the bastard!" the counter lady shot back.

A reasonable-looking man in a light gray suit, a little wedding band on his right hand, tried to make the drunk shut
up. "Enough with the shouting, let the lady work!"

The fight grew; people in the line were already beginning
to take sides. The waitress forgotten, people were cursing
Gorbachev, *perestroika*, the democrats, and each other. It was
almost like a street demonstration, but one that Bukin
wanted no part of. He only spoke once, when the drunk began
to shout Stalin's praises, punctuated with, "I'm going to fix
that dirty bastard, don't think I won't!"

The best Bukin could think to do was to bellow at the
drunk's neck, "They ought to put you in the ground alongside
your precious Stalin!"

At this, the drunken workman suddenly turned, smiled,
and almost politely, said, "No, it's not me they ought to put
inna ground, s'you, the whole fucking buncha you fucking
eggheads."

Bukin dropped the exchange because by then he had managed to seize a hard, cold meat patty, which he carried happily
away to one of the café's little plastic tables, all of which
were sticky and covered with crumbs. The drunk plainly took
Bukin's silence as a sign that he had won.

Bukin was so enjoying his food that he didn't even notice,
a bit later, when the drunk crept up beside him to mutter the
last word aromatically in Bukin's ear. "They ought to hang
all you shits on a meat hook, know what I mean?" Then he
studied Bukin's face with intelligent, almost sober eyes.

The cold meat stuck in Bukin's throat. His enormous, im-
portunate appetite suddenly vanished. The drunk braced himself against Bukin's table, cocked his arm, and gave Bukin a
light whack on the back of the head. Then he laughed happily
and disappeared through the filthy glass doors of the café.

Stunned and startled, Bukin leaped up and started to follow
the man, but after a step or two he understood that continuing the fight was pointless, and he came back to the table.
The other people in the café looked at him in disappointment;
they had wanted a fight, and now they would be denied one.

The filthy table, the lone fat-frosted patty on the white
plate, the empty salt shaker, the two flies (not so big, it's
true), and the people chewing, faces down, above their dingy
trays suddenly filled Bukin with such fantastic despair that if
he had been a woman he would have burst into tears. The
incredible poverty of everything he saw around him, of what
people wore, ate, said . . . it was all suddenly totally unendur-
able. He felt like leaping up, stomping the meat patty under
his foot, kicking the glass out of the doors, and then running
away. He'd catch that damn drunk, knock the man to the
ground, and stomp him to a pulp, shouting, "Swine! Swine!
Swine! You want a master? You'll get a master, you swine!
You'll get order, and Stalin, and socialism . . ."

Instead of doing that, though, Bukin got up and, eyes rigidly
staring forward, abandoned the field of battle.

Life on the street hadn't changed during Bukin's brief ab-
sence. People were shuffling about pursuing their own affairs,
a hunter's gleam glittering in every eye. Everyone seemed
always to be scouting for food. Successful foragers were carrying away their trophies in cardboard cake boxes, while
crowds of young men jammed in around the private cooperative stands, all of which seemed to have foreign names. The

trolleybuses, sagging with age, engorged crowds of silent, sullen passengers. Up at the crossroads, a militiaman was lazily perusing the driver's license of the unlucky swarthy Caucasian he had just nabbed, no doubt on a minor technicality. The driver was nervous and flustered, probably trying to decide whether or not to bribe the militiaman, and the militiaman was waiting patiently until the Caucasian had the brains to realize he should.

Now hungry again, Bukin half jogged along the sidewalk, musing sadly on the pointlessness of life, especially his own life. Oleg's life. Soviet life. He couldn't force himself to decide on any one course, to *do* something. When he passed the yellow-and-blue militia Zhiguli, Bukin overheard the driver shouting at somebody on his car radio. That's how they make order, he thought gloomily. Or maybe they're just following somebody. Maybe there's an alert out about me. All-points bulletin for Oleg Bukin, born 1955, nationality Russian, non-Party . . . Then he began to wonder what *was* written in the file they must keep on him. What did his socialist fatherland know about him?

Now it was completely dark, but Bukin still couldn't decide what he should do. Should he save himself, save the democrats, or even beyond that, save the whole country from the danger that threatened it?

He knew that he was being stupid, that the smartest thing of all would be to run somewhere far away, immediately. Bukin stopped in the middle of the sidewalk feeling tired, awkward, and ridiculous in his indecision.

And suddenly he knew what he should do.

Cooper! Dale Cooper! God, how could he have forgotten about the grinning, sleek American who had interviewed him last week as part of his article "Moscow Mosaic"? Dale was the Moscow correspondent for one of the world's most famous newspapers, and was also writing a book about the new generation of Muscovites. Of course, Cooper was the one who should be told about all this, and the sooner the better. Then this news would immediately be on its way *out*. It would be published *over there*. Then the good guys would find out about it and the bad guys would run away. And he, Bukin, would immediately become famous. And safe. The KGB would never bother a man who was famous in the West.

Bukin liked that thought so much that he even laughed. And there was almost nothing he had to do to make it happen, either. Just get to Cooper's apartment and then talk to him. The information he was carrying was like money in the bank for Cooper, the more so because the correspondent was undoubtedly also working for the CIA. Like most Russians, Bukin was convinced that all American journalists were attached to the CIA.

Bukin decided it was better not to phone Dale; instead, he would just show up at his apartment. The extraordinary nature of his news seemed to fully justify an uninvited visit, in Bukin's mind at least.

It was only when he got to the building where the journalist lived that Bukin realized it would not be so simple just to drop in on Cooper. The building was guarded, and Bukin had to telephone from a public box around the corner to request that he be met. As they talked, Bukin was certain that the line was tapped, but now he was no longer afraid. It was just a few steps from the telephone to the door, and *they* would scarcely dare do something to him right here, so close to all the foreigners.

When he let Bukin in, Dale looked distracted. He offered Bukin a chair, poured two mugs of thin, cold coffee, and nodded. "Very well, I am at your disposal."

The correspondent always spoke painfully correct Russian, moving his lips so strenuously and consciously that he looked like some kind of android robot with a state-of-the-art translation program. It wasn't bad to listen to that sort of machine, but it was awfully difficult to converse with it. Bukin was rattled because he had not intended to simply come in and report, then leave. He also wanted to test some of his theories about what precisely all this meant.

Dale drank the last of the coffee, mostly grounds, then craned his crew-cut head slowly. "So, what is new? What is happen-ing?" he asked, articulating with extraordinary precision.

After which, Oleg, who had been so certain he would give his "interview" with weighty self-assurance, suddenly hunched forward and began blithering.

The American listened, watching Bukin intently.

"So, you would like your words to be published in our newspaper tomorrow?" he asked when Bukin sputtered to a close.

"You mean this interview?" Bukin asked.

"What interview? There has been no interview! We have had what you might call a private conversation. In addition, I don't think I can say that you have told me anything wholly new in nature. My dear Oleg, in America the papers write every day about your coming revolution."

Bukin gathered himself, tried to stand up.

Cooper continued. "That's right, you know. Both the revo-lution itself and when it will come. Now, if you had brought in those papers that this girl you mention picked up, that would be different. Or if perhaps it was the son of this Georgi Alekseevich who was telling me what his father said . . . But you don't bring me the girl, and it seems unlikely that the son would give away his father. So, I will have to beg your pardon, but—"

"What you're telling me, then, is that none of this is of the slightest interest to you? You don't believe any of this?"

"For argument's sake, let us say I believe. And let us also say that I will be lucky enough to convince my bosses that this is true. So let us say that everything you just told me is published. Then what happens if there is no revolution? And what if we are accused of meddling in internal affairs? Or worse, of inciting them? I will be expelled from the country, and then the coup really comes, a month after that. Except that it will be another man who writes about it, not me."

"The coup is coming within three days."

"And if it doesn't?"

Bukin opened his mouth to argue, but he couldn't. Suddenly he was seized by an enormous apathy, a vast indifference to everything that was happening. He recalled Nadya's call, and thought that he ought to have met her immediately, as she wanted. And not because of those stupid papers, but just to get together, to "watch the news." Instead, Nadya would be mad at him. And this damn Yankee was no doubt correct. Andrei had just had another big blowout with his father because his father, as usual, had been cursing Gorbachev, threatening him.

Dale's indifference was reflected in Bukin's expression. Bukin quickly finished his coffee, but he had no desire to simply confess his defeat, to recognize the pointlessness of his visit. He had to save face somehow.

"Well, maybe you could notify . . . you know, the CIA. . . ."

"There's a great many more notices of that sort there than you or I imagine. I have to say that I understand what you want, and in your place I would probably have done the same thing. Still, you must agree that none of this is solid, somehow. This isn't how such things are done, with typists and daddies and . . . well, you understand what I mean."

"You mean it was a waste of both our time, my coming."

"Why ever so? I always enjoy my contacts with the intelligentsia of Moscow. I am especially pleased when the best people of the city trust me, an ordinary reporter. And anyway, don't worry, Russia isn't Panama. Somehow I just can't believe all this talk of coups and revolutions. Maybe it is just a hunch or something, I don't know. But just for a moment try to imagine Russia and . . . a coup? Tanks on Gorky Street—or Tver Street, I mean, the old name? Right, you see? Tanks on Pushkin Square or around the Kremlin? Kind of hard to picture, isn't it?"

Oleg had just about given up, but he offered one last argument.

"How about what happened to Khrushchev?"

"Listen, that was never considered a coup. Just your Communist party decided to change its leader because it didn't like the old one. That's all. But now they would have to get rid of the president, and that's a different thing, don't you agree?"

"Sure, but even so, they're up to something."

"Now there I agree with you. And if I knew just exactly what it was, I'd be the first to publish it in the paper myself."

"Well, so you'd better go out looking." Oleg knew that the conversation was over, and he stood up.

As soon as he was back outside, though, Oleg Bukin was once again seized by terrible fear from all sides. He tried to shake off this unpleasant sensation by hurrying toward the well-lit and always crowded Garden Ring Road. The talk with Dale hadn't gone well. He hadn't been able to convince the journalist about anything. He should have; he should have argued and begged and cried and shouted and whined. Maybe he ought to go back? No, as they say, that train had already left the station. Well, maybe this Cooper was right, then? Wasn't he right that if they really were up to something, something serious, they would have been as silent as the grave? And this was all so out in the open. If Andrei was to be believed, his father was prepared almost to go out and shout the coup at every crossroads. Indeed, it was all sort of insubstantial somehow—for a coup.

Bukin had already reached the corner of a side street from which he could see the lights on the Garden Ring Road. He looked both ways, then stepped into the street, to cross. A car flew around the corner. Bukin noticed that its headlights were off, in spite of the darkness.

Accelerating, the car hit Oleg, who felt a sharp pain in his legs, then blacked out. The blow flung his body several meters along the street, where it hit the asphalt with a thump. The car disappeared. A passerby walked over to the crumpled Bukin, bent closer. A black, turgid puddle was oozing under Bukin's head.

The lone passerby straightened up and continued on his way.

8

Georgi Alekseevich in a Fury

The president of the State Committee for Machine Construction got up just a little later than usual. The empty apartment was quiet; its thick walls kept out the noise of the city. Sunlight washed the light-colored furniture, the soft armchairs. Georgi Alekseevich listened carefully. Yes, absolute silence, meaning his son hadn't come back. He had spent the night at his Tanya's. Well, he knew best. And things hadn't turned out so badly. Georgi Alekseevich didn't feel like thinking about yesterday evening.

Instead, he got up and went into the kitchen. He set the blue teapot on the stove, fished a bright red tomato out of the refrigerator, then two eggs and a hunk of sweet-smelling cheese. He glanced out of the kitchen window, from which he could see his Volga and the driver slouched indolently against it, smoking. Georgi Alekseevich was running late. Except, as people said, bosses were never late; bosses had "been held up."

Today the boss was held up an especially long time.

When Georgi Alekseevich finally got in to his office, there were several bald men waiting outside, looking like some sort of child's toy set called "Middle Management." To judge by the sour expressions on their faces, they had all come to complain about their problems, or else they were going to try to squeeze something out of the committee.

There had been a time when Georgi Alekseevich had loved petitioners like this. He could help them or refuse them help. He could feel his power over them. Now, though, his power to punish or reward had been sharply curtailed. He even felt guilty somehow before these "generals of the fatherland's industry," because now it was he who most often had to throw up his hands in powerless despair. Out in the provinces, it was years now since orders from Moscow had been met with unquestioning salutes and instant obedience.

His secretary, Vera Petrovna, got up from her desk to tell him what had happened. Zhuravlev had phoned from the Council of Ministers, and Boris Petrovich had called from Party headquarters over on Staraya Square, and there had been calls from Sverdlovsk and Karaganda. And any minute Major General Khokhriakov was going to come by.

"Thank you," Georgi Alekseevich said, smiling at Vera Petrovna, congratulating himself again on having a secretary with such a lithe young figure, such elegant clothes. Say what you like, the perfect secretary isn't just some girl, even if she's gorgeous, like Kulik's Nadya. What you wanted was a smart, serious woman who was beyond the age of silly flirting. No question, he wouldn't have minded courting Vera Petrovna himself, but really *courting* her and not just sneaking the odd grope or squeeze, as a lot of his colleagues did. He remembered that once, when he was in Kulik's office, Boris had given his Nadya a pat practically up her skirt.

Vera Petrovna was standing with her head inclined, ready to listen.

"If General Khokhriakov comes, then show him right in. I'll interrupt whatever I'm doing."

Then he went into his huge office with the incredibly long conference table and shut the door behind him.

Now he ought to gather himself, put all his problems and worries out of his head. *All* of them, even those that were connected with General Vitya's visit. He had work he ought to be doing. Work for his *job*, what he *should* be doing. Georgi Alekseevich sighed, trying to decide which of his visitors he ought to see first.

The phone rang: Vera Petrovna.

"Georgi Alekseevich, your son would like to speak with you."

"Andrei?"

"Yes, he's waiting downstairs by the guard. He wants a pass to come up."

"I'll talk to him on the phone. Make the connection."

A minute later Georgi Alekseevich's phone rang again.

"Papa, I have to talk with you right now."

"What's wrong? Is something wrong with your mother?"

"No, I just have to talk to you—right now. It's important."

Georgi Alekseevich absolutely hated it when his family bothered him at work. He had categorically forbidden his wife and son to telephone him at the office, so he wasn't happy about this visit of his son's. Still, it was obvious that something highly unusual had happened. He was going to ask Vera Petrovna to write out the front door pass for Andrei, but even so he asked, "Well, all right, but still, what's happened?"

"This is important. . . . You remember what we were talking about yesterday? What you told me yesterday?"

"I always remember what I talk about!"

"Papa, I'm sorry, but I have to tell you something."

"What?"

"Father, you don't understand what's happening. . . ."

Georgi Alekseevich could feel irritation rising in his throat. He didn't want to quarrel with his son, and he didn't want to continue this pointless conversation.

"Enough, son, enough. We'll talk at home. I'm busy right now, very busy. I'm sorry, but I've got to work now. I'll see you this evening."

"Father—"

Georgi Alekseevich hung up. Then he pressed a black button on the desk next to the phone. Thirty seconds later his door opened and Vera Petrovna came in.

"Georgi Alekseevich, now can you see—"

"I beg your pardon, Vera Petrovna, but I must ask you in the future to not let any of my family disturb me while I'm working. Is that clear?"

"Quite clear. Georgi Alekseevich, General Khokhriakov has come to see you."

"Sorry, sorry. Show him in."

However, he had not even finished the sentence before General Vitya shouldered the secretary aside and bulled through the door.

Khokhriakov glared sternly at Vera Petrovna. The secretary glanced questioningly at her boss and then left the office.

The general shook Georgi Alekseevich's hand and then, still silent, almost ran to an armchair, where he plunked down. Georgi Alekseevich studied his visitor closely.

Khokhriakov was wheezing, meaning that he was winded; the man must have been hurrying. He was almost panting, in fact. His round general's eyes stared fixedly ahead, and his fingers were clutched tightly around the arms of the chair. At length his breathing grew more normal and he released his grip on the chair. He slapped himself lightly on the knees.

"All right, so what's going on out there?" Georgi Alekseevich asked impatiently, nodding his head toward the window.

"Georgi," the general said, rising from the chair, "Georgi, what I have to say is of the utmost importance. They asked me to talk to you because you and I are supposed to be friends. . . ."

Supposed to be, but you're no friend to me, Georgi Alekseevich thought to himself.

"Georgi, I don't have to tell you how important everything that's about to happen is. You're always saying yourself how the main thing in our life is work, the cause . . ."

Whenever Khokhriakov was upset he talked in circles, repeating himself constantly, because he was always afraid of getting down to the meat. However, Georgi Alekseevich didn't require that the general say it out loud; he understood that the subject would be Andrei, his son. He scowled, ready to leap to his boy's defense. He regretted that just a moment ago he had refused to see Andrei, because that meant that he would now have to find out what his son was up to from this slobbering hippopotamus of a general, who had now heaved himself out of the armchair.

Georgi Alekseevich had forgotten the men who were still waiting out in the lobby for him. His only thought was of Andrei, but Khokhriakov was still beating around and around the bush. Finally the general sighed.

"We've reached the conclusion that it would be better for the time being to ... well, isolate the boy. For everybody's good. His, ours, yours. So I've come to ask you to help us."

For a moment Georgi Alekseevich thought he had misheard. What the general was really trying to say took a while to filter through the meandering, confused way in which he was saying it. As soon as Georgi Alekseevich heard the word *isolate*, though, everything became clear—they simply wanted to get rid of his Andrei, put him away somewhere, and then, depending on the circumstances, they would decide what to do with him. And they didn't even have the guts to tell him, the boy's father, directly that that was what they'd decided. Instead, they had sent Vitya over, after the thing was all decided among themselves.

"Who's decided? Who was it sent you here?"

"Boris decided. Kulik, I mean. And believe me, he's doing the right thing. He had ... *we* had reason to do exactly what we're doing."

"So, you decided? Did any of you ask me about it? And just who does this Boris Fedorovich Kulik think he is anyway? He's just like you, Khokhriakov, damn you! You and he decide whatever the devil you want about your own children, and I'll worry about mine. And meanwhile, why don't you all go fuck yourselves!"

Then he shut up, trying to think about this mess. While he was shouting at Khokhriakov, Georgi Alekseevich had suddenly understood that, in fact, it was he who was wrong, and Khokhriakov was right. All of them were roped up in this, very tightly. The whole business was very scary indeed, and no doubt his son really could do them all a lot of damage. Georgi Alekseevich suddenly caught himself thinking about Andrei more distantly, like someone he worked with, not like a son.

Meanwhile, Khokhriakov was grunting and puffing, growing seriously angry. "If that's the way you want it, the hell with you, too. Don't take my word for it. Talk with Boris or somebody else. I came to see you because you're a pal, but have it your way." The general pulled himself up with ponderous dignity. "So, good-bye."

He left.

That was the end of Georgi Alekseevich's working day. Besides, who could think about work when in just a couple of days there were going to be such important and radical changes? How could he talk with those men out in the hall when he didn't know himself what tomorrow would bring, for them *or* for him? He could imagine those poor souls, who had jammed themselves into his lobby from the early morning on, hoping to get his decision. Oh well, let them wait a little bit longer. After all, everything he was working on right now was for their good anyway.

He strode vigorously about his office, breathing deeply. All right then, he thought, things are coming to a head. But what *assholes* those guys are! They don't ask me, they don't tell me, they just decide to pick my Andrei up. To *arrest* him, essentially. Just to tie up loose ends, make things look neat. Not that they'll *do* anything to him, of course. There's no chance of that. They were right to send Khokhriakov so that I wouldn't get angry. But he's wrong. Completely wrong. What possible grounds do they have for *doing* something like that? Would my son really have galloped right off to tell somebody else about our little chat? Not that our *chat* even amounted to anything. All right, so I cursed those fucking goddamned democrats and their beloved Misha up and back, and even said that the lot of them were done for pretty soon. Yes, he had said that, and even said when. He had talked too much, like the old fool he was. But he had said it to his *son*, his own son. And then his son had gone ... or at least that's what Khokhriakov said. Was he lying? No, Khokhriakov wasn't lying. Could Andrei really have gone off to tattle to that Bukin of his? If he did, then the hell with everything.

The hot line connected to Party headquarters on Staraya Square rang. Georgi Alekseevich knew it had to be Boris Kulik. He picked up the receiver.

Kulik spoke softly but very forcefully, trying to forestall any anger from Georgi Alekseevich.

Instead of answering immediately, though, Georgi Alekseevich waited, pausing for several seconds after Kulik finished. Then he said, "Well, Boris Fedorovich, do what you think is necessary. I trust your judgment entirely." Then he paused a bit longer, and then, remotely, as if he were speaking at an official conference and not chatting with a personal acquaintance, he said, "I am in full support of the Party line."

9

Dale Cooper,
American Reporter

After his Russian acquaintance left, Dale began to wonder. People talked to him about a coming coup almost every day, and there was constant discussion of it at the embassy. Plus, at the most recent reception at the Iraqi embassy, one of the French advisers had been arguing that a coup was inevitable and that he had even been told how the coup would proceed. True, no one had said *when* it would take place. But it seemed as though coups were in fashion now. Not a novelty, exactly, and certainly nothing that could be called sensational. Of course, he probably ought to inform the embassy, but even if he did, they probably knew everything anyway.

It had taken Cooper until his second year there to come to love this country. The first year he had hated everything; it was simply for his career that he had agreed to the posting. Before that he had been in Nicaragua, Poland, and Czechoslovakia. Those postings had been interesting, too. But somehow he had always been conscious of his own superiority over the Czechs and the Latins and the Poles. Of course, he'd felt it here, too—immediately, as soon as he saw the empty windows of the Russian stores and the fat, squat-legged women in their impossibly ugly jackets and their gray overcoats and their huge bundles slung front and back over their shoulders. He felt awkward around the lower-rank intelligentsia, who seemed always to be smiling timidly, as if constantly begging his pardon for their shabby apartments, for their joy at the foreign foods he brought when invited to their tables.

He felt sorry for the Russians, but he couldn't fight off the revulsion that had gripped him during his first trip on their famous Moscow metro; the whole place stank of sweat and unwashed bodies. His revulsion had lasted a year, maybe a little more. The constant sensation that Moscow was more like some backwoods South American village than a world capital kept Cooper at home more than he should have been. He didn't go out on the streets, although he faithfully attended every one of the innumerable press conferences and presentations that had become such a rage in recent years. Not that these presentations ever had much to present.

The change in his thinking had come on without his noticing. He really didn't even know when it had happened.

Simply, one day Dale Cooper suddenly realized that he was beginning to sympathize with the eternally melancholy and frequently drunk intellectuals (what the Russians called "the flea-bitten intelligentsia") his job demanded he keep company with. His feeling wasn't pity; it was something else. He still felt superior for being an American, which made him stronger than they and more self-assured. More important, he also felt himself freer than they. And richer. It was funny to say, but while he lived in Moscow he felt as though he were incredibly rich. The longer he lived in Moscow, the more grateful he was to Providence that he had been born in his ugly, triple-decker-packed Boston suburb of Quincy instead of in this vast, windswept Moscow.

But, strange to say, he began to be thankful that these people *had* been born here. Once he had dreamed that he was a Muscovite, a native Muscovite. Nothing *happened* to him in the dream, but he remembered the sense of incredible claustrophobia he felt at having been born in Moscow. He was more powerful and more experienced than the Russians, more able to live a normal human life. Even so, many times he felt naked and insignificant in Moscow. He couldn't have survived there as the Muscovites did. That's what they did, too. Survive.

By degrees Cooper learned how to listen to their confessions, learned how to take account of their defenselessness, and even learned how to respect them. He understood that a Russian in America would find a place for himself, but an American in Russia—never.

So Dale began to "learn" Russia.

Now this course of study was in full swing. Cooper had come to understand some things, some of them very well, and some things . . .

Well, for example, this Bukin visit.

The man had come by to warn him that there would be a coup attempt against the state by the end of the week. Then he had said he was sorry and left. Not quite right in the head or something, probably. So what was Dale to do? Naturally, he didn't believe Bukin. Or, more precisely, he believed him but thought it odd for Bukin to name almost a precise *date* like that! And then to ask help besides. Yes, it was a weird country. You never got used to the place.

His doorbell rang. Dale got up to open it. Two correspondents were standing there—Art from Holland and his friend, a Finn with the weird name Akhti. They were already pretty well into their partying.

" 'Scuse us, Dale," Art began, "but we're running out of stuff. We wanted some more booze and we figured you've got some, you always have some." Not waiting for permission, Art slouched into the kitchen, where he began rummaging in Dale's refrigerator. Akhti stood where he was, hesitant. He wasn't as drunk as his friend, and so felt a little embarrassed.

"Akhti, Dale, come here immediately." Art's voice boomed like a loudspeaker.

Akhti was still vacillating. "In this heat," he murmured, "drinking vodka isn't so—"

"I keep the vodka in the freezer," Dale said, surprising even himself.

"Well, that's a different story, then."

They gathered in the kitchen. Art immediately poured each of them a glass of frosty ninety-proof. The shot glasses had little piggies on them for some reason. They lifted their glasses, then Dale drained his with a grimace. Art drank his vodka as if it were water, and Akhti just sipped and then put his glass down. After the vodka Art opened a can of beer, which he poured into his vodka glass, then drank with relish. Dale grimaced again.

Art poured another round; Dale and he drank, but Akhti passed again.

"He doesn't drink." Art nodded at Akhti. "Even though everybody says that Finns are all drunks. Come on, drink while there's drink!"

They were speaking a bizarre Russian peppered with English words and phrases. Then they switched to English but continued to swear in Russian.

They had a third glass. Art burped and said that he had an urgent telephone call to make, but the number was in his address book so he had to run back to his apartment for a second. He stood, then staggered toward the door. They heard him fumble his way out, the front lock rattling.

"He's gone to puke," Akhti said. Dale suddenly realized that the Finn was absolutely sober.

"So let him puke. You want coffee?"

Akhti nodded. Then, while Dale fussed with the coffeepot, Akhti began to talk. He discussed his feelings about Russian women and the idiotic Russian weather that nobody in his right mind could get used to. He cursed the Moscow militia, which recently had begun to operate on one very firm principle—respect for big bribes, which was why they had begun snaring any car that bore foreign plates. Next the Finn started cursing Art, the Dutch alcoholic, after which, without skipping a beat, he started on politics. Dale was surprised to learn that his uninvited guest was a supporter of strict rule who, if he were Russian, would definitely have supported the Stalinists. Akhti was convinced that a military coup was coming soon; in fact, he was willing to bet a bottle of whiskey right now that the coup would come before winter. His reason for that was that machines work worse in the winter, even Russian machines; in very cold winters not even Russian tanks would start right away.

Akhti finally fell quiet, finished his coffee, and then asked Dale what he thought about the chances for a coup.

Dale said firmly that he didn't believe a coup was possible in Russia.

That surprised Akhti, and displeased him, too. He was certain that the time was ripe for a coup, and that all that was needed to put everything back the way it ought to be was three smart generals.

For a second Dale thought that Akhti was simply jerking his chain a bit, but the Finn continued to insist on his point, listing reasons that, in his opinion, a coup was inevitable. He became so passionate in his arguments that you might have thought this Finn Akhti was personally in charge of the coup.

Dale argued back, very precisely laying out why he thought a coup was impossible. They argued back and forth for about thirty minutes, during which Akhti became utterly sober. The Finn finally scratched his head, stared at his host, and said, "Well, maybe you're right. What do they want a coup for anyway? Besides, the Russians are all too lazy for something like that. Lazy, like their great big fat women, the ones you see waddling around. You know how come I hate the whores here?" Akhti seemed to be returning to his earlier themes. "They aren't ever fun, you know? They don't laugh; they just giggle. That's disgusting, don't you think? And the regular women, not the whores, just women, they're so damn slow on the uptake. Then there's how funny they look when they start to undress. The nice girls, I mean. I was with this one girl, and she started taking off her panty hose, like *this* . . ." The Finn contorted himself, giggling.

Dale scowled, still thinking of the earlier conversation. "There isn't going to be a coup. I'm positive about that."

"What?" the Finn asked. Dale noticed that a shadow had seemed to flash through the Finn's eyes.

Bastard, you're stone-cold sober and always have been, Dale thought. So how come you're pretending to be drunk? Some sort of stupid game?

Akhti got up.

"All right then," he said, "since you're so convinced that there's not going to be a coup, I guess I can go to bed without worrying. You're right, there's no Pinochet here, and no Stalin, either. That's what they need. Anyway, this girl takes off her panty hose that way—she's nervous, I guess—but she rips them. And then she gets so upset that she forgets all about why it was she came to my place to begin with. And I . . . Oh yeah, where's Art? I'm going to go have a look, see what's become of our poor drunken friend."

"Go ahead, go check."

Dale shut the door behind the Finn and then collapsed, exhausted, onto his couch. Akhti had worn him out with all his blather about coups and panty hose. Dale lay staring at the ceiling for about ten minutes and then went to the bathroom, where he washed his face in cold water. Then he stared out the window at the murk of the tiny side street, which was empty in the late evening, a silent and indifferent typical Moscow street.

After he left the American's apartment, Akhti went to Art's apartment, where he found the Dutchman sleeping peacefully on an unmade bed. Not wishing to wake his friend, Akhti closed the door quietly, then went downstairs and got into his car. Instead of heading back to his own apartment building, he cut across the Garden Ring and ducked into an alley near Trubnaya Square, leaving his car near the front door of an old, seven-story building. He walked up to the second floor and rang a doorbell.

The door was opened by a short, mousy girl with a pleasant

face. She took him back to a room where a solid, dark-haired man was working at a desk; he greeted Akhti heartily and happily.

"There you are! We were wondering what happened to you! We were getting nervous. No telling what might happen in Moscow at night nowadays. So, what have you got to tell us?"

Akhti glared at the man. "When are you going to leave me alone?"

"We'll leave you alone, we'll leave you alone. You've done your job. But remember, it wasn't us that betrayed you, right?"

Akhti said nothing.

"Zina, sweetie," the man said to the girl, "get the two of us some tea, would you?"

"Thanks, don't bother," Akhti said. "I've already had coffee. Let's get down to business. I did what you asked. I don't know what you wanted to know for, but the American doesn't think that there's going to be a coup. He thinks it's all nothing but talk. He doesn't take the coup seriously. Is that enough?"

"Thanks, you've been a good friend. You see how nice things work out? That's détente, you know? I mean, it's important to have people thinking of us properly."

"I hope this is the last time, then. It is, isn't it?"

The man at the desk slowly fished a cigarette from his pack. "It's my personal opinion that we have no more right to bother you. But remember, I'm not the one who does the deciding. Naturally, I'll pass on what you say, and I'll be sure to tell them, too, that you always cooperate in whatever we ask you to do. I can't make any promises, but ... Well, I'll do what I can."

"But you told me yourself that this would be the last time!"

"That's what I thought myself. I also didn't think that what I gave you to do was such a ... mmm ... a *complicated* burden. After all, you really ought to be grateful that you're not in jail, you know? I mean, you know yourself that getting caught with three hundred grams of heroin in your suitcase, that ought to be jail for one hundred percent sure. And here you are, running around free. You work, you write. You meet girls. I mean, you *do* meet girls, right? And for that . . . powder, well, you have to pay somehow. Either go to jail or help us out. So you're helping us, and thanks."

God, when will this end? Akhti thought in despair. If anybody had told me a year ago that I would be *their* agent, I wouldn't even have been offended, I would have just laughed. Why in the hell did I let myself be talked into carrying that damned powder? Idiot! What a complete *idiot*!

All he said, though, was "I'm tired. I'm leaving."

"Of course, buddy, of course. Sorry to have troubled you," the man said, getting up to accompany Akhti out into the corridor. "Once again, I apologize for the trouble. See you again."

Zina, sweetie, opened the outer door and Akhti left, descending the stairs without looking back.

After he had seen the Finn off, the man made a telephone call. "Good evening, Nikolai Ivanovich," he said softly into the receiver. "The Yankee didn't check any of the story. He has no plans to do anything or to follow up."

Nikolai Ivanovich replied, and the man nodded.

"Yes, yes, you're quite right. The story has hit a dead end."

10

Georgi Alekseevich

The workday was rolling smoothly toward its midpoint. Sometimes Georgi Alekseevich could even let himself believe that there was nothing going on beyond the walls of his office, that Khokhriakov's visits, Kulik's phone call, and all that nonsense with his son were all nothing more than a bad dream, one that he had finally been able to shake off. Now he was trying to help a factory in Krasnoyarsk that had been waiting for more than two months for delivery of a vital steel alloy, which distracted the president of this all-powerful committee from any other problems. Georgi Alekseevich simply worked. Today he even gloried in his work.

Beyond the walls of his office the huge city hummed smoothly. Georgi Alekseevich could imagine the way, right now, that the polished black Volgas were pulling up in front of the tall building, its entrance decorated with cast-iron banners; here and there among the Volgas, like cruisers among lesser boats, enormous Chaikas would be maneuvering for berths. Around the corner, people were scurrying for the metro. There was a trolley stop near the metro, but Georgi Alekseevich had not had to wait for a trolley for about fifteen years; even that had occurred only because his car had broken down and, for reasons he couldn't recall now, he hadn't wanted to phone the garage for a replacement.

None of that seemed too long ago. Who had destroyed that

smooth, sure flow of unchanging Soviet life? How had they *dared* to disturb it!

Georgi Alekseevich scowled.

His secretary came in without knocking and, as usual, reminded him that it was lunchtime. He realized he was hungry. When he was in a good mood he always had an appetite.

However, he didn't get to take lunch in the building.

Just as he stood to leave the Kremlin direct line buzzed. Georgi Alekseevich had a pretty good idea who would be calling him, and it didn't make him want to answer. He did, though. He couldn't refuse to answer. It was Kulik, inviting him to come over to the Kremlin for lunch. *Inviting* wasn't quite the word. *Ordering* would be closer. And Georgi Alekseevich obeyed.

Kulik had five men at his lunch. Spread out on the conference table in his office were open-face sandwiches—bologna, gray caviar, bright yellow cheese. A second oval-shaped plate had salad greens, still damp. There were also dark green bottles of Borzhomi mineral water and two bottles of cognac. A separate table had blue cups with clear bouillon.

The dignified gray and balding guests settled down comfortably, looking forward to a friendly chat.

Georgi Alekseevich was greeted with happy exclamations and the growlings of empty stomachs.

He sat at the table and grabbed a sandwich, saying nothing.

"Hey, that's not how we do things here!" Kulik barked. "Georgi comes in last and sits down first! No, first you pour for all of us. A nice brotherly drop for all of us, we have a drink or two, and *then* we go to the table."

They poured for one another, into plain glasses. Then they drank, each draining his glass. Kulik paced about his office.

"I asked you here, my dear comrades, to give you some . . . news. Not that I have to tell you anything, because you know everything as it is. Don't get the idea that this is a meeting or some kind of council or something. I just wanted to get a look at all of you again. A look, understand. We've each done our jobs. Now it's time for our armed forces and the KGB to have their say. Our national defenders, you might say."

They had another glass each. It was plain that everyone was hungry, impatiently chewing to get at the sandwiches. Only one of them, the baldest and skinniest, who had been in finances all his long life, had given Kulik a hearty, "Brave lads, the lot of them!"

Brave lads, indeed, Georgi Alekseevich thought to himself. Can they really be getting ready to do it? They aren't afraid to move against the boss?

"Hey, Boris, did you replace that little Nadya of yours?" the finance man asked Kulik.

"No, this girl's just temporary, I let Nadya have a day or two off. She had to go someplace."

"Yes, a girl like that would probably always have someplace she had to go. A sweet piece of work, that one!" The finance man guffawed.

"Where's Marshal Vitya?" Georgi Alekseevich asked the fellow who was sitting next to him on the divan; the man was in charge of transport and loved to repeat endless stories about how in his youth he had worked as an engineer on a real steam locomotive.

"Right now Viktor's doing something very, very important. You might say he's on duty, at his post," Kulik replied weightily.

"Come on, what kind of post could Khokhriakov have? He can't tell a tank from a refrigerator!" the transport man objected with a derisive snort.

"No, it's true, right now Khokhriakov is doing something of the utmost importance. If you don't believe me, ask Georgi."

Georgi Alekseevich shuddered when he heard his name. He didn't understand why he should know what exactly it was that Khokhriakov was doing right now, but to be on the safe side he nodded, and even muttered, "Whatever the general does, it's always of the utmost importance."

The conversation meandered along. Out of habit, each of

the men complained of how hard things were now, that no-body gave a god damn, nobody respected authority. Here and there could be heard "But where am I supposed to get the money for them?" and "I'm not going to give them any of my funds, you can bet on that!" and "I'll just lift the quotas on them, that's all!"

Who the first "they" were wasn't made clear, but the other "theys," that was obvious: they were the "they" who had ceased respecting the bosses, who had ceased to obey. It was for this that "they" had to be punished.

"So how's your boy?" the railroad man asked Georgi Alekseevich.

"My boy? The boy's all right. He's writing, thinking . . ."

"Not married?"

"Keeps saying he's going to."

"He's got somebody to marry, at least?"

"There's a girl. A woman, actually. Not a bad one at all. Smart, calm. If she actually marries my boy, I'll consider him lucky."

"Your Andrei's not a bad bit himself. Quick on the uptake, you know? My wife reads all his stuff. He's famous, did you know that? Not like you and me!" The man guffawed.

Georgi Alekseevich couldn't suppress a self-satisfied little smile. Whatever the kid might think of him, and no matter how much they might fight, even so, Andrei had turned out all right.

Then Georgi Alekseevich felt as though he had just been stabbed with a burning cigarette: Precisely what job *was* Khokhriakov doing right now? Not putting his Andrei "out of harm's way," by any chance? Georgi Alekseevich thought of himself here, eating and drinking, while out there some-where they were . . . with his son . . .

He got up and went over to Kulik.

"Come on, where is Khokhriakov really? It isn't safe to let an idiot like that out of your sight. He'll make some huge mess of things, and here it is practically on the eve of . . . well, you know."

Kulik looked sage. "Don't you worry. The job we gave him isn't anything complicated. We know well enough what Khokhriakov is like. I do have to say, though, that the guy is decisive, and he'll do what you ask him to. The only thing you can't do is put him in a spot where he's got to think."

"That's the truth." Georgi Alekseevich sighed. "Khokhriakov thinking is even scarier than Khokhriakov not thinking. What I was wondering though . . ." He stopped speaking and stared at Kulik.

Kulik smiled back pleasantly, already guessing what his "comrade-in-arms" was thinking. "Listen, Georgi, without your say-so, nobody is going to dare touch him. I give you my word on that. It would be better if you whipped him into line without us, actually."

Georgi Alekseevich nodded.

Their lunch—if this strange meeting could be called a lunch—was rolling smoothly to a close, but still Georgi Alekseevich couldn't quite make out why it was that Boris Kulik had wanted to get them all together, today, here, now. They hadn't talked about anything serious. It was all just chatter. Nervous chatter and nothing more. Everybody was tense. They talked about nothing, all of them, but they were thinking about the same thing. In a few days they would either all be given a second life—one that would return to them everything they had lost and give them new power—or they would all be gone. Completely gone, never to return to this life, these offices, those waiting cars, the direct telephone lines and pretty secretaries.

Another question none of them knew the answer to was whether the people would follow them. Would they be cheered or cursed? Georgi Alekseevich kept finding himself thinking about how afraid he had been of the people at the bus stop, how he hated and feared the reeking men who clustered in their lines in front of the vodka stores. He still had not shaken the almost animal fear he had felt two springs ago when he had chanced to be strolling around his neighborhood and had come out onto the Garden Ring for some reason; he had bumped right into a demonstration by Yeltsin lovers. It would have been one thing if the marchers had been just a gaggle of hysterical women in their home-knit hats, but there were also lots of young men in the crowd. Calm, thoughtful, serious types. Georgi Alekseevich had ducked back into the side street to avoid them.

Just then Kulik got up and stood in the middle of the room. "I think that soon we will be seeing each other in somewhat different circumstances. The professionals are going to do what they are good at, and you have to do what you are good at. The most important things are calm and order. No sudden moves. Everything is to be done in the name of the common good. I hope that the president will support us. If he wavers, it's his privilege to do so, I think. I'm certain that in the end he will come over to our side. Society must return to a state of calm and then begin to move forward again. *Perestroika* will continue, but in a more sensible way, one that is better suited to our people."

Somebody near the window choked on his cognac and began to cough.

Kulik hated to be interrupted. He scowled.

"So, as I was saying, in a more sensible way, one that is better suited to our people. That's right. So . . . And the people who get in the way of stabilization, they will have to be moved aside, and in some cases they will have to be isolated . . . temporarily. We will have to move quickly and decisively in this area as well."

Everybody nodded.

"Our country has experience with resisting destructive elements, and I hope that experience will be put to good use, in the full measure. Those bearing direct responsibility for realizing our main goal are decisive people. But I repeat, all of us must act energetically, since there are also a lot of people, even among those who are closest to us, a lot of people who do not understand the danger of the present moment."

That's a dig at my Andrei, Georgi Alekseevich thought.

Kulik went on. "In general, we must be vigilant, decisive, and ready for any unexpected eventuality."

"Always ready!" the finance man barked, like a Young Pioneer. "What you say about vigilance, that's right, that's one hundred percent. And we ought to keep our tongues in our heads a bit more. Do more, talk less, that's what."

"Hang on, I'm still talking," Kulik said; being interrupted a second time had obviously shattered the whole pace and structure of his pep talk. "What I'm trying to say is, there's nobody we should be afraid of. Everything depends on us. All right, I'm done. Who else has something to say?"

Nobody had anything to say. The meaning of Kulik's veiled words was sufficiently clear. It was also clear now why he had gathered them all together. This would have been an ordinary Communist party "locker room talk" if not for the fact that they had gathered not just to mouth support for the Party line or to organize the next "voluntary Saturday" but rather to undertake something considerably more serious and important.

Georgi Alekseevich glanced at Kulik, who had apparently intended to say something else but then changed his mind.

Kulik contented himself with saying, "Comrades, I hope you will forgive me for the modesty of today's lunch. I also invite all of you to a big banquet at the end of next week." He laughed.

"Is the banquet going to be in the Kremlin?" somebody asked.

"And where else would it be?"

Georgi Alekseevich recalled, unfortunately, that in 1941 the Germans had also planned to celebrate their victory with a big feast in the Kremlin, and even had printed up the invitations.

"So," Kulik continued to meander, "we'll be ready for anything unexpected, but we have to believe we're going to win."

Everybody was a little bored by Kulik's speech, particularly since none of it was necessary; they all understood without it. All these "big bosses," these "captains of industry," shifted impatiently, wriggling out of their chairs. They said quick farewells to one another, almost getting stuck in the doors in their scramble to get out of Kulik's office.

The finance man left with Georgi Alekseevich, who had decided to take the stairs and not wait for the elevator. Glancing over his shoulder, the finance man asked quietly, "So what do you think, really? Is it going to come off? They aren't going to break our necks, are they? I mean, I'm what they call hooked up in this, but I came into it late. What you all were thinking about when you started this, I don't actually even have any idea. I believe you all, of course. There is no other way out. But on the other hand, who knows? Maybe those guys have something up their sleeve, too? They're not idiots, after all. They want power, too. What's the army got to say for itself? Have you heard anything from your friend Khokhriakov?"

Georgi Alekseevich's face soured with disgust and dislike. It's a bad thing, to get mixed up in a dangerous business like this and be so halfhearted, he thought; all he said, though, was "We're all 'hooked up' in this. *All* of us are going to answer for it. If we get a kick up the backside, then the winners are going to put all of us behind bars!"

The finance man understood his mistake.

"No, no, I didn't mean that, we're all in this together, of course. And it's not going to be easy to break us. The people are with us," he added after a pause. As soon as he said it, he could feel how phony his words sounded.

"Listen"—Georgi Alekseevich turned to the man—"*what* people? When was the last time you saw this 'people'? Talked with 'the people'? You know where the nearest metro stop is, eh? Where you're most likely to find cheese for sale now? Come on, tell me where they sell cheese in the city now, eh?"

The finance man sniffed, offended.

I shouldn't have done that to him, Georgi Alekseevich thought to himself. To tell the truth, I'm not much better myself. Most of what I know about the people is from Andrei. I should have kept my mouth shut. Georgi Alekseevich repented inwardly, then, trying to sweeten the "medicine" he had already administered, he said, "None of us understand anymore what's going on in this country, who the people living in it are or what they want."

They went on down to the ground floor. At the door they shook hands and then got into their separate cars.

Left alone in his office, the important Party and government figure Boris Kulik kept glancing up at his door, even though he knew that nobody could ever come through it without his permission. Finally he opened the top desk drawer and dug out from under some newspapers three color photos of his secretary, who was lying naked on a floor, her legs flung wide. Nadya's eyes were wide open, and her corpse reminded him of a store dummy for advertising women's underwear. He had seen a pretty dummy like that once in Hamburg, when he had been one of the dignitaries at the opening of a trade fair of some sort.

Studying closely the pictures of what as recently as yesterday had been his secretary Nadya, Kulik clicked his tongue. Then, finally, he put the photos back among the newspapers.

In no hurry, he picked up the telephone, dialing seven digits. It was an outside call, to somewhere in the city.

They were slow to answer, but when at last they did, the person who spoke sounded sleek, well fed, and confident.

"Yes?"

Kulik said nothing.

"Is that you, Boris?"

Kulik was impressed by the quickness of the person he had called. "It's me."

"So, what do you think?" It was as if the owner of the voice knew what Kulik had just been doing, and furthermore, could not conceal his own pleasure at knowing so much. "You happy? Everything just like you wanted? All secrets kept secret? What, no thank-yous?"

"All right, but how come *that*?"

The voice coughed. "That? Well, first of all, you might call it a report from the field. And in the second place, you were always a man who liked cherry. And in the third place, pal, I wanted to give you some idea of just what kind of work it is we have to do over here." The speaker laughed. "All right, let's let the boys go, all right? They're tired and awfully cranky. And anyway, isn't it pretty much all the same to you, eh?"

"You know, there have to be limits in everything."

"Now, there you're mistaken. Incidentally, if you'd like, I can also send you over a file on a certain car accident."

"No," Kulik refused sharply. He added, after a moment's silence, "Oh well, nothing to be done. It's all just fate, I suppose. See you later."

Then he hung up.

11

A Little Stroll

The photos of poor Nadya put Tanya into shock, so that for a while she completely forgot about the order—"Silence!"—that had come with them. The photos were almost professional in quality, Polaroids. Tanya had never seen this woman before, had not even dreamed she existed. Still, the picture of the dead, naked body filled her with dread. Whatever had happened to this unlucky stranger, it was all too easy to imagine the same thing happening to her.

"You see?" Andrei said quietly.

"What do you mean, 'You see'? I don't get this. You want to tell me now what the connection is between your damn secret and this woman? Now I have the right to know everything. I do have that right, you know."

"All right, I'll tell you. But not right now. Wait until this evening. I have to meet a man, and then I'll tell you everything."

"All right, I'll wait until six."

"One more thing. Don't go out until I come back. And . . . to be on the safe side, don't open the door for anybody. Let people think you're out."

Andrei understood perfectly well how stupid his advice sounded. No doubt if those people needed to do so, they could easily get through a locked door. Still, he would breathe easier knowing that she was at home with the door locked. Even if it wasn't much different than being a kid and thinking that the best antidote for fear was to hide under the covers.

Andrei kissed Tanya on the forehead, then left. He still hadn't decided where he should go. He could look for Bukin, but Bukin was already better informed than he, no doubt. There wasn't any point in trying to telephone him; Oleg wouldn't have spent the night in his own apartment. In a normal country, a person who got an envelope like the one that had been in Tanya's box would probably go to the police. But here in Russia even the thought of doing that seemed so stupid to Andrei that he grunted. And as for going to his colleagues from work, to try to tell them this incoherent story . . .

Andrei's despair grew deeper and blacker. His intense desire to find something to lean against overwhelmed any possibility of logical thought. His head swam and his legs, for all that it was morning, would scarcely carry his body. His fingers trembled involuntarily, and even a stranger could have told from a glance that Andrei felt terribly ill.

His eye chanced on a taxi coming toward him. In the morning it was still possible to get taxis.

Andrei raised his hand, and the taxi stopped. He plunked down on the backseat and named the first downtown street that came to his mind. It wasn't far; in fact, he could have walked, and the driver looked at his passenger in amazement. Andrei didn't even notice. He sat limply for the few minutes that the ride lasted, which seemed to be long enough for him to pull himself together again.

The taxi let him out at Soviet Square, near the Aragvi restaurant, which Andrei had last visited when somebody or other had celebrated the defense of his stupid dissertation. For some reason, all that Andrei could remember about the banquet was some guy with a three-day beard who had been hanging around the toilets, offering cheap watches for sale.

Now the restaurant was closed, surrounded by cooperative kiosks dealing in stale meat pies and flat Pepsi. Andrei bought a cookie at one of them and did what he could to chew it,

washing it down with some cherry-colored fluid, which left
a sort of squeaking sensation in his teeth for a while.

Not far away was the statue to honor Yury Dolgoruky,
founder of Moscow, who sat majestically astride his fat horse.
Clustered around the pedestal was a shabby group with excited faces. They were waving homemade placards and banners with the red, blue, and white of the Russian empire.
One of the banners demanded: "THE COMMUNIST PARTY MUST
ANSWER!" Answer *what* wasn't spelled out. Actually, it didn't
have to be, because everybody knew. Harried-looking men
with plump briefcases scurried up and down Gorky Street,
darting through the lumbering women with their empty shopping bags. The working day of the crowded city had just
started, people were just beginning their affairs, and these
people who were gathered for their demonstration were of
little interest to anyone. Except themselves, of course. They
had come to "struggle," and their mood was very aggressive.
One of them had brought a megaphone. He was exhorting
people to chant "Nuremberg trial for Communists!" right
there beneath Prince Dolgoruky's feet.

The morning was getting hotter. The next speaker cursed
Gorbachev for his willingness to compromise, and Yeltsin for
his excessive caution. Andrei bought a second dust-dry cookie
to complete his meager breakfast. Passions around the monument were growing more intense. A couple of hundred people
milled, no longer listening to the speakers but simply shouting at one another. A door opened out onto the balcony of
the Moscow City Council, on the other side of Gorky Street,
and somebody in a white shirt stepped partway out, apparently trying to decide whether to come out and see what was
going on. A little Moskvich honked furiously at the crowd,
which had spilled over into the side street and blocked its
exit onto Gorky.

Maybe I should go up to the megaphone right now and tell
them what I know, just me alone, and not worry whether
they think I'm nuts or not? Andrei wondered. At least my
news would be common knowledge then. They would go tell

everybody. I could ask them to have everybody they know broadcast it, pass it along. It's stupid and naive, of course, but at least I wouldn't be keeping the news bottled up inside me, like some expensive wine in a fancy bottle that will probably evaporate before anybody works up the courage to drink it.

"And I have proof, I have facts," the megaphone bellowed. "Proof that the Communists are preparing to rise up against Russia. They want to crush us. But we will save Russia. I'm not afraid of their informers! I am going to tell everything!"

Another man, standing on the sidewalk not far from Andrei, was snapping incessantly with an old camera, grinning as he did, as if savoring revenge, as if each click of the lens was the tightening of some ratchet—on a gallows, perhaps. When he turned around suddenly, Andrei caught a glimpse of his steel teeth. The man's thick veins bulged from the tight grip he had on the black body of the camera, and his eyes raced around the crowd as if he were looking for somebody he knew.

"I'm going to tell!" the speaker went on. "They are preparing a coup. The newspapers are writing that. Where I work the Party committee is in constant session, and they are always threatening those who left their Party. They are always saying that they will show those who left. My boss even just says it straight out: 'What you need is a Stalin!' Higher up they are all in on it, too! They've raised the prices of everything to stir people up!"

"Citizens of Russia!" A tall, scrawny man interrupted the speaker; apparently he was one of the organizers. "Friend! Everyone is writing and talking about a counterrevolutionary coup. I agree with this! But today that is not what we should be talking about. We have come to support the mayor of Moscow, to give him our support and at the same time to petition him."

The photographer took a final snap and carefully placed his camera into a case. Then he came to stand near Andrei, where he began to listen attentively.

Andrei had already decided against making his "important

announcement" at this meeting since he understood that no one would pay the slightest bit of attention to him. He was beginning to move off when the photographer turned to him and asked, in an unexpectedly young voice, "You like it?"

"Like what?"

"That, what they're saying?"

"I don't know." Andrei didn't like talking to strangers on the street. He considered them beneath him. But he also feared that he would not be able to sway his opponents in street debates, which would cost him authority in his own eyes.

"They're scum, the lot of them, and they're all going to pay for this." The photographer squared himself. "Nothing scares me. That whole lot of them are going to be in deep shit. Everything is going to come back like it was. We're certain of that. And these guys, they're going to get what's coming to them. The army won't allow it; the Party won't allow it. And the people don't support them." The man suddenly began to spout slogans from *Pravda*: "The people are for justice, equality, fraternity."

"So why are you photographing them then?" Andrei asked.

"What do you mean why? For a record, so that later we'll know who was where, to help later when they clear all this up."

"Ahh," Andrei said, feeling both frightened and repelled. "So, you think that everything is going to go back to the way it was?"

"Pal, I don't 'think,' I *know*. There's a revolution coming, just like in 1917. That's what's coming, all right. And we've got to be ready for it. You're young yet, you don't understand a lot of things, but we're never going to give up socialism. Just let somebody say the word and we'll support him to the end."

"And then you'll send your snapshots to the proper authorities?"

"You might say that. I'll send them on."

"Well, well . . ." Andrei said, wondering for a second whether to punch the man in the nose—or at least snatch the camera.

There was now a young man in a white shirt and yellow sandals standing in almost precisely the spot the photographer had just vacated. He was studying the crowd with a pleasant but very attentive look. Not so much gazing at them as peering. There was something elusively familiar in his modest little smile, too, something that Andrei had just recently seen. In the car outside Bukin's apartment, his memory prompted. Yes, it was the same shy smile of a man who was wholly convinced of his boundless ascendancy over the mere mortals around him. It was a professional smile.

Andrei felt his guts twist. Not bothering to listen to any more of the communist photographer's maunderings, Andrei headed down Gorky Street toward Manege Square without any idea of whether he should go that way or not.

I should go see my father, he suddenly realized. Of course, he had to see his father. In spite of everything, his father would be able to understand, maybe even *do* something about this hell, this sense of being trapped without exit. Even if his father was mixed up in the conspiracy, he still didn't know about those photos. He didn't know that Tatyana was being threatened, or that his son had been threatened either, for that matter. Of course, he would understand everything.

As he left the square, Andrei looked over his shoulder out of instinct. He saw that the photographer now was pointing his black camera directly at him. Farther up the sidewalk, the pleasant-looking young man in yellow sandals was also smiling at him.

Nearer his father's committee building there wasn't much crowd. Andrei ran up the handful of stairs to the door. At the guard's desk he asked for the phone; the guard knew the boss's son by sight.

"Of course, please."

The father-son conversation was very short, and Andrei had no idea what he had said or done to so offend his father. Why had his father not understood how important it was that they talk right now? Andrei was sure that the militiaman who had had no choice but to listen to their conversation had chuckled.

Andrei turned his back to the guard and slowly went back down the stairs. At the glass revolving door he saw General Khokhriakov.

The militiaman at the entrance saluted smartly, and Khokhriakov waved indifferently. The general glanced in Andrei's direction, met his eyes. Both of them immediately looked away.

Then Andrei was back outside, and for the first time he noticed how hot it was.

There is a special quality to Moscow heat. It is not the heat of the desert, which can be endured because the air is so dry, and it is not the heat of a seashore in summer, where the cool of the deep salt water cuts the heat. Moscow heat is sweaty, horrible, and endless. There is nowhere to escape from it, not outside, not at home, not in the parks. The only cool place is the metro, which isn't so much cool as dank, so that it makes you shiver.

Leaving his father's office, Andrei first walked back up Gorky, which was jammed with dusty, stinking automobiles. Threading his way through the anxious, preoccupied crowds, Andrei was jostled and shoved; he gritted his teeth. When he got to Mayakovsky Square he stopped, lost in thought. He simply couldn't decide what he ought to be doing. The huge angular monument to the poet for whom the square was named was casting a thick, almost inky shadow. The McDonald's restaurant across the street had an advertising sign on the roof that was illuminated so brightly that it stood out even in the sun. The entrance to the restaurant was jammed with crowds of unshaven, dark-haired, impudent-looking southerners who stared smugly at passersby.

Andrei sighed and then set off decisively for the metro. The Mayakovsky station had been built sometime before the war. The fretwork ceiling was decorated with oval mosaics of bodybuilders and gymnasts, ships and airplanes, all held up by a double row of columns extending the length of the platform. In general the station recalled a simplified version of a Catholic cathedral; all the place needed was some statues of saints and a pipe organ.

The station was both beautiful and clumsy at the same time. Its grace and luxury were of absolutely no moment to the people scurrying about within it. He had heard, though, that the subway train engineers liked the decorations, and so did the Moscow Party functionaries. Probably that was true.

Studying the various pictures on the ceiling distracted Andrei for a bit from his own problems. He remembered coming here as a little boy with his father, before his father had become a big boss. Uncle Vitya had brought him here, too, around the time when he had just been promoted to colonel; Andrei remembered how Khokhriakov had kept sneaking glances at the shiny new third star on his epaulets.

Finally Andrei jammed himself into a subway car. Right behind him, a man rushed in wearing a pink shirt with a bright red spot on the chest. Despite the man's obvious familiarity with the metro, it was clear he was a foreigner. His movements were too free; no Russian would behave like that. That sense of personal freedom made any foreigner stand out immediately, marked him as different from somebody born and bred in any of what used to be called "the fraternal family of Soviet peoples."

The foreigner settled himself near Andrei, caught his eye. Absolutely mechanically, Andrei answered with a little grin. At the next station the crowd of people leaving the car was so great that Andrei and the man were forced out of the car. Between ebb and surge there was a moment of silence, in which the fellow who looked like a foreigner whispered to him, "Your name Andrei?"

"Yes," he answered, also whispering.

"Caution, the doors are closing!" the melodic recording fluted from inside the subway car, and both men, obedient to Moscow "metro instinct," jumped back into the train.

Crushed against the door, they continued to smile at one another, already with a sense of conspiracy.

"So, you're Andrei?" The man's accent was virtually unnoticeable, but Andrei could still tell that this unexpected companion's native language was English. "Oleg told me to contact you."

"Is that right?"

"If you don't mind, maybe we'll get off the metro. I think it's worth us having a chat."

Crushed against the doors, they had to speak directly into one another's ears, as was natural in the din of the Moscow underground.

Andrei thought that if he was still being followed it would be relatively easy to shake whoever was tailing him in the crowds of the metro. At least if the person following them wasn't the pretty, thin girl who was jammed up against him on the other side.

"Let's get off, then," Andrei agreed.

The doors parted again, and they were on the platform. The girl fought heroically against the tide of people exiting the car, trying to stay where she was. Finally she was victorious, and remained in the car.

The two men headed for the escalator and the exit.

As the escalator whisked them upward they said nothing to each other; it was only when they were fully out in the cloying summer air that the stranger said, "I didn't introduce myself. I'm a friend of Oleg Bukin's, a correspondent."

Miraculously, because he did not have a good memory for faces (a weakness in a sociologist), Andrei remembered this man. He had seen this face in his own institute, when the man came to pick up the preliminary results of some questionnaire that a colleague of Andrei's had promised him. Andrei strained to recall the man's name.

"Mr. . . . Cooper?"

"That's right, Cooper, Dale Cooper."

They both sighed, relieved. Now Dale was spared having to

prove that he was not some man from Mars, and Andrei was spared having to decide whether or not his new acquaintance was an agent of the KGB. Nor was there a need to explain why Dale would want to talk to Andrei.

"When did Oleg talk to you?"

"Yesterday."

"Did he tell you about . . ."

Dale hesitated, trying to decide how to convey the content of their discussion. Unable to do so, he simply said, "Yes."

Now it was Andrei's turn to wonder whether he needed to find out any more about what Oleg had told the correspondent.

"I suppose you can guess why I want to see you?" Cooper asked.

"Yes."

"I should tell you straight off that I didn't believe our friend. In general I think . . . or thought would be more precise, that the Russian intelligentsia is so excitable that they are inclined to exaggerate certain circumstances. That's probably true. But our friend now . . . well, I repeat, I didn't believe him. I thought I was even able to convince him that he was wrong. It's ridiculous, of course, to ask me to inform somebody about something that's going to happen . . . that there's going to be a coup, that Gorbachev is going to be overthrown."

Dale was talking smoothly, not worrying about speaking correctly as he moved toward the major point he wanted to talk about. Andrei could sense this, and was prepared to be surprised.

"So if you didn't believe him, then why did you go to so much trouble to find me? You wanted to hear it all from me?"

"That's it, hear it from first hands, as I guess you say it. But that's not the main reason."

"How did you find me?"

"That's my little secret."

"No, come on. . . ."

"Luck, actually. Today one of my colleagues wanted to interview your father's assistant, and his car broke down, so he

asked me to take him. When I was in the car I saw you
coming out of that fancy building, and there was some sort
of general going in. I left my car and followed you."

"So why didn't you come up to me right away?"

"Andrei, I'm pretty sure that right after Bukin left my place
something bad happened to him."

"What?"

"I think he was hit by a car."

"Are you serious?"

"That's what the concierge in the building said. That there
was an ambulance in the middle of the night, and the doctor
asked to use her telephone to call the hospital. She went out
to look in the ambulance, and she thought that the man she
saw lying there was the same fellow who had come to see
me earlier in the evening. The doctor said that he was already
dead."

"How could she know all this?"

"She asks every visitor whom he's visiting. Also, that
wasn't the first time that Bukin had been to see me."

Andrei felt as though he was going to faint. Even after the
business with the photos he'd still had an infantile hope that
everything that was going on around him was a series of stupid, terrible coincidences. He had done everything he could
to resist believing that some huge universal horror was quietly but inexorably bearing down upon them.

Dale walked beside him, silent. The correspondent could
not know what was boiling in the soul of this Russian, who
on the surface seemed scarcely to have heard this news about
the death of his friend. Perhaps he was just feeling fear, frightened that Bukin's end would be his as well.

"All right, all right, but what to *do*?" Andrei didn't notice
that he had begun to mutter to himself.

"What?" Dale asked. "Did you say something?"

"Me? Yes, I . . . No, no, I didn't say anything. What is this?
What should I do?"

"You're asking me?"

"No, Dale, I'm asking *me*. Dale, you didn't believe him,

but what he was saying to you was God's own truth. He learned about it from me."

"And ... uh, you found this all out from your ... mmm, relatives?"

"Yes."

"You see, the thing is ..." Dale paused, uncertain how to put it to Andrei; after a bit, he said, "You see, Andrei, all the newspapers write so much about your coup that in the first place everybody is sick of it and in the second nobody believes it. Then there's the third thing, which is that he said you wouldn't want it printed in the paper. What possible good is a correspondent whose material can't be put in the paper? Really, what good is a journalist like that?"

Dale was going to continue, but he fell silent after a look at Andrei. The Russian was walking along beside him, expression wooden and head bobbing up and down, like a swimmer who was making heavy going against a choppy sea. Why am I telling him all this? Dale wondered. I didn't come after him to justify myself. All I wanted to do was *clarify* the information I got from that poor Bukin fellow—plus, be able to file it so that they would believe me, so that I wouldn't just be reporting more rumors about an impending coup but would actually be reporting the real coup itself. I have to get as much out of this kid as I can. And instead here I am excusing myself or something. . . .

Andrei suddenly turned to him. "So what should we do?"

"You want my advice? What you and your people should do?"

"No, you didn't understand me. I asked what should *we* do, what should *all of us* do?"

Now Dale understood him. Andrei didn't want to give an interview to a journalist. He wasn't even asking for help. Rather, he saw Dale as one of his own, a man on his side who could and must help him and everyone, which meant also himself, to find a way out of the situation.

The American frowned. "What should *we* do? We should make sure of all this, and the faster the better. Get all the news you can to me as quickly as you can. I'll send it to the paper. Right away, to get the wheels moving. Understand, though, I have to make sure that all of this looks absolutely reliable. No feelings and emotions, just facts, dates, names."

"So I should give you top-secret material?"

"You don't want to be an American spy?" Dale spat on the soft, warm asphalt. "You want to play fair and square with those guys?"

"Dale, that's my father!"

"So you don't want to be like Pavlik Morozov? That's the kid, isn't it, who turned his old man into the GPU? See, I know your revolutionary history pretty well, don't I?"

"Shut up, Dale." Andrei scowled. "What if they're following me? Or somebody runs us down with a taxi? 'The Tragic Death of an American Correspondent . . .' You like the sound of that?"

"Enough, Andrei old buddy. Don't make a nervous wreck of yourself. They can still fix up all of *us* easily enough." He stressed the "us" portentously, for which he was immediately rewarded by a grateful glance from Andrei.

"All right, if that's how it is, I'm going home. We'll meet tonight at ten precisely at the Pushkin monument. And Dale, I'm counting on you. We have to stop them. They won't dare do it if you can get this in print. Or at least send out a serious warning for everybody. And don't think I'm just talking big if I say that it probably wouldn't be good for the States, either, if they got rid of Misha."

"It wouldn't be good for anybody," Dale said with finality. Then he added, "Except Castro and the Chinese, of course. And Qaddafi."

"And your friend Saddam," Andrei added.

"Well, then"—the newspaperman smiled—"it seems there's a fair number of them."

"There's a whole *lot* of them. And that's why *we* have to be especially careful today."

"You're right there, Andrei. Take care of yourself."

"You too, Dale."

"Don't worry about me. In the entire history of Soviet-

American relations there hasn't been a correspondent from our side who didn't get home safe and sound."

"God grant."

They said good-bye and parted.

Andrei had decided to go back to his father's. Dale was in a hurry to get back to his apartment. He figured, though, that to be on the safe side he would invite one of his friends to visit, as insurance.

Dale walked along the broad street, the sidewalk cut by the sharp black shadows of the buildings. Somewhere up above the roofs the sun was sliding toward evening, cooling just slightly. The sun was still plenty hot, but not quite as ardent somehow, as if it had already decided it had done enough work for the day. The city was preparing to change its cast of characters. In another couple of hours the crowds on the streets would be totally different, languid, not darting from store to store but just strolling along. And it would be a crowd with money, too, casually slamming the doors to its many cars. A crowd that could simply visit a restaurant, where the prices were so high that none of the morning or afternoon crowd could touch them.

Then, amid the remote stage set of the Moscow streets, life would be acted out as quite a different play, for the pleasure of the actors themselves.

Dale was tired, and he regretted not having his car. He used public transport in this country only in the most extreme of circumstances. He still had not forgotten his horror on his second day in Moscow when he had seen how people jammed themselves onto the trolley. It had seemed rude, even lewd somehow, to press so close to women and men who were complete strangers. He had gotten used to a lot in the Soviet Union, but this intimacy with complete strangers was more than he could bear.

He decided to take shortcuts, and so set off down an alley toward his apartment. There were little houses with broken windows and doors huddled close about on all sides. In between yawned waste spaces that once had been inner yards, now choked with the abandoned discards of former apartments. The alley was empty, save for two old women on the other side who struggled slowly along with thick red shopping bags.

Two fellows stepped out of a derelict yard and came toward him. As they passed Dale, one of them shouldered him sharply. Dale inhaled mechanically.

"Hey, what's with you, man?" the man who had shoved him asked Dale threateningly. "Something bothering you, eh, man?"

"He must want something," his pal said, stopping and reaching a long arm toward Dale.

Dale lost his head. He had no idea how to get rid of these hooligans, whose appearance right now could not have been more poorly timed. He wondered whether he shouldn't maybe give them some money—dollars, even—to get them to leave him alone. He put his hand in his pocket.

"Hey, man, give me your shirt. And your watch," the first guy said.

"I'll take the jeans and the moccasins," the other said. "Come on, we'll trade. You give us your clothes and we'll give you a couple in the face." He reared back and punched Dale in the nose.

The journalist staggered backward, and then somebody else—apparently there had been three of them—gave him a terrific blow on the base of his skull. Dale waved his arms weakly and then blacked out.

12

Scenes Played
in Papa's Apartment

Andrei unlocked the door and went into the apartment. His father still had not returned. The apartment was absolutely still, the air smelling faintly of dust and domestic life. Andrei closed the front door carefully, then locked it. After the past few hours, during which Andrei had slowly but fully come to understand the dimensions of the danger that had overtaken him, that locked apartment door represented absolute safety. However, it was no lock that guaranteed the safety of that apartment; it was his father, the all-powerful head of the all-powerful committee, which was an arm of the all-powerful state, from which Andrei wanted so badly to hide.

Maybe my father is right? Andrei wondered. Maybe that power really is necessary, the one Bukin hated so much? That strong, unchecked power that even the Americans have to respect, half a world away? Isn't life easier when you lock yourself up behind iron curtains and concrete walls, because then you don't have to think seriously about anything?

Andrei turned on the television. Some beaming stout fellow appeared on the screen, smirking at the audience and talking about famine, or perhaps political crisis, or perhaps both at once. Then there was a hectic, bright-colored advertisement for some new, imported perfume, the unfamiliar Western-style commercial making the perfume so unworldly that it was as though nothing like that actually existed; certainly that perfume, the ad, and their world were utterly alien to Andrei, his father, Bukin, and everyone else he knew.

The phone rang. Andrei answered it.

"Yes?"

"It's me, Georgi." Andrei heard Khokhriakov's sharp voice. "Georgi, everything is as we agreed, but still, don't you get mad, because we had to—"

"I'm not angry, Uncle Vitya," Andrei interrupted, smiling into the phone.

"You mean it's you? What are you doing there?"

"Where should I be, Uncle Vitya? You called our home number."

"Your home number, of course, it's your home number. I dialed without thinking. I meant to call Georgi at work."

He was obviously trying to cover up; Andrei knew very well how Khokhriakov's voice sounded when the general was lying. The interesting question was *why* was he lying?

"So, that means you're at home, and that means, well, you're home. And here I was thinking that I was phoning your father."

There was something in the general's voice that Andrei didn't like. A falseness, as well as some sort of agitation that he didn't understand.

"Well, all right, then, see you. . . ."

"Anything you want me to tell Papa?"

"Your Papa? Nothing. He'll be home in a bit, and I'll phone again. Or say hi. Tell him I said hi, of course. See you."

Then, not waiting for Andrei to say anything, Khokhriakov hung up.

The television was showing a cartoon of a wolf chasing a rabbit. No matter what the wolf did, he never caught the rabbit, and the rabbit always tortured the unlucky, melodramatic wolf, who was always a failure, fated ever to endure the taunting of the big-eyed, unpleasant little rabbit. Didn't anybody ever feel sorry for the poor wolf? Couldn't they let him catch the rabbit at least once?

Andrei decided to telephone Tanya to say that he would be late coming over.

There was no answer. Andrei hung up and dialed again, but the result was the same. That disturbed him; how could he have left her alone all day after she had found such photos in her mailbox? Really, what he had done in effect was lock her up in her burrow, order her not to go anywhere, and then go off and disappear himself. What if she was out looking for him? Or what if *they* had come to her place, and she had opened the door for them?

Andrei could picture the three photos with appalling vividness now. He frowned; was this really happening to him? It was incredible; sometimes he could understand precisely, as a reality, what was happening to him and what *could* happen, but then at other times suddenly everything would seem so strange, so fantastic and distant, that he might have been at a play that he was watching closely, even intently.

After repeated attempts, Tanya's telephone remained stubbornly unanswered.

Andrei heard a noise out in the hall. It was his father, using his key to open the brass double-bolt lock, which had been imported from Italy.

Andrei jumped up.

"Ah, it's you. Thank God. I'm glad." Georgi Alekseevich said warmly.

"What do you mean, 'thank God'?" Andrei was puzzled.

"That you made it."

"Made it where?"

"Home, damn it, home!"

"I come home every day. Why is that suddenly worth a 'thank God'?"

"What are you doing, picking at every word?"

Andrei shrugged.

His father started fussing about, changed his clothes, then

went into the kitchen. Andrei heard the refrigerator door open, then slam.

The scene they were playing out was almost an exact replay of the one of the day before, save that now it was the older half of the family who wanted to make peace, smooth things over. Andrei was more inclined to keep needling his father. He no longer remembered what he had wanted to talk to his father about that afternoon. He decided instead to take full advantage of his father's good humor and put off for a half hour, or even an hour, any unpleasant conversation. After that, come what may.

His father was already carrying white china plates from the kitchen, and antique cups, and long-tined forks. He put two tins of fish in tomato sauce on the table. Two years ago such tins had been the dinner of choice for gutter drunks; now they had become such rarities that they rated as a staple of the high Party grocery supplements. His father also set a white and clammy-skinned cold chicken, tomatoes, cognac, and two glasses on the table.

Father and son sat down across from one another, and Georgi Alekseevich poured for them both—more for his son, less for himself. He long ago had ceded his son superiority in capacity for drink. They both tossed the liquor back and then set about eating the fish, to which they added fresh, bright red tomatoes.

They ate a while in silence, then had a second glass each. Only then did Andrei remember. "Khokhriakov called you. He was sort of stunned that I was home. Did you tell him I was supposed to be out of town or something?"

Georgi Alekseevich got such a thunderous look on his face that Andrei dropped the topic immediately. "All right, Papa, no Khokhriakovs. We won't spoil our dinner."

Then he tugged free a drumstick, biting with pleasure into the soft flesh. After more silence, though, he tried again.

"So how was work?" Andrei asked. "How are things with the administrative-command system?"

"Absolute shit," Georgi Alekseevich answered without even a hint of a smile. "Complete and utter shit that the devil should cart off to hell."

Andrei studied his father with wonder and despair. Georgi Alekseevich very rarely cursed his office and what it did, especially these past months, when he had done the opposite, in fact; he saw his committee as one of the few things holding the state back from collapse. Now suddenly this. "Shit" was normally reserved for the Moscow City Council or the Supreme Soviet.

Andrei ached to ask why suddenly his father had spoken so, but he didn't. He simply coughed, cleared his throat.

"What're you squeaking about?" his father growled. "There's nothing strange about it. The whole damn place is rotting, falling apart. And us with it. We're not any exception. We have to save—"

"Save?" Andrei interrupted, knowing they were drifting into politics again. "Save whom? Save what?"

"Save you."

"Save *me*? Why save me? And who's going to save me?"

That was it; the peace feeler withered. They stared at one another, each daring the other to go on. Andrei glimpsed a strange fear that he didn't understand flit across his father's face. He also got the clear impression that something wasn't being said. It was as if there was something his father was dying to say, something very important for Andrei, but he wouldn't let himself say it.

Is he going to just blurt out what they've been conspiring at? Andrei wondered, knowing that that was too unlikely to be believable. Still, there's definitely something on his mind.

"Why save you?" His father shrugged, then suddenly sighed. "Because you talk too much, that's why."

That put some more cards on the table. No doubt his father knew that after their supper yesterday Andrei had gone to see Bukin, and it was also quite likely that he had been informed of the meeting with the American. His father had been warned, and probably even frightened. Now he wanted to save his son—from his own colleagues. Surely, though, his father didn't know about the woman, the one in the photos. In the first place, her death had no direct connection to him, Andrei, and in the second, *they* would know about his father's character and his strict morals. They would know how he would take the news of some unfortunate girl who was first raped, then murdered. So, if Andrei were to tell him about the rape-murder and then show him the pictures . . .

Then what? His father would renounce his friends and spit in Khokhriakov's fat face? Switch sides and run off to embrace Yeltsin?

"What is it that I talk too much about?" he asked, almost insolently.

"Quit repeating what I'm saying. You know perfectly well what I'm talking about. By now your fine friend Bukin would undoubtedly already have repeated your story to every fucking democrat in the city. Except he was stopped in good time, thank God."

"You're sure he was stopped?"

"Positive. The boys told me they were going to hold him a while, to let him cool off a bit. He's no dummy; he can figure out when something's hopeless. The Russian people would never support the likes of him."

"Do you know where they're keeping him?"

"That's not my department. In a safe place, of course."

"Safe, all right, but even so, do you know where Bukin is?"

"Don't ask me stupid questions. I don't know . . . probably some guardhouse someplace."

"He's in the morgue, Papa. The morgue is where they're keeping Oleg Bukin. He was run over by a car yesterday. Run down and killed. You think I'm making it up?"

His father said nothing for a while; then, "Well, so that means it's even more important to save you."

"I wouldn't worry about saving me. Don't bother. Better take a look at these instead." He took out the horrible Polaroids and held them out to his father.

Georgi Alekseevich studied them closely, then shoved them away. "What is this you're poking in my face? Who is it?"

"These were in Tanya's letter box this morning. Inside the envelope was a letter addressed to me that had just one word on it. 'Silence!' "

Georgi Alekseevich took the photos back again. The pretty face, which death had not disfigured, was somehow familiar. However, her nakedness, her legs flung indecently akimbo, the thin trail of blood from her nose, all that made it more difficult to recall the circumstances in which he would have seen her. He checked memories of Andrei's girls. A nurse at one of the high Party clinics. The girls from the secretarial pool at work who flitted about the corridors. Then he tried to recall girls from the offices of his friends.

That was when he suddenly recognized her.

But this *couldn't* be Nadya, dead? He remembered his last conversation with Kulik. The man had said that Nadya had asked for some time off from work. Then Georgi Alekseevich recalled the strange way the man's eyebrows had twitched when he said it.

Georgi Alekseevich looked closely at the first photo again. Yes, this was Nadya.

"What happened to her? Who did . . . that to her?"

"What happened to her is what it seems is supposed to happen to me. She knew too much. As for who did it . . . better you should ask your colleagues."

"Watch your tongue, son. You know that I have nothing to do with degenerates like that. Thank God. Just keep that in your head, you understand me?"

"What kind of degenerates do you prefer to deal with, then?" Andrei knew that he should let his father assimilate some of this. Catch his breath, get his bearings. But he couldn't let up. "Come on, tell me. If not these degenerates, then which ones, eh?"

His father tried to say something but instead just opened his mouth, then sighed deeply and looked away, unable to meet his son's eye. These photos were like a blow below the belt. Kulik had apparently upped the stakes considerably, and now was going to drag the rest of them down along with him. Saving the country was one thing; cutthroat, nasty murder was another. And no doubt Khokhriakov knew all about this murder. Possibly he was even in charge of the whole thing. Maybe Kulik was the one who had called in the "iron" from KGB headquarters over on Dzerzhinsky Square. God, how could anyone *do* that to her? And they hadn't even had enough decency not to rape the poor girl, defile her before they sent her off to the next world. Poor unlucky Nadya. What he ought to do was make damn sure that whoever had done this got what was coming to him, what he deserved, and then he should break off dealings with all those . . . assholes. Then he remembered that the photos had been sent to Andrei at Tanya's apartment. His Tanya. Khokhriakov was keeping his word—they weren't touching Andrei. But would they touch Tanya? These photos certainly spelled out what might happen if they did, didn't they?

"Where's Tanya?" Georgi Alekseevich snapped.

"Papa, isn't that something I should be asking you?"

Just then both the telephone and the front door rang; Georgi Alekseevich snatched the first; Andrei leaped up to open the second.

Not even asking who was there, Andrei flung wide the door to have a weary but beaming Tanya leap into his arms.

"Where *were* you? I told you not to leave your apartment!" he snapped.

"You know, if you were so worried about me, you could have tried telephoning maybe once or twice. I was bored at home, so I went out for a walk. What could happen to a person in broad daylight, eh? Is Georgi Alekseevich home, too?"

There was no need to reply because both of them could hear the man's angry voice booming from the other room. "Why are you always threatening me? You've warned me already a hundred times! I know all about it, you don't have to worry! Yes, I agreed to do it! What more do you want? What spy?"

"Let's go into the kitchen; I need some water. And we'll get out of Georgi Alekseevich's way. You hear how mad he is?" she said, pulling Andrei off to the kitchen, where she took water straight from the tap, then suddenly turned and hugged him, hard. "God, I was so worried. . . . I missed you terribly."

"All right, all right, you don't have to look at me like that," Andrei said.

"Like what?"

"You don't know? I'd say it's not problems you're thinking about right now but maybe something else? With pillows, hmm?"

"You're right. I really was thinking about that something else. I mean, I know that it's not such a great time, but I thought you'd still be home alone—"

They heard Georgi Alekseevich bellowing from the next room. "What Americans? What in the world are you talking about? What, did you see him with your own eyes?"

Andrei began to listen to his father; he could guess what the call was about. Jesus, first they follow me, and then they call my father to tell him about it. It's disgusting. And now they're making me out to be the next best thing to a spy. I hope my father doesn't try to talk to me about it now, lecturing me and shouting.

"All right, all right," they heard Georgi Alekseevich say. "Do what you have to do. But make sure you do it the way we agreed."

The older man hung up.

Andrei waited a bit longer before going back into the room, and when he did he brought Tanya.

"Hey, Tanya!" Georgi Alekseevich greeted her affectionately. "Good to see you. How are you?"

"Hello to you, too!" Tanya said, so happily that both men smiled.

"We were just having supper here, see? Come on, join us, pull up a chair."

Tanya nodded her thanks and sat down. Andrei sat next to her. Silence hung heavy in the room as each of them thought his own thoughts. Or hers. Or, more exactly, each of them thought he or she was mulling over private thoughts, but, in fact, they were all worried for each other—and for themselves. Andrei fished around in the tin with his fork. Georgi Alekseevich cut tomatoes with exaggerated care, laying precise portions on each of their plates.

Georgi Alekseevich sneaked a sidelong glance at his son, almost stunned by his son's appearance of indifference. *If what Khokhriakov told me just now is true, then my son is nothing more than a bum. Running off to tattle to some foreign correspondent, to spill the whole story. But what could he have spilled anyway? What does he know about what's to come? Who could have told him? Me, that's who. I'm the one who told him, old idiot. I'm the one who caused the whole thing, ruined what we were doing* and *put my son's neck on the block.*

Tanya didn't need feminine intuition to sense the general tension in the room. Nor had she completely shaken the fear and disgust that had sprung up that morning after she found the letter in her box. Maybe the fear had dulled a bit, though, not cutting quite so deep now. But she still wanted to clear up all these mysteries, to find out what was going on, so that she could stop worrying about all this. Besides, she was also very hungry.

She hesitated over the meager pleasures of this bachelors' table before finally choosing a hunk of bright pink bologna, after which she poured herself a small glass of cognac from the bottle Georgi Alekseevich had gallantly moved nearer to her. She sipped delicately.

"Tanya, you're very pretty when you drink cognac like that," Georgi Alekseevich said, pleased with his own compliment.

Tanya smiled, said nothing.

"Sure was hot today!" Andrei pronounced after a while.

"Very hot," Tanya agreed.

"What do you expect?" Georgi Alekseevich joined in. "It's August, almost the end of August. I remember, about ten years ago I was bringing a new factory onto line at about this time. Believe it or not, Tanya, at the ceremonial banquet . . . they had to hold it outside . . . my assistant came down with sunstroke!"

"God, I'm tired," Andrei said, apropos of nothing, "and I still have to go visit somebody tonight."

"Visit who, Andrei?" Tanya asked. "I thought we'd go back to my place after."

"It's for work, but I don't think it'll take too long. It's what you might call an official visit."

"Well, if it's an *official* visit," Georgi Alekseevich muttered, "then you'd better go." He gave Tanya a strange look.

Which Andrei saw. "I'd probably better go right now. As they say, 'Sooner begun, sooner done.' "

"Well, you come back to my place after your visit, you hear me?" Tanya insisted.

"You bet. All right, Papa, see you later. Until tomorrow."

Georgi Alekseevich got to his feet. "Run along, then. Take care of your business. And I hope it all goes well." He even stepped toward Andrei as if he wanted to shake his son's hand farewell, but then seemed to change his mind.

Tanya waved her fingers good-bye. "See you later!"

Andrei made a fuss out of leaving, going the long way around the table before finally exiting smartly out into the hall. He looked back into the big room, then nodded his head and left.

When the door had slammed, Tanya raised her head and said, "Georgi Alekseevich, it's all so horrible!"

"What's horrible, Tanya?"

"We're in danger, all of us. I don't know for sure what the danger is or where it's coming from, but . . . I'm sure it's coming. Andrei knows, but he won't say. He shouldn't be going where he's going."

"You know where he's going?"

"No, but I know he shouldn't go there. He shouldn't go anywhere. This morning . . . this morning I got a letter. Or he got a letter, actually, but it was sent to him at my place. It's pretty embarrassing to talk about, but . . ."

Georgi Alekseevich wasn't paying much attention. Instead, he had gotten up and gone to the window, was looking down at something outside very intently.

"Did you hear what I'm telling you, Georgi Alekseevich?"

"I did, Tanya. And I swear to God you have nothing to worry about. Everything is going to turn out all right. Everything, honest."

"For Andrei, too?"

"For the two of you. For Andrei."

Georgi Alekseevich was distracted, watching through the window as Andrei went out of the building. Just outside the door a man approached him, said something. Andrei shook his head sharply and tried to brush past, but the man stepped in front of him. A Zhiguli pulled close, and the man stepped smartly forward, right into Andrei. Georgi Alekseevich's son sagged, falling against the car door, except that at just that precise moment it opened and Andrei disappeared into the backseat.

13
Preamble

Nothing was happening, nothing at all. What *could* be happening in Moscow in August? Everything interesting in Russia always happens in the fall, or in the beginning of winter at the absolute latest. Revolutions, plenums of the Central Committee, uprisings . . .

Summer, that's go-to-the-country time. The dead season.

What kind of news could there possibly be in the summer?

The politicians were weary. Some vacationed at their old summer homes, others at their new ones. Some just borrowed the neighbors', but everybody was out in the country, napping away the hot afternoons and strolling in the cool of evening. Their assistants, of course, were still back in the city; half stunned with heat, they kept sending out the same tired reports, going through the motions of sounding warnings that uprisings were coming. Lazily the politicians waved these warnings away as if they were so many torpid flies. The politicians' wives clicked their tongues and shook their heads, fretting over the newspaper stories written by greedy journalists who kept gnawing at the prospects for a future "Russian rebellion, mindless and cruel," against which Pushkin had warned so long ago in one of his poems. The politicians rolled their eyes in exasperation; they agreed with their wives and the journalists but nodded knowingly to one another.

Sometimes there were phone calls from the politicians' friends—writers, journalists, even artists—warning darkly of catastrophe. The politicians invited the Jeremiahs out to the country for a visit, and sometimes the Jeremiahs just turned up on their own.

The "patriotic" newspapers thundered about attacking hordes of Jews, the "democratic" papers roared about the return of Stalinism, and all of them sang in chorus about famine in the winter to come and the collapse of the "great power." Everybody warned everybody, and nobody believed anybody.

Unbearable, dusty, summer torpidity hung over the huge Eurasian capital. The only things that seemed to be moving downtown were American and European tourists, snatching up Russian stacking dolls—gaily painted crude caricatures of the Soviet president that still managed somehow to look an awful lot like the grinning man with the birthmark on the right side of his forehead—from the street vendors.

Yet this summer was not like other summers. The country was like a lumbering train, "CCCP" in bright red on all the cars, still thundering along at full throttle, but the brakeman was unaware that the brakes had already burned out, and there was a steep downgrade up ahead. The passengers bounced along in their seats, watching the passing scenery indifferently, with no idea of what lay just ahead on the tracks.

However, not every passenger in the CCCP sleeper cars was serene in ignorance; there were also some who sensed that something was amiss, that the train was racing along out of control, and on the wrong track besides. These passengers tried to convince the conductors to stop the train, or to switch to another track. It had happened before in the country that passengers had forced a change of engine drivers. On those occasions the drivers had let go of their throttle switches meekly, passing the train to other hands.

Those changes had happened without fanfare, and most of the passengers had discovered them only by chance. "Well-connected" friends had told them, or the newspapers had passed the information on, well padded around with lies; simply, the jungle drums had passed the news along.

Nowadays, though, changes of that sort would never occur in silence. Such a crew change would require the participation of people who always remained quiet and who were accustomed to viewing everything that happened as the very things that *should* happen. In this way, too, that summer was unlike other summers.

These so-called ordinary people still had not come to understand that their opinion mattered, that indeed it could become decisive. Even after their victory—electing Yeltsin as president of Russia—they still had no sense of their own power, even though they had managed to elect as leader the very man they wanted. They lived as they had always lived, and the pleasures of having backed a political winner were small compared to the joy of finding a store that had cheap bologna to sell.

Boris Fedorovich Kulik had not understood the complexity of what he had conspired to do. He was frightened. Frightened that he was actually doing this, and frightened that if the conspiracy failed an abyss would yawn open before him so deep and dark that he would be afraid even to glance into its bottomless black. Kulik's earlier conspiracies had all been to get himself a promotion, or to elbow a rival aside; had he failed at any of those—which he had not—the only cost would have been some unpleasantness. Maybe little unpleasantness, maybe big unpleasantness. Maybe even very big unpleasantness. The game he was taking up now, though, would have absolutely unpredictable consequences, in part because he didn't know what the game's rules were.

Kulik couldn't even be secure in thinking that the Party supported his rear—"the Party" meaning that mix of personal friendships, family connections, and common material interests that some of the impudent wags in the ranks of the democrats had profaned Marx by calling "class interests." In fact, there was something in what the wits said. Those Jew professors wouldn't have been so willing to hammer Marx into the

people, even for free, if there hadn't been something to it. To
Leninism, too. Class interests were a serious sort of a thing.
But now even his "class comrades," Kulik's brothers in the
nomenklatura, had begun to turn yellow, afraid to take responsibility, making round eyes and hiding their faces like
teenage flirts at their first dance. This old Party man was
making come-hither eyes at Yakovlev, that one was playing
kissy-face with Shevardnadze, another was trying to hold
hands with Yeltsin.

Naturally, Kulik also had some "boilerplate" kind of guys
on his side. His sort to the bone, prepared to do whatever it
took, whenever. However, it was exactly their readiness to
do *anything* that Boris Fedorovich found hardest to get used
to. He found it even harder after a couple of them had been
sent to "see to" the poor little secretary Nadya.

Of course, Kulik scolded himself, the rest of us, we're nothing but sissies. *We* just talk and talk, while those guys are
doing something.

If the "average Soviet man" had been told anything about
the men who had killed Nadya and their sort, this "average
Soviet man" would have scoffed, disbelieving. To the average
man, no matter how cruel and unprincipled it became, the
government was still the government. The *state*. The average
citizen believed in the state, even if he hated it and feared it.
He believed in it because he never—or at least very rarely—
saw what the state actually did and what the men who ran
it were actually like. The "powers" that the average man saw
close-up were the manager of his apartment building, and the
militiaman walking the neighborhood, and the surly salesgirl
slouched in the shop, and his boss at work. Those were people
you could complain to, or shout at, at least. This same average man, though, loved and revered the hidden government,
the state he never saw, the big bosses in their black Zil limou-
sines or their Chaikas, zipping in and out of the Borovitsky
Gates at the Kremlin, or in and out of the yard at Staraya
Square, Party headquarters.

What a disillusionment it would have been, had this average citizen known just how cynical and capricious the big bosses really were!

Boris Fedorovich Kulik considered himself part of the state structure, but he would have been deeply offended if anyone had said to him honestly that all he was representing was himself. He would have been equally offended by anyone who called him a primitive womanizer, since he considered his attraction to young women to be a form of life affirmation. And he would have been equally offended to be called a cynic, for he thought that, having reached the supreme heights of power, he would remain forever in the ranks of the high communist nobility. Kulik felt certain that he knew what ordinary people needed and wanted in their lives, and what they didn't need or shouldn't have. He felt equally certain that he was not one of the ordinary people.

At the moment Kulik was racking his brains, trying to imagine various ways the future might develop. He was trying to keep calm and confident because he was so frightened of the unknowable future that he trembled on the lip of panic.

General Khokhriakov had no such misgivings. He knew one thing perfectly—his was but to serve. The gold epaulets on his fat, thick shoulders were second cousins to the sort that head waiters sometimes sported, or the doormen in the better sort of hotel. Khokhriakov was the kind of man people called by nicknames, and he was used to it; it didn't even bother him to have people use these names when strangers were in the room. He was the sort of general who had no ability whatever to command, because he had spent his entire career within the "heaven" of the General Staff. He was what they called a "package general."

At the moment Khokhriakov was ferociously proud to have been trusted to participate in the upcoming events, even though he understood virtually nothing about them. However, he did like talking weightily with the others, hinting, giving veiled warnings, even growling obscure threats. In secret he dreamed of seeing himself on the television during the press conferences to come, when he would be able to interrupt some impudent journalist . . . he hoped especially it would be that long-beaked one from *Nezavisimaya Gazeta,* the one that seemed to care fuck-all about everything, thinking that he could do whatever he liked.

Not to mention the epaulets, of course. Big new epaulets with a large star and the seal of the U.S.S.R. If he had them now, he would have gone straight up to Pushkin Square, where all the democrats hung out. Just a little stroll—say, from the Pushkin monument to the Rossia movie theater, less than a hundred meters—and everyone in sight would have just about turned to stone. A living, breathing Soviet marshal, right there among them! All right, it was all kind of petty, but couldn't a marshal have his little whims? How many times had just plain General Khokhriakov enjoyed the glances of men who understood the insignia on epaulets when he stopped to buy cigarettes or something at a kiosk. Then it had been a mere general buying cigarettes, but soon it would be a *marshal!*

Khokhriakov was just a few steps away from being a marshal. And he would take those steps. In fact, he had all but taken them already.

Was Khokhriakov frightened of what he was doing? No. How can a servant feel fear? A servant fears nothing as long as he is doing his assigned job properly, doing his duty for his boss, and doing his duty to his own ambition.

There was one other thing—Khokhriakov was also honest. Only extremely stupid and extremely self-confident, never-mistaken people can have the kind of honesty that Khokhriakov boasted. People like him are always utterly convinced that their every action brings only good to those about them. Such people are not even being vain when they think themselves to be blessings bestowed upon an entire nation. Vitya Khokhriakov was prepared to suffer for his beliefs, so convinced was he that all of his difficulties and "torments" would be repaid three-fold.

Not that there had been so many difficulties in Khokhriakov's life. Which made the general even more convinced of his own virtue.

Until recent years, that is, when Khokhriakov's sense of being right had not so much been shaken as it had simply faded. Even Khokhriakov had begun to notice what a great number of people seemed to live and think in ways other than they should. Differently from how Khokhriakov did. Too many people, really, and their numbers were growing. And they were loud, too, not at all shy about shouting out their own convictions out there on the streets. People weren't afraid anymore. That was worrying. It used to be that such people would be branded as dissidents and would be chucked into jail or out of the country.

Lately, though, people like that had started to get some power. It almost seemed as if they were being *permitted* to gain power. Khokhriakov vividly recalled Marshal Kuritsin's words at a conference of army political instructors. Everyone there had assumed that the marshal had gotten far too old, that he had outlived his own brains. However, the old marshal had glared down at all of them from the podium and said, "Don't be afraid. The people have to think about things, talk things over. Give the people time to talk. In my division every sergeant used to think that he was the commander-in-chief, but that made him fight well. People like to think that they're what the world rests on. . . ."

The old marshal's words had reassured Khokhriakov. Sure, give the people a chance to think and talk things over, even give them a chance to run the show a little—under the strict eye of the Party, of course. And then everybody would be happy.

Now, though, the Party was losing its grip on things.

How it had all begun no one could be sure. They thought at first that the changes were jokes, for fun. Some kind of game. It was Georgi who had been the first to get alarmed. In fact, it really had been Georgi who had gotten them started on all this. And while they were all mulling things over, trying to make up their minds, the situation had gone from bad to worse to terrible. What had shaken Khokhriakov more than anything was the day when some pimple-faced lieutenant colonel had shown up in Khokhriakov's office, just barged right in, and had begun to demand all sorts of rights. Khokhriakov had gotten ready to dress him down properly, as he deserved; he had risen heavily from his chair, even drawn a huge lungful of air, but while he was gathering his thoughts the impudent lieutenant colonel had just left, disappeared.

Power was slipping through their fingers. General Khokhriakov could tell even from the way the junior officers saluted, the way the cab drivers in the city cut off his well-buffed, glistening Volga. He was stunned at the absolutely open, impudent way the newspapers had begun to write about the country homes that the generals were building for themselves. What had finally convinced Khokhriakov to join the plot, though, was the morning when some curly-headed Jew photographer had popped out of the bushes to snap a picture of the general leaving his own house, and then Khokhriakov's bodyguard was too cautious even to chase the louse away.

By degrees it began to seem to him that he was almost the last screw in the sole remaining mechanism that could put some brakes on for this ever-accelerating disaster. General Khokhriakov was fully aware of his own class interests, and he had no intention of betraying them to anybody.

As for the fact that they were doing all this planning, as it were, *around* the president of the country, behind his back . . . well, General Khokhriakov didn't think about that. He didn't even like the word *president*; something in him protested against it. It wasn't a Russian sort of a word. Foreign, somehow.

As ever, though, Khokhriakov felt right doing what he was doing. He went about his duty honestly, openly, fearing no one, betraying no one, and even trying to assist friends of his who in these difficult times had fallen into difficult straits. Today he was delighted for this chance to help his old friend Georgi Alekseevich, whose son was in grave danger.

The general was an honorable man. There was just one thing that he didn't enjoy—having to worry about how some of his orders and assignments were actually carried out. He didn't like to think about the people who actually followed the orders, either.

There were a lot of flunkies around to actually carry out what the big bosses dreamed up. Some of them were very . . . out of the ordinary.

Maksim was tired. He and his partner, Snegirev—whose name Maksim knew only because the man had said it when they met—were in their third day of fiddling around in the city. Maksim wanted a nap, or a cool shower, or a chance to just lie on the couch and stare at the ceiling. He could hardly wait for the order to stand down, when he would be released. The people back in the office already owed him for a lot.

Sometimes he felt as if he were working alone, that this old pest Snegirev was just tramping along behind him—or, even worse, had been assigned to him, with orders to get rid of him after he had done what he was ordered to do. When that possibility flitted through his head he tried to study his partner's face out of the corner of his eye, but the man's face was as flat as a blintz. His eyes were half closed, and he looked like some leading man from the provincial theater where Maksim's mother had once worked, eternally angry with her son, the director, and life itself.

Snegirev had shown initiative just one time, when they were doing that girl, the one they had liquidated. When Maksim had offered her to Snegirev, the man had seemed excited, which made Maksim even more disgusted with himself. Then there was the drooling pleasure with which Snegirev had photographed her naked corpse. Gets off on dead bodies, I wouldn't doubt, Maksim had thought. He had heard that there were perverts like that.

Maksim always enjoyed his work. Or not his work, exactly, so much as the sensation of his own strength, his power over people. Even when he was just a stakeout man, "herding" some fellow, he still felt a full dose of pleasure in his sense of superiority over the man he was following. He had almost come to see every person on the street as his, somehow, to follow.

Of late, though, the pleasure of that superiority had begun to slip. People didn't seem to feel that holy shiver of fear so much anymore, didn't wonder whether the man standing next to them was "from the organs." More and more often now Maksim felt insulted; instead of pride and a sense of his own greatness he often nursed a dull anger.

Once, when he chanced on a militia cordon surrounding one of those straggling, typical demonstrations, Maksim had started shoving some guy who was carrying a shopping bag. After a bit, he punched the man. For what, he couldn't really have said himself. Well, he could, actually. Because of the look the man had given him when Maksim had muttered something like "This is getting out of hand, damn it." The old man had glared at him, not quite with disgust, not quite with condescension. Whatever, it drove Maksim mad to have somebody look down on him. On him, who was *somebody*!

However, when he attacked that poor girl, suddenly he had been ashamed of himself. And disgusted, too. He had never thought that he could turn into the most common sort of criminal. He had always respected the law. Now, though, when everything in the world was beginning to fall apart, he turned out to have lost his inner spine, whatever it was that had held him back from reprehensible acts. Now he had ceased in his own eyes to be a "man from the organs." In fact, he had ceased to be a man at all.

Maksim didn't know what exactly that girl had done, what sort of crime she had committed. The fact that they had to "disappear her," though, said a great deal about the seriousness of her crime. Then there was the great secrecy of the talk the boss had had with him and Snegirev; they had been briefed separately, both told that a great crime against the state was involved.

What sort of crime, neither Maksim nor Snegirev had asked.

Maksim had counted on getting a few days off after the "operation." A little vacation or something. They had even promised him. But he hadn't been given a break. The very next day they had asked his "help" in another little matter. . . .

Not that it had been terribly complex—to spend a little time with a guy at a "guest house" and make sure that he didn't go anywhere. First, of course, they had to convince the guy to go to the rest house, or simply just take him there. Nothing very tough, really.

However, the boss who had given the orders had asked them to be as gentle and tactful as possible with the "patient"; this wasn't a criminal, just a man who might be in a fair spot of trouble, which he had to be spared at all costs.

Maksim had agreed, of course. Especially since they had to take care of this "guest" for only two or three days.

Now they had this guy in the car with them. He was still a little stunned. Andrei was his name, which Maksim and Snegirev had learned only about a half hour before they went to pick him up.

Andrei sat on the backseat, the two KGB men in front. He knew why he had been shown this great "honor," but he had no idea what the next few hours held for him. On the other hand, he was the only one in the car who had the slightest idea what parts they were all slated to play in the events to come, and when they would begin.

Only Andrei knew why Nadya had been killed—and Oleg Bukin, too.

However, not even he knew that the famous American journalist Dale Cooper had just regained consciousness in a narrow iron bed in a semiprivate room in the Botkin Institute.

14

The Country Place

They rode in silence.

They had nothing to say to each other. Maksim had been expecting hysterics and was braced for dickering and wheedling, but this one whose name they had said was Andrei kept his mouth shut, staring straight ahead.

So Maksim relaxed, forgot about the man. Without even thinking he dug in his pocket for a cigarette. The fellow they had picked up leaned toward the door, and Maksim realized that if this Andrei had wanted to just hop out at some intersection, he and Snegirev would have had trouble stopping him.

The cigarette smoke drifted toward the backseat and then flowed in a blue-gray stream out the rear window.

Andrei leaned forward, hands clasped on his knees.

It was Snegirev who broke the silence; apparently he, too, had lost track of things a bit, and so was no longer entirely sure whether they were bringing in somebody who was in custody or had simply been agents of a particularly extravagant way to invite someone for a visit.

"Won't be long till we're there," he said to the car in general.

"Is that right?" his partner asked, surprised because he had thought he knew this route as well as he knew his own fingers.

"Yeah. See, this is the Ring Road now, and that's just about home. It's just a bit farther along the highway in that direction."

What in the hell is he blithering? Maksim wondered, knowing that their destination was at least another thirty minutes out along the highway.

"So it won't be long until we're there."

"Where's there?" Andrei asked automatically.

"Where we're going," Snegirev said. "Where we're supposed to be. . . ."

"Of course," Andrei said as a sort of answer.

"It's a nice place we have there. Good air. You can get a good rest, relax properly out there."

Snegirev was precisely, even punctiliously, executing his instructions to be correct and deferential with this "guest"; they were not to make a scandal.

Maksim sneaked a peek over his shoulder at their new ward, the man with whom he still had to spend a couple of days. His preliminary estimates of the man were not at all comforting.

This Andrei person was intelligent, educated, and obviously self-confident, even though right at the moment he was naturally off balance. More precisely, the man seemed rather stunned to have been treated in the way he had been. No doubt he had been expecting something rather different. Maksim and Snegirev were of absolutely no interest to him, and he seemed not even to be very interested in their eventual destination.

It certainly looked as though this Andrei really had not done anything, that he was, in fact, being put out of harm's way or hidden from someone. For the moment Maksim didn't care; however, the strict order not to let the "patient" out of their sight, that presented certain problems. There was no way of keeping him within four walls by force, which meant that there would always have to be somebody at his side. Maksim didn't much care for that idea, especially since the fellow clearly wasn't much used to the idea of obeying "requests."

Snegirev's happy shout interrupted his thoughts.

"Hey, a squirrel ran across the road. A little squirrel!"

Andrei sat forward to study the little creature that had hopped to the edge of the road.

"There's a lot of squirrels here," Snegirev said. "But there used to be even more."

"When 'used to'?" Andrei asked.

Maksim noted that their "guest" had begun to speak; he wanted to know what was happening after all.

"This is more or less a nature preserve. Like it's always been. But now there's lots more cars, and noise, and people . . ." Snegirev explained distractedly.

Andrei's eyes were weary of the endless white stripes of the highway bisecting the narrow, tree-overhung road right out to infinity. Infrequently they overtook light trucks, and a couple of times his driver squeezed their car to the side to let big red-and-white buses pass.

The two men sitting in the front seat were correct in their behavior, polite, and even tried to please him, or so it seemed to Andrei. Where were they taking him, though? To prison? An interrogation of some sort? He had no idea. And why were they taking him out of Moscow anyway? Wouldn't it have been simpler to just chuck him in jail somewhere? And why did they have to seize him right there, by his building, practically under his father's nose?

Lord, what am I thinking? Andrei suddenly realized. Tatyana's still there, at my father's. What's going to happen to her? Not that she knows anything, and besides, she's in my father's apartment. He loves her. But then again, he loves me, too. . . .

"We're here," one of the men said. The older of the two. "Now we can do some serious resting."

The car came to a halt next to a small booth; a high, solid green fence stretched away from the booth in both directions.

A tall man emerged from the booth and came over to the car. He checked the driver's papers, then glanced at the backseat and went back into his shelter.

The gate, which had a green star welded to it, slid back, and they went through.

On the other side there was only the same road through the wilderness, different only for being narrower still, and without a white stripe in the center. After about five minutes the car pulled up on an asphalt square next to a two-story building faced with five thick, freshly painted columns.

Maksim was the first to leap from the car. He was stiff after the long ride and wanted to shake himself out. Next was their "guest," who stood silently next to the car.

Snegirev lazily pulled himself out last, plopping his long legs down on the asphalt, then at some length sticking out his head.

"We'll show you where to go," he said to Andrei.

Andrei simply nodded.

The silence of their guest was beginning to irritate Maksim. Maybe he really doesn't give a fuck about us? He obviously didn't expect to get invited for this drive in the country, but . . .

Andrei turned and headed for the building, not waiting for the other two.

"Hey, where the—!" Snegirev started to say, but then clamped his jaw and trotted after his prisoner, who had gone ahead.

Maksim gloomily brought up the rear, liking this role of silent guard less and less. He recalled how he had brought somebody else here six or seven years ago, a geologist, or maybe a physicist; the guy had shaken the entire way, blabbering on about the beauties of the scenery, as if that would make his guards more sympathetic to him. The first thing he had done when they arrived was ask to be taken to the holding pens, promising that he wasn't going to break any rules.

This one, though, just walked in ahead of them, as sure of himself as if he came here every day of the week.

Inside, Andrei stopped in the cool hallway, its floor covered by red carpets. He looked inquiringly at Maksim, who he guessed was the senior of the two. Maksim jerked his head to indicate that they were to go upstairs.

They climbed the broad staircase, walked down the wide corridor, which wafted the pleasant mix of smells to be expected in an elite vacation complex. They crossed another stair landing, then turned into another corridor. The same thick red rugs covered the floors. There wasn't another human in sight.

Maksim stopped beside a door.

"Please, in here."

Andrei strode in, noting that the door didn't lock.

Andrei was growing increasingly certain that there was no threat for him here. If they were going to interrogate him there was no point in taking him so far out of Moscow. Most likely they just wanted to have a little chat with him, in as cozy an atmosphere as they could arrange, to convince him not to do anything else that was "stupid." Maybe they, in fact, wanted to save him from serious trouble.

Of course, Andrei reassured himself, of course. His father had fixed this for him; in fact, he had all but told Andrei so. And then there was that conversation with Khokhriakov. Everything was in order, Andrei decided. This is nothing special, everything is fine. . . .

Still, though, he had lost. Nobody would be there to meet Dale, and the people who had sent the photographs would never be punished. And Oleg had died for no reason.

So Andrei was saved, but nothing more.

"Something wrong?" one of his guards asked politely.

"Excuse me, you talking to me?"

"Yes, I was wondering . . ."

"Wondering what?"

Maksim realized that the boy was beginning to feel like fighting back a bit. He made a bet with himself, that the next thing the boy would ask was why he had been brought here.

"Would you mind telling me what the meaning of this is?"

"I'm afraid I have to disappoint you, but I haven't the au-

thority to inform you of the reasons for your presence at this
post." Maksim pronounced the word *post* with particular
care. "You'll get all the information you want in a moment,
from . . ." Maksim fell silent, because he didn't know himself
who could tell them anything about the reasons for this journey together.

"There's a toilet and shower here," Snegirev put in.

"What?"

"What I mean is, there's everything you need. And they'll
feed you like anywhere. Three squares a—"

"Oh, I'm pretty sure that we'll get this cleared up in good
time," Maksim interrupted in an offended tone.

"I'm not clearing anything up," Snegirev shot back, also
offended. "The man has to understand that—"

"He'll find out—"

"You both may go," Andrei cut them both off, savoring his
own presumption, which, he noted, left both of them speechless. "I said, you both may go. And as for this 'information,'
I'd be grateful to receive it as quickly as possible."

Then he sat on the couch and looked out the window.

There was a silence. The guest had clearly seized the initiative, which his guards could not permit. Even Snegirev, who
had sort of liked Andrei, was now angry. Both of the KGB
men froze next to the couch with no idea what to do next.

Their orders had contained only the two points, to "arrest"
and "deliver," both of which had been done. They had even
brought him up to his room. So what were they supposed to
do now? Maksim had expected to be met, but there hadn't
even been a duty man in the hall. Certainly he couldn't just
go out and look for somebody to give them further instructions, not with their prisoner right there; Maksim considered
that to be beneath his dignity.

All three continued in silence. Andrei was enjoying the situation enormously.

"Well, then . . ." the senior of the two drawled.

Andrei didn't react.

"So then," Maksim said decisively, "I wish to inform you that you will stay in this room, which will be locked, until such time as you will be allowed to leave it for the purposes of—"

"Purposes of what?" Andrei asked, not bothering to turn around.

"Purposes of eating supper," Snegirev said, and then the two men turned on their heels and marched out of the room.

Andrei listened carefully, but nobody turned a key in the lock. There wasn't even a click when the door was closed. He got up and tiptoed to the door. He tried the handle; the door opened slowly.

The long hallway was deserted. The closed white doors somehow reminded Andrei of a rank of soldiers standing at attention in a narrow barracks. Maybe he should walk around this place, bang his heels a bit and let everybody know how independent he was? As soon as the thought came, though, he rejected it. He looked up and down the deserted hall again, saw nobody, and went back into his room.

The room was clean, comfortable, pleasantly cool. And absolutely unreal. Everything, every aspect of this, was unreal. The trip here, the conversation with the American journalist, the morning at Tanya's, and the time with Oleg Bukin. Unreal, all of it. And at the center of this absurdity was Andrei, who was trying to decide something, do something, but remained unable to cut this knot tied around himself.

He walked back and forth in the room. He was silent, even though normally when he had to think through some complicated problem he usually talked to himself out loud. Here, though, he didn't let himself forget for a minute that he was among enemies. He was certain that his room was bugged, that even now, when he was all alone in his room, those horrid little tape recorders were continuing to spin, recording even his silence. No doubt some agent was sitting hunched over the tapes, listening to what was going on in this room. Andrei cursed as foully as possible. He regretted doing so immediately. Naturally he wasn't the only one to have been so daring in the face of this all-powerful, invisible enemy. So all he was really showing was his despair and powerlessness.

He bit his lip, drummed his fingers on the bedside table. They'll be getting that on their tapes, too, he thought.

He sat, got up, sat again. He couldn't concentrate. Maybe he didn't even want to concentrate. After all, as soon as he concentrated, he would have to make a decision of some sort. But Andrei didn't want to decide anything. He was like a criminal, exhausted by the chase. He had managed at last to reach his prison, and now he didn't want to leave it.

Just when he had decided that nothing would shake this feeling of melancholy, unpleasant dreaminess, the door suddenly flew open.

Andrei leaped up.

The man at the threshold was about fifty, wore a crew cut, and had on a white shirt with the word *Johnson* embroidered on the pocket.

He strode over to Andrei and greeted him heartily, though without extending a hand.

Andrei smiled.

"Andrei Georgievich, I'm very sorry that we will have to have our little chat here. I understand that you probably don't find this much to your liking, that you were brought here without your permission. I'm sorry, but you understand yourself that . . . well, that we had to . . ."

Andrei was silent, but looked skeptical.

"Excuse me, but I would like you to understand us properly. You also must help us."

Andrei found his voice. "In the first place, no, I don't understand you. In the second place, I don't know how I can help you. And then"—Andrei laughed—"both you and I know that our conversation is being listened to and recorded, that you haven't come to me simply to visit. This is your job. I'm merely a detail for you, something you have to deal with. Your 'object,' you might say. So let's do things this way—you tell me what you need, in as few words as possible, and I will

answer. I think I will answer. By the look of things, you and
I won't agree about a great deal. But whoever's listening will
know we tried."

The man with the crew cut nodded in happy agreement.

"By the way, what's your name?" Andrei asked.

The man excused himself, held out his hand. "I'm an
Andrei, too."

"More formally? Your patronymic?"

"Andrei Pavlovich. Psychologist, in a manner of speaking."

"Very well then, Andrei Pavlovich, you have my attention.
Sit down, please."

"Would you like me to order some coffee?" Without waiting for an answer Andrei Pavlovich dashed out of the room,
forgetting to shut the door behind him.

Andrei was certain that the man had gone into the room
next door, where the equipment had been set up already. It
was just seconds before Andrei Pavlovich returned with a
round black tray on which were two cups, steaming lightly.
There were two lumps of sugar on a little saucer.

Andrei Pavlovich carried the tray easily in one hand, then
set it on a side table before sitting down himself in an
armchair.

Andrei took one of the cups and sipped.

His opposite delicately plunked a sugar cube into the coffee
and stirred it with a small spoon, the handle of which was
shaped like the Salvation Tower of the Kremlin.

Both of them finished fussing with their coffee and looked
at one another. They smiled.

"Andrei, you're pretty impressive," the man began.

The prisoner looked quizzical.

"Well, what I mean is . . . I mean, you know yourself—"

"Andrei Pavlovich, whether they are recording this or not,
you're still going to have to report, so let's get a few things
straight between us right from the start. I know more or less
why I'm here—"

"All right, all right, but let's at least finish our coffee. What
do you say?"

"All right, let's."

"Right now you don't like me. I can understand that. If I were in your spot I'd feel the same way. My degree is in philosophy, after all. I graduated in 1967."

"What branch?"

"You'll laugh, but it was Russian religious philosophy."

"So what are you doing here?"

"I'm not sure how to tell you. You wouldn't know, of course, but in the 1960s there was a Professor Melnikov. He was trying to get the religious philosopher Nikolay Berdyayev rehabilitated, but he was slapped down pretty quickly. He published his work in West Germany, and there was a scandal."

Actually Andrei did know, because he had chanced not long before to read an article about the man in *Izvestia* or someplace. The article had intrigued Andrei, and he had decided to try to look Melnikov up, only to discover later that the professor had died about three years before.

"So anyway"—Andrei Pavlovich scowled, furrowing his forehead—"that's when the circus began."

"Excuse me, but what's the connection to you?"

"I was Melnikov's student. I defended him in the department. Just me, nobody else. It was stupid of me, of course. So they decided to squash me, too, just before final exams." He made a sweeping gesture with his hand. "So I went to see Melnikov, to ask him how things stood, what I should do. Melnikov said I should repent."

"And?"

"And I didn't."

"You didn't repent?"

"That's right, Andrei . . . uh, Georgievich, I didn't repent. But they didn't force me out of the department, either. For a year I got to be a big hero, and then suddenly they called me in for a little chat, trying to convince me to take up 'another line of work.' "

"This line?"

"That's right, this line. They said that . . ."

"That it was a great honor, right?"

"That too. But the main thing they said was that an honest, principled person such as myself could be a great help to the Motherland. That our battle with the enemy requires probity and courage. That I had been brave when I stood up for Melnikov. That the KGB needs people like me now. They spent the entire fall trying to recruit me."

"They succeeded, apparently."

"They did."

"Listen, why are you telling me all this?"

"I don't know."

"I know."

"You do, do you?"

"They teach you to do these things. Ways to make prisoners speak frankly, because you have been frank. I've read a thing or two, you know; this isn't something you people have invented. The tsar's police did the same thing. They were also supposed to be open, gentle, and generous with their prisoners."

"Well, it worked for them, didn't it?"

"Sure, but they didn't have tape recorders then, did they?"

"There aren't any here, either. They're turned off. Or maybe you don't believe me?"

"No, I don't."

"That's your right, of course. Pay attention now, though. I have to know who else you talked to. You know what I'm talking about. However, it wasn't because of that that you were brought out here. That was simply to save you."

"My father?"

"That I don't know. But the orders are that you aren't to be touched. And we're supposed to find out who else you talked with, if we can."

"That's your assignment?"

"That's my assignment. Now, moving on . . . you have a day, maybe a day and a half . . ."

"To do what?"

"To help the people who need to be helped. I don't know

how you're going to do it. But you should know that your
Cooper has already been mugged."

"Why in the devil are you telling me all this? I don't believe
anything you say. Plus which, I'd have to say that the tsar's
police were a bit more subtle."

"Andrei, you can do what you wish. You're a free man here.
You haven't been arrested, just 'sent away for a rest.' I've told
you everything there is to tell. Oh, there's one more thing.
Don't try to get anything out of Maksim and his pal."

"You mean the pair that brought me here?"

"That's right. Their instructions are to not do anything to
you, but the situation could change."

"I'm kind of confused," Andrei said, although the words
surprised even him. He caught the other man's eye and repeated, "I'm kind of confused."

"Well, then, why don't you go take a walk around the
grounds? Before you do, though, I'm going to just nip out. I'll
be right back."

Andrei Pavlovich left, this time shutting the door. Immediately Andrei heard voices in the corridor. Andrei Pavlovich's
voice was angry, and the other voice—unrecognized—sounded
apologetic and upset.

The door opened again.

"Whether you want it or not, I'm going to give you some
company on your stroll," the man said to Andrei with unexpected severity. "Come on, let's go."

They went out past flower beds full of red and orange flowers. Only then did Andrei Pavlovich break his silence.

"Now they're going to be recording your room 'round the
clock. I gave them hell for being so sloppy. You can believe
me or not, that's your business. My business is to warn you."

They went down a straight path planted on either side with
young pines. Mushrooms peeked up among the fallen needles;
clearly nobody here bothered to pick them. Overhead they
could hear a jet, which the trees made invisible. They passed
a neatly made bench, then a second one. The path made a

sharp turn and went for a ways along the high fence, freshly painted green.

"This place is guarded 'round the clock, too. All the way along, and very carefully. However, at nine in the evening the senior office is called to get special instructions. That call lasts about fifteen minutes. Now the road bends to the left. You walk about five minutes and it comes back to the fence again. There's a mark scratched on one of the panels there. Better not make any noise on the highway. Cut across the road. The Lesnaya train station is right there, and there's a lot of summer people around. There's a train at nine-thirty that'll have you in Moscow in twenty minutes. Right now it's supper time."

15

The Ward

Dale was in a fury. Not that anyone could have known.

It would have been hard to notice. Impossible, even.

To say that Dale's head felt as if it were splitting open was so inadequate to his pain that it almost didn't describe it at all. If he lay perfectly flat on his back, immobile, then he felt no pain. But as soon as he tried to move, even the slightest bit, then pain lacerated his head, his neck, and even his shoulders. Finally, with a great deal of creaking and grinding (or so it seemed to him), he managed to open his eyes.

He saw a white ceiling, badly cracked, overhead. One of the cracks began beyond his eyebrows and ran past his nose and down his lips, far beyond the horizon of the ceiling he could see without moving. Dale squeezed his lids shut again, waiting until the pain passed. It finally did. He concentrated, listening for noises about him. There was only thick silence, as if everything were packed in cotton. He couldn't even hear traffic. There was virtually no place in Moscow where you couldn't hear traffic. So he must be in a big park someplace. Probably the park around a hospital. Yes, he was in a hospital. A good one, actually. He knew that because there was no one in the room except him. If there had been a neighbor Dale would have heard him breathing.

All right, so he was in a hospital, where he had been put

after that strapping young mugger clobbered him. The one who had taken a liking to Dale's moccasins.

By degrees Dale reconstituted what had happened. He had been going home. After talking with—

Hold everything! Dale froze; more exactly, his thoughts froze. His body remained as it had been, motionless on the bed underneath the cracked white ceiling.

He had been heading home so as later that evening . . . or this evening, that was . . . to go meet that Russian guy, the one who had told him news he more or less already knew, but because of the way he had put it this news had suddenly seemed extremely interesting. Dale was going to get more information from him.

So, Dale decided, that meant he had to get out of here, and as quickly as possible.

He fumbled around the bedside table, looking for the button to call the nurse. He thought he had found it, and even pressed it. Now he had but to wait a bit. Lord, how his head did hurt! He must have taken a terrible blow. A professional blow.

The silence continued unbroken.

Finally he heard footsteps; they were so light that the person making them must have weighed almost nothing. Dale sensed someone watching him. He tried again to move his head. That made him black out.

The whole thing started again when he came to. Consciousness, the slow attempt to open his eyes, studying the long crack in the ceiling, the call button.

Then, cautiously, he flexed and relaxed his fingers, his toes. He was able to move his lips. But his head—my God, his head . . . It felt as if someone had nailed it to his pillow.

But at least he could think now. Not remember. Think.

And what he thought now was that his "tennis shoe muggers" weren't just ordinary street riffraff. If they had been, they would have at least bothered to look at his feet. What he had been wearing was, in fact, a ripped-up, old, worn-out pair of cheap Keds. So it wasn't moccasins they had been after. They had wanted to put Dale away in here. Meaning it was no coincidence that those people had bumped into him. He had been followed. And the Russian kid, he'd been followed, too. Meaning that like it or not Dale was now in the middle of this Russian mess, as a result of which he had taken one on the head. All right, but there was a limit to everything. . . . And where in the devil was the nurse? How long did a person have to ring to get someone to come?

Again he heard the quiet footsteps. Whoever had made them was now standing right up against the head of his bed.

Dale shifted position. He wanted to turn his head, but he failed. Whoever was behind him was in no hurry to bend over the victim, either.

He opened his mouth, but he had no idea what he was going to say.

"Ahh," he heard his own voice saying, "ahh . . ."

Then, suddenly, the white ceiling was replaced by a very pretty female face with upturned green eyes. The eyes looked at Dale sympathetically. A moment later he felt something wet on his lips; he was being given a drink.

"Can you hear me? If you can, close your eyes."

Dale did.

"You are in a hospital. Everything will be all right, but right now you have to rest. Just take it easy, everything will be fine."

The woman disappeared. Dale licked his lips, enjoying the moisture.

A low conversation began somewhere near his bed.

"Leave him be," the woman's voice said.

"I'm not going to talk to him. I just have to have a look at him. We're looking for the perpetrators. I understand that he won't have anything to tell us right now, but I have to at least have a look at him. What do you think, can he hear us?"

"He's terribly tired. He's confused. You have to leave him alone for a while yet."

"Days even, right?" It wasn't clear whether the man was asking or checking.

"We'll have to see. Right now, though, he needs rest."

The voices stopped. Dale assumed the people had left the room.

He opened his eyes. How many hours, or days, would he have to spend staring at this crooked line on the ceiling? They'd suckered him, and without much trouble. Yes, of course there was going to be a coup. Today, tomorrow. And the one who broke the news wasn't going to be Dale Cooper but instead that fat fool from the *News*. Still, maybe not everything was lost. They had said "several days." It seemed as though that woman doctor—or nurse?—wasn't part of this business; she didn't seem even to know who he was. They apparently had just told her that he was another victim of Moscow's street hooligans. So all Dale could do was think and try to get his strength back up. Lord, if only he had listened to poor dead Oleg Bukin! But everybody was always saying what he had said, and nothing had ever come of it! All right, but what was he supposed to do now?

Suddenly Dale felt a wave of weakness, consciousness departing his beaten body. He had no strength to fight against it. Oh well, there's still time to deal with this, he thought, and then sank into oblivion again.

When he opened his eyes the next time it was dark. He could make out a window in the wall, lit by distant streetlights. Dale moved around; he felt almost no pain. He twisted his head about; it didn't hurt. He flexed his hands, moved his feet. His body did what was asked of it. He raised himself slowly, slowly, to his elbow, terrified of setting off that terrible piercing pain again, the one that had tortured him for that first attempt at moving.

He lay there a few minutes more, savoring the incredible weakness of all his parts, glad that he could turn his head to the side. It was true that things were far from normal in his body. He felt around for the places where the pain seemed to radiate from, threatening to erupt again at any second to overpower his body. For the moment, though, all was quiet.

He could hear women talking outside the window.

"Katya, give me a coin. I'm going to call and tell them I'm on the way home."

"You think that booth is working?"

"Last night the nurse said that it was working. The one that's by the front door, she meant."

"All right, let's try that one then. I'll go with you."

The voices moved away.

Dale gathered all his forces, then sat up on the bed.

The pain exploded upward, chewing along his nerves. Dale groaned and returned his head slowly to the pillow. He lay resting a while longer, then repeated his attempt. This time he sat up slowly, leaning on the headboard. He rested for a while, then tried to stand. Surprisingly, that was easy. Maybe he had learned how to handle his body so that it didn't hurt him? Emboldened, he tried a new experiment—he inhaled deeply. Nothing, no pain. So he took a step, another, several. He made it to the door, then grabbed the handle. Just then, though, his knees seemed to turn to porridge. Dale turned slowly and shuffled back to the bed.

He lay there again, resting. After a bit he fingered the bandages on his head. He must look like a smooth white ball, he decided. He had bandages across his chest, too. They had hit him from the back; he could have sustained spinal damage.

He rose to a sitting position again, glanced at the bedside table. He was surprised, and very pleased, to see that his things were on it. He recognized his notebook in the dark, his shoulder bag that had contained a few rubles before the mugging, a handkerchief. Dale picked up the bag and shook it; the coins clanked.

He knew that he had to dig in the bag now, without turning on the light in the room, to find one-kopek or two-kopek coins for the telephone. After that would come the hard part—getting to a phone and calling. Obviously he couldn't use the nurse's phone or the phone at the duty desk. They'd never let him, and besides, they were doubtless being guarded by the KGB. However, the guards would be sure that he was still lying motionless. Unless they were sitting right outside his door, he had some chance of getting to the pay phone and calling the embassy.

Dale got up, went to the window. The window was latched, and he clearly didn't have the strength to get up onto the windowsill and undo the lock. Anyway, the window was too far off the ground, not that he could have managed to jump off even a matchbox right at the moment.

Dale managed to shuffle to the door and open it a crack; the door swung out into the hall. He peeked out. His room opened onto an empty corridor, at the other end of which he could see two glass doors, a strong light burning on the other side. There were two narrow leather couches in the hall, as well as an armchair and two plant stands that held some sort of dark green plants that looked like close-shaved cactus.

The journalist examined the corridor again and then, certain that he was alone, moved cautiously out of his room.

He was afraid to go along the hall toward the glass doors, but not because he thought that whoever was beyond the doors would grab him. Rather, he was afraid of his own weakness; the corridor was too long, and the risk was too great that he wouldn't have the strength. As it was, he had to hold on to the wall to walk, and before very long he found himself forgetting why it was he had ever left his cozy dark little cubicle in the first place. Now all he knew was that he had to keep his back to those backlit doors.

Suddenly he was startled to feel his hand sink into thin air—there was a shallow recess of some kind, with a door, painted gray, like the walls, which is why he hadn't seen it before. He pushed on it with both hands and felt the door open. A cool fragrance struck his face. The injured man all but gulped this fresh air.

The door took him directly from the hospital corridor out into the garden, which was lush with August, but the path was already scattered with the first fallen leaves of autumn. Overhead the moon had no doubt already begun to glisten.

Dale couldn't actually look at the moon, though; to do so would have meant moving his neck.

He had no idea where the pay telephone was, and he was almost at the end of his physical resources. But after its slow start, fortune had decided to smile on him. Not two steps from where he now stood was an ancient garden bench.

He could hear noise of some sort from the hospital. Shouting. A man's voice, Dale decided before losing consciousness entirely.

When he woke up he was in bed again. The same green female eyes floated over him, now looking frightened and guilty. Her lips were moving, too, but Dale couldn't hear whatever it was the woman was saying.

Then a man's face appeared over him. This face was studying him closely, sizing him up.

Dale didn't enjoy that. He was unable to move, absolutely powerless. As powerless as Oleg Bukin had been when he came to Dale for help.

"He's better now," Dale heard the man's voice say. "I can tell, he's feeling better. He's seeing and he can hear."

"But he's very weak." The woman was speaking as if she were trying to save Dale, to spare him something that was very, even incredibly, unpleasant.

"If he's so weak, how did he manage to walk out of here?"

"That was right after the shock wore off, when he was just starting to come to. You can't move him right now."

"I don't want to move him. I don't even want to touch him. I just don't want him to hurt himself."

"But he's not going to be getting on his feet anytime soon."

Looks bad, Dale thought to himself. I would have to guess I'm done for. He tried to open his mouth, because he had to say something right now, while the woman was here. He didn't know why, but she seemed to be on his side, sort of. She had to know at least that he was a foreigner. If he could at least say his name . . .

"Look, he's moving his lips."

"But he can't talk."

"He can talk, he can!" The woman seemed overjoyed with

Dale's ability. "Can you hear me?" she asked Dale. "If you can, then blink twice."

"He doesn't have any reason to talk."

"Wait, look, he's blinking! He understands us. He hears what we're saying!" the woman almost shouted.

"That's good; we have to ask him a thing or two."

Dale remained stretched out in his hospital bed, waiting for the outcome of this battle between the nurse and this man who seemed so interested in the state of Dale's health. That was for sure, anyway; this stranger was awfully interested in Dale. Interested enough to make sure that he got what he wanted out of Dale, regardless of what the medical signs were.

The pair continued to spar.

If the woman knew who I was, whom she had lying in her ward, would she fight so hard for what she thinks should be done? Dale wondered. The weakness was terrible. Absolutely terrible, because he couldn't talk. He was physically incapable, no better than a vegetable. But even if he had been in a condition to say something, the only people to hear whatever it was he said would have been this green-eyed nurse and the other guy, Dale's own personal observer.

"What makes you think he can't speak?" Dale heard. "Look, you can see yourself, he's trying to talk, he wants to talk, he must be able to talk."

The man didn't reply. He was deciding what to say, how to say it.

This is the scariest thing I know of, Dale thought, to be absolutely defenseless. To understand everything that's going on around you and not be able to do anything at all about it.

Dale concentrated, gathered all his strength, and opened his eyes wide.

"Look!" the woman shouted. "He has something he wants to say!"

"No he doesn't!" A heavy hand wiped over his face, closing the eyes it had cost Dale so much effort to open.

"What on earth are you doing? Listen, why are you doing that? What are you doing?"

Dale could only imagine how the stranger's hands had passed over his face, how this unknown person had used his strength and his impudence to force Dale to submit to his will. He, Dale Cooper, was entirely in the hands of some nameless KGB agent. One of those guys Dale had always insisted to his colleagues he wasn't afraid of.

Dale gathered what strength remained to him, used it to make a fist, squeezing tightly enough to drive his nails into his palm. Then, in precise English, he said, "I demand to see my consul."

"My God, he's a foreigner!" the woman shouted, surprised.

"That's right, that's why we have to be extra careful with his health," the man answered.

Dale felt a small, almost pleasant jab somewhere on his shoulder. Then the voices faded away, and Dale fell asleep.

16
Suburban Train to Moscow

Andrei didn't believe the other Andrei; this Andrei Pavlovich had been too frank with him. He'd been too quick to take him to the hole in the fence, too. Even so, there'd been something in that unexpected move that Andrei simply couldn't understand; why had the KGB man laid his cards out so quickly?

Could Andrei Pavlovich and whoever was above him really be counting on his running away from here? What did they think—that he would make immediately for the apartments of his fellow conspirators (who didn't exist) to fill them in on what he had heard from his father and also to boast about how he had been able to slip away from the almighty KGB?

That seemed unlikely, but that left only the wildest and even more unlikely variant—that Andrei Pavlovich had been speaking the truth. That he was honestly trying to help Andrei.

Andrei drank tea in his comfortable room, checking his watch incessantly. It was still hours until nine P.M. Well, he could at least use the time to do some thinking.

Andrei began to pace, from corner to corner, from window to door, and back again. It would have been a good time to get advice from his father, except that it was also an obviously stupid idea. It was his father's fault that he was in this spot in the first place. Andrei wouldn't have minded knowing how this place was guarded and whether anybody would come after him if he decided to "check out" of this "hotel" on his own.

Andrei Pavlovich had shown him where to slip through the hole in the fence, but he hadn't given him any idea of how to slip out of the building.

Just then the door opened. A woman came in, her face framed by long reddish hair; she put two plates on the table. One held tomato salad; the other, goulash and noodles beneath a sauce of ill-defined color and character. There was also some glistening silverware of a sort available nowadays only in extremely elite cafeterias and lunchrooms.

Andrei wasn't hungry at all, but he wanted to get some sense of the local cuisine. He nodded politely at the woman's "Have a nice dinner," and then bent over the plates.

The goulash wasn't bad, and the noodles were properly cooked, but the sauce proved to be mostly Bulgarian catsup. Andrei ate slowly because the food took his mind off his thoughts. His stomach gradually gained ascendancy over his brain, and a pleasant warmth washed over his body.

After supper, after the woman had gathered up his dirty plates, Andrei lay on top of his precisely made bed just as he was, in pants and shirt. He didn't feel like thinking, and certainly not like doing anything. He really felt as if he were "in the country," vacationing. There were people to look after him, and the quiet, obedient serving people seemed ready to satisfy his slightest wish.

So this is how people become traitors. I should be trying to run away, to get out of here. I have to, I must. . . . But I don't want to. I don't want to go crawling through some fence and chasing after the train. I don't even want to get up off this bed and go out to the hall. Andrei cursed himself stiffly but couldn't make himself want to get up.

Hey, wait, maybe they wanted to knock me out, so they put something nasty in the noodles. That wouldn't have been hard. If they did, then there's nothing I can do about it. Let Andrei Pavlovich play his little tricks with somebody else, then. I wouldn't mind knowing what he's going to write for his report about our first meeting. For that matter, what kind of reports do they write here anyway?

He continued to lie there, panting in the light breeze that blew into the room.

Then, suddenly, he leaped up from the bed.

What had made his drowsiness slip away was a mental picture of himself as fat and sleepy, dozing here in the intoxicating August forest, indifferent to the entire world, pleased with himself, and secretly glad that he had been forced into not having to fight *them*.

In that light the conversation with his "benefactor," Andrei Pavlovich, didn't seem so stupid. And anyway, why would the man have been trying to set him up? What would that have accomplished? So they could follow him again? Why? How could they imagine anyone would be dumb enough to lead them to the apartments of other conspirators? Not that he could have, because even if there were any, he didn't know who they were or where they lived. Or maybe they were expecting him to put them onto the trail of some secret anti-Soviet underground, of which he surely had never been a member and he doubted even existed.

No, this Andrei Pavlovich's game was a lot more interesting than that. It might even be that he had given Andrei what he needed to take a chance and escape. If that was so, then there were only two reasons for it—either Andrei Pavlovich supported Oleg Bukin and his pals, or he was convinced that the Communists were on the verge of defeat, and so he wanted to build some great alibi for himself in case there was ever some kind of "Nuremberg trial" for Bolshevism. Either way, it seemed likely that Andrei had, in fact, been given a chance to get out of his captivity and so continue this strange game, which had started with that conversation with his father.

Andrei glanced out the window. The parking lot in front of

the building remained empty. Naturally the lot was visible to anybody in the building, making it impossible to leave the place and not be noticed. Andrei had no idea what might be on the other side of the building, although he supposed that it would be the domestic guts of the place, kitchen and boilers and the like. He still had no idea of how the building was guarded.

Two men walked out from the porch. Andrei recognized them at once as his kidnappers, who were arguing fiercely about something, constantly looking back up toward the windows. They went along the front of the building, then disappeared around the corner. Andrei looked at his watch; eight-thirty. He wondered whether the other Andrei had actually lured them away to improve his chances for escape.

Making up his mind on impulse, Andrei slipped out into the hall and shut the door carefully behind himself.

It was growing dark already, but he had little trouble finding the path, following it to the necessary bend. He pushed aside the loose board, then stopped, stunned by the incredible ease with which he had wriggled out of this bastion of the state security forces. Then he dashed across the road, swifter than any bounding hare, and ran through the forest toward the place where Andrei Pavlovich said the station lay.

Nobody remarked his presence on the platform once he got there. A few obviously important couples paced the platform, discussing signs of impending changes in the weather. There were also some old men on the benches, waiting for the train with expressions of extreme gravity and complete indifference. The station was lit by powerful electric lights, pitching everything beyond them into gloom and turning the whole scene into a frame from an old black-and-white movie. In his simple shirt and rumpled pants, Andrei fit into the movie just fine.

He took a place in the center of the platform, so as not to stick out from the other passengers. He didn't have a long wait, but in his situation every second seemed to drag on for a good quarter hour. From time to time he looked along the platform, trying to figure out who, if anybody, had been sent to follow him.

Andrei could imagine the way the guard would shout when his disappearance was discovered, how Andrei Pavlovich would curse the guard, and how a general alarm would be sounded—or maybe even "battle stations." Or maybe they had some other sort of alarm to be used in such situations. There would be a real fuss, though. . . .

Unless, of course, they had set all this up.

Two youngish girls came onto the platform leading a cute spaniel. The dog ran over to Andrei, sniffing him. One of the girls leaned over to her friend, said something. The other raised her nose in the air, and both went haughtily past. A huge rustic-looking fellow came onto the platform from the other end carrying a tire.

The spaniel started barking, making Andrei glance around. He saw a young man trying to climb onto the platform from right off the tracks. The fellow clung by his elbows, quivering and shaking, but then kept slipping back onto the track.

"Careful, young man, the train is coming!" a nicely dressed, middle-aged woman said, worried about him.

"Fuck you, lady. Mind your own damn business," the man said from underneath the platform. He was obviously drunk as a Dutchman.

The suburban train, like some round-eyed beast of the evening, was already gliding toward the platform.

Andrei waited while the girls with the spaniel and the tire carrier got into one of the front cars, then watched the drunk pour himself out from under the platform. Finally, just as the doors were shutting, Andrei jumped into a car himself.

It was a bit chilly in the car. The evening air was rushing in through the lowered windows, blowing away the accumulated smells of a hot summer day. Not even bothering to spread out among the empty seats, the passengers were drowsing sweetly; almost all of them were going to Moscow, the last stop, and so weren't afraid of sleeping through their stations.

Andrei wondered feverishly whether anyone would be waiting for him in Moscow, and how he might escape them if they were. Not to mention the other question, where to go if he actually made it. The closer the train got to Moscow, though, the more urgent it became to come up with some sort of answer. Certainly Andrei couldn't simply rely on the will of God.

"Ticket," somebody said above him.

"Pardon?"

"Pardon my ass. You have a ticket or are you deaf?"

"A ticket, a ticket. God, I . . . You know, I forgot."

Andrei realized just then that it was true; in his haste he had forgotten to buy a ticket. Now he would have to pay a fine.

He dug around in his pockets, felt a couple of threes, and held them out to the stout little ticket lady.

"What? You think that's all the fine is now? Come on, let's have the rest."

"I'm sorry, I forgot. I don't really know what the fine is," he said, digging feverishly through his pockets for more money.

"If you don't know how to use public transport, then stay in your private car. Fellow thinks it's nighttime so there's not going to be anybody checking on the trains. But there is. There's me. Come on, I'm waiting. Or maybe you'd rather go see an official?"

But Andrei had already found a hundred-ruble note, which he handed the ticket lady with an air of independence. Sleepy passengers were beginning to stir in the car, searching worriedly for their own tickets.

"And just where am I supposed to get the change for that?" Andrei shrugged.

"I said, how am I supposed to make change for that?" the woman repeated.

"Listen, figure that you got your fine and just . . . go away."

"You hear that? 'Go away'? Listen, big shot, I don't need your money, I've got plenty of my own, that I *earn*! 'Go away'! You're a hooligan, that's what you are!"

"I can make change, young man," a gray-haired man sitting close by, in badly worn jeans, said wearily.

"Thanks," Andrei said, glad to have an end to the incident.

It was now completely dark outside. The forest was petering out. The train rattled across a bridge, then passed a group of new sixteen-story apartment buildings. Those blazed with thousands of lights, and people walked hundreds of dogs near the still-new-looking entrances, the old women on the benches by the doors finishing up their evening gossip. Occasional cars raced along the nearly deserted streets. These were the inhabitants of Moscow's fringes, who spent their days crushed in the metro and the buses and their evenings in front of the television.

Andrei got up from his seat and went to look at the train schedule because he had decided to get off somewhere before the last stop, then take a bus into town. That seemed safer, somehow.

There were still three stops in the city before they got to the end of the line. Andrei decided that he would get out at the next stop, which looked particularly promising because it was next to a new bus park. Or he might take a taxi, and then *they* would never find him.

And tomorrow was Saturday. Nobody gave a damn about anything on Saturday. At least that was how it used to be. So it would be a good time for him to start to act. The first thing to figure out, though, was where to spend the night. Surely the KGB couldn't have put a man outside the apartments of everybody he knew?

Andrei pushed open the inner door, went out onto the platform between the cars. The train was crossing a big switching point, and the cars rocked and swayed badly. Andrei grabbed the wall. Two militiamen came out onto the platform from the next car.

"Well, well, look at this," one of the two said. "A drunken citizen. It's against the law to ride the suburban trains in a condition of insobriety."

"Good heavens, comrades, what are you saying?" Andrei gaped, for a moment not realizing what was happening.

"Bet you this is the fellow who refused to pay his fine and then was rude to the ticket collector, Comrade Sergeant," the other militiaman said.

"You may be right. Doesn't hurt to check."

"I paid my fine, you can ask that other passenger," Andrei protested.

"Which passenger?" The militiaman's voice already sounded mocking.

"The old guy with gray hair." Andrei nodded back at the car, then froze. The old man was standing in the doorway, staring through the dirty glass at the three of them, the two militiamen and Andrei, who now seemed to be a hooligan under arrest. The expression on the man's face made it clear that he was not only watching what was going on but was in charge of it. Andrei's eyes met the old man's. The gray-haired fellow shrugged his shoulders ever so slightly.

Andrei turned back to the militiamen.

"Well, all right, shall we go?"

"You talking to us?"

"Who do you think I'm talking to?"

Both of the militiamen looked puzzled. The train was pulling into the station.

"Are we getting off here?" Andrei asked.

The militiamen were shifting from foot to foot, not certain how to react to the behavior of this odd "hooligan."

Andrei stepped off the platform. A moment later so did the two militiamen, galloping to catch up. Then the old man with gray hair got off, too, hurrying.

"So, we're here?" Andrei asked him.

"Yes, Andrei Georgievich, we're here," the older man answered. Then, paying no attention to Andrei's presence, he barked at the militiamen, "Just exactly where were you two ordered to pick him up?"

The pair was silent, with hangdog, guilty expressions.

"Well, hop to it now. Go get the car. If it's not here in fifteen minutes . . . And you two call yourselves operatives!" He spat on the asphalt in disgust.

17
Return

The one who seemed happiest about Andrei's being picked up again was the younger of his two guards. Maksim.

"Why'd you do that, huh?" Maksim snapped immediately, as soon as they'd put Andrei back into the room he already knew by heart. "Night, it's dark, it's damp already, and you're running around on the suburban trains? Besides which, you don't bother with a ticket? Well, let's be friends anyway. My name is Maksim Petrovich, and from now on you aren't going anywhere without me, except up and down this room. You hear me? You hear me? I asked you."

"Yes, sir. I heard you, sir. Yes, sir," Andrei managed to say with weary sarcasm.

"You'll have lots of time for that sort of joke now. We brought you here like a person and treated you nice. We did treat you nice, didn't we?"

"Yes, sir, very nice."

"And what did you do? Let us all down, that's what. You caused a . . . well, you caused an emergency. You know what an emergency is, don't you?"

"Yes, sir. An emergency is . . . well, an emergency. Sir."

"Well, every time there's an emergency, somebody has to take responsibility for it, you know? And who's going to answer for this one, eh? Come on, speak up."

"I don't know, sir."

That enraged Maksim Petrovich. He could let himself rage now; before, they had ordered him to hold his temper, to endure. Now that order had been changed. The anger that had been building up all day against this enemy of the people had finally erupted.

"How'd you find the hole in the fence?" he snarled.

"What hole?"

"Who turned off the alarms for you?"

"I don't understand what you are talking about, Maksim Petrovich."

"All right." Unexpectedly even for himself Maksim suddenly cooled off. "We don't need you, we've got lots of information already, Andrei Georgievich. And this can wait until morning. Everyone's tired, even me. Well, what I'm trying to say, see . . . well, it's just that all of us were really worried about you."

"I'm deeply disturbed to have been such a bother," Andrei replied, the very picture of gallantry, wondering at the same time whether the man was trying to apologize.

"I imagine that everything will work out all right," Maksim said. "I think we'll be able to come to a meeting of the minds. For now, though, I'll wish you good-night. Incidentally, the last train has already left, so you won't have to worry about going anywhere." Then he turned around and left, grinning hugely with his own cleverness but wondering at his loss of heart. Could he be losing his taste for such work?

Andrei slept like a baby. He didn't even hear the efficient Snegirev tromping up to his door every hour, opening it a crack to check on the prisoner. And he would have been very surprised to hear the precise little KGB man muttering, once when he came right up to the bed, "My God, how can he sleep like that after everything that's happened to him?"

There was hot, very sweet tea waiting for Andrei when he woke the next morning, and an omelet with thin slices of sausage and bright red tomatoes. Andrei took a shower, ate his breakfast with appetite, and then went to peer out the window.

The day before had vanished with almost no trace, as if the day had simply never been. Especially, there had never been that idiotic attempt to escape on the suburban train, with the two militiamen on the car's end platform or that stupid ticket woman. Or maybe she wasn't so stupid. The whole thing had been executed masterfully; he had believed her to be exactly what she had meant him to. And that gray-haired gentleman in blue jeans! No one would ever have believed that he was KGB. All these people must take acting lessons taught by real masters of the craft, Andrei decided.

The only real question remaining was what was going to happen to him. Nothing, probably. He would sit tight here until whatever was to happen happened. Whatever it was, he would be watching it on television now. He would see the declaration of a new Soviet government. And then he'd go back home to his father. Under his daddy's wing. To write his little sociological articles. True, it was hard to say what kind of sociology there would be in the new government. Probably whatever sort Khokhriakov needed—or wanted.

Well, even so, Andrei wouldn't have minded knowing what had happened yesterday after he was discovered missing. It was clear that Andrei Pavlovich had indeed meant him to escape using that route. That's why they were sitting on him so tightly now of course. Or maybe not. There was another explanation: some of the men here wanted to let him go and follow him, so as to net some new people, while the other KGB men preferred just to follow their orders and not let Andrei get free. Secrets within secrets within secrets, the left hand having no idea what the right hand was up to. So between them they had messed things up. They must have such mix-ups all the time. It would be impossible not to have them.

Andrei found himself wanting company badly. Even the company of Maksim the guard would have done, as long as it came right that second. But no one came in. Maybe they had decided he was too scared to try another breakout. More likely the perimeter guard had simply been beefed up, put on alert.

Andrei grew more and more depressed, glancing continually at the door. An hour went by. In the bedside table, he found an old copy of *Pravda*, which he read with interest. He waded through a profile of a leading factory worker, then carefully read the lies about the state of the economy (which everyone knew was disastrous), glanced through an endless article by some philosopher who explained at vast length why socialism was the only possible intellectual choice. The man was clearly either an idiot or a totally unprincipled careerist. Likeliest of all was that he was both. The most interesting things in the paper, of course, were the letters from readers, which one after the other demanded that order be brought back to the country. The letter writers raged against the universal immorality and permissiveness. Some pensioner rhapsodized about how his father used to knock him to the floor if ever he chanced to use a coarse word.

Andrei was going nuts with boredom. Simply to have something to do, he went to the toilet for a third time, washed his hands with the precision of a surgeon, and then dried them bone-dry with the ancient, threadbare towel.

Then he flung the window wide open and began bellowing out the Stalin-era song "My Motherland Spreads Far and Wide." He hadn't picked the stupid song for any particular reason; it simply was the first one that popped into his head.

He heard a noise behind him. He whipped around.

"You at it again?"

"What again?" Andrei almost added "Your Grace," but managed to stop himself.

"You're supposed to be a grown-up, but you're carrying on like . . ."

"Like what? Come in, come in, Maksim . . . uh, Petrovich."

Maksim did so, but somehow made it plain that the room

might be Andrei's, but *he* was master of the house. Andrei didn't like that.

"What, need a little sugar on this?"

"What do you mean, Maksim Petrovich?"

"I mean you, friend. I mean you."

"What do you want?" Andrei's good feeling was scattering as he studied his guard despisingly.

"I don't want anything. You, though ... We're going to show you a man, and you have to confirm that he's the one who helped you escape."

Andrei said nothing.

"Did you hear what I said?"

"Quite clearly."

So now there's another guy gets his foot stuck in this, Andrei understood. If that crew-cut namesake of mine really meant to help, then this is not looking so pretty. More like I'm supposed to throw him overboard.

Three people came into the room: the gray-haired man from the train, a young guy in a bright blue tight shirt, and one more. Andrei scarcely recognized yesterday's proud Andrei Pavlovich in the pale, crumpled man with haunted, fear-dulled eyes.

"So, we're old friends," the man he had seen on the train said. "Andrei Georgievich, do you know this man?"

"I do."

"You met him yesterday."

"I did."

"He told you how to get out of here."

"He did not."

"You're sure?"

"I am."

"You're lying, Andrei Georgievich."

"No."

The crew-cut psychologist stood silently, his head hung low.

"There's nothing you want to say?" the gray-haired man asked Andrei again.

Andrei said nothing.

"Andrei Georgievich, your silence isn't going to help. We've already sorted things out with this one and his chums. We've been watching this piece of shit for a long time. But if you were to tell us what we want to know, well, you might say it would wipe out your guilt."

"My guilt with whom?"

"Us."

Andrei laughed loudly. "You guys, I've got nothing to be guilty about."

"Well, then, guilty with your father. You like that better?"

Andrei sobered, watchful. This reminder of his father seemed unexpected in these surroundings. Had they done something to him? "Father of an enemy of the people," like back in Stalin's day? It sounded funny, maybe, but also scary.

"Well, then, Andrei Georgievich and Andrei Pavlovich, there's nothing more either of you wants to say? All right then, that's how we'll play it. Ask Comrade Snegirev to deal with him"—the senior KGB officer nodded at Andrei Pavlovich—"and we'll continue our chat here."

The young man stepped close to Andrei Pavlovich, gave a quiet command: "About face!" When they got to the door the young man suddenly punched Andrei Pavlovich viciously in the back of the head. He gave a gasp and collapsed face forward. Then the door was shut from the outside.

"They'll get to the bottom of things just fine without us."

Andrei could hear a scuffle in the hall, then a stifled shriek. The gray-haired officer got up, opened the door. "Quiet, damn you! You're bothering us. And hurry it up, will you?"

"Fucking assholes!" Andrei muttered with bitter impotence.

"Who?"

"You guys. You're assholes."

"And you're angels, of course."

"What do you want now?"

"Just an honest little talk. You know that's what we stand for, don't you? Honesty?"

"Silly me, forgetting that. Like in the song about the KGB, right? 'Clean hands, ardent hearts, and icy heads'?"

There was another shriek, this time from the next room.

The gray-haired man cursed. He stalked out of the room, and a minute later Andrei could hear him shouting through the wall.

He came back into the room. "Well, as I was saying, they won't bother us anymore. Idiots never stop being idiots, you know? They figured that our talk would go better if it had a little, what would you call it? Mood music? Although I guess it doesn't make much difference to you, does it? But me, the older I get, it's started bothering me."

"You have that sort of music a lot?"

"Good heavens, what do you take us for? Almost never anymore. It isn't done nowadays."

"What *is* done?"

"All right, now we're coming around to what you and I have to discuss. And before we do, I ought to stress again that this is an absolutely frank and open discussion. So, first thing, Andrei Pavlovich was trying to hurt us. That wasn't a staged escape."

Pity then, Andrei thought. If I'd been a bit smarter I might have gotten away from them. Taken a suburban train outbound, for example, and then got off somewhere, walked through the woods, and flagged down a truck to get back into town.

"Still, you couldn't have gotten away from us." The gray-haired man was speaking. "Everything in this district is closed, watched. If we hadn't stumbled on you at the station, then we'd have gotten you out on the road. Inbound or out," the man added judiciously, as if guessing Andrei's thoughts. "Anyway, that's all in the past. Pretty soon you'll be set free, but for right now it's better that you're here. There's not much chance that your sticking your nose into things would change how this will turn out"—here he smiled, showing two rows of perfect white teeth—"but it never hurts to make sure, does it? And it gives us a chance to chat. Who knows? Maybe we'll like you, and you'll like us."

"You think so?"

"More or less. But there's more. I can tell that you're a decisive sort. Even maybe a little too decisive. But our dear Andrei Pavlovich here, it seems he still has some comrades-in-arms. That's why we had to take steps to protect ourselves, and you and . . . well, you and yours."

"What do 'mine' have to do with this? Especially since my people can perfectly well take care of their own safety?"

"Not all of them. The girl, for example . . ."

Clearly the gray-haired officer enjoyed effects, and knew how to stage them. Just as he said that, the door was jerked open and Maksim shoved Tanya into the room.

18

On the Eve of Victory

Georgi Alekseevich slept very poorly. Not because his conscience was bothering him; no, he felt he was doing the right thing. But that last scene, the one with the car, and Andrei, and that thug who was plain and simple shoving his son into the automobile . . .

Tanya had left soon after Andrei. She could tell that Georgi Alekseevich was upset about something, and she didn't want to be a burden to him. She promised to call him when Andrei got back to her house, and then she left.

However, it was Georgi Alekseevich who phoned her. He lied, saying that Andrei hadn't been able to get through to her number and so had called him, asking that Tanya be told he had been delayed and so rather than bother her coming in he would spend the night at home. It was a feeble lie, so transparent that Tanya might well get mad. She hadn't sounded offended, though.

The next morning he expected her to call, so to be on the safe side he unplugged the phone. That way he could lie again, if need be; he could say he had been summoned to some emergency at work, or just that he and Andrei had gone out for a walk.

He only plugged in the phone again around noon, even though he promised himself that if it rang he wouldn't answer. The telephone remained stubbornly silent, though.

Tanya must be mad, Georgi Alekseevich decided, sitting in the armchair next to the silent receiver.

He had nothing to keep him busy, keep his mind off things. He had stopped reading the newspapers months ago, and he didn't like the new television programming. All the radio ever seemed to have on was either rock and roll or endless complaints about how bad everything was, punctuated by confident, expert assurances that things were going to get even worse.

Trying to find something to do, he went out on the balcony. Ragged clouds straggled across the sky, and a gusty, unpleasant wind slithered against the walls of the building. The weather seemed undecided, uncertain whether to let go with a real rain or perhaps instead to clear away all this confusing overcast and give people the pleasure of a real hot August day.

Georgi Alekseevich hated the look of the sky and the clouds, and his long, empty balcony and the squeaky wicker chair on it, and his apartment, furnished with all the luxury of a high Party hotel. He hated himself, too; he felt useless and evil.

Maybe that's truly what he had become?

He leaned over the balcony railing. It made him dizzy, and the rough benches by the front door seemed to rock. I wonder what's the last thing a man sees when he throws himself out a window? Or maybe he shuts his eyes? People say that in a plane crash everybody loses their mind instantaneously, so that nobody knows what's happening to them.

Georgi Alekseevich pushed himself away from the railing and went back inside. He flopped down in the armchair. President of the all-powerful committee, and he didn't have a blessed thing to keep him busy at home!

He thought of his son. What was the boy eating there? What was he talking about, and with whom? What he really wondered, though, was what the boy was thinking about his father, who had sent him away to that "summer house," as Khokhriakov loved to call the place. Summer house, summer house . . .

What if his son had put up resistance? Shouted, fought back? What would they do to him then? Khokhriakov had said that it was like a rest cure there, but if Tanya were ever to find out that Andrei's father had sent his own son to such a rest cure, she certainly would never speak to him again. Although who's to say? Maybe she'd thank him afterward for having saved the boy, for not letting him fling himself bare-chested onto the barricades.

That's if . . . if . . . if what? If we manage to chuck Gorby out by the scruff of his damned neck? But what if it's our necks, our scruffs?

He continued to sit and brood, feeling nastier and nastier. He began to wish for somebody to vent his anger on.

The doorbell rang.

Georgi Alekseevich figured it must be Khokhriakov, and he went to the door savoring the fact that he was going to jump down the general's throat, demand an account of what the devil they were doing to his son.

Except, when he unlocked the door it was Kulik who was standing there.

"Surprise, Georgi. You expecting me?"

"Can't say I was, Boris Fedorovich. Come in, put up your feet. You've come on business, I suppose, because you hardly ever come as a guest."

"On business? We're all on business now. The same business. And we're going to see this business through to the end, all of us at once, right?"

"Is this a joke, Boris Fedorovich?"

"We're just about through joking, Georgi. I was going by, coming from our soldier boys over at General Headquarters, and I look up, see you hanging your head over the railing. So I figured I'd drop in and give the old war-horse a little bucking up."

"Thank you. I'd have to say honestly, Boris Fedorovich, that things could be better in the spirit department."

"All of us could be better in the spirit department, Georgi."

"Come on, all of us?"

Kulik was already on his way into the room when he suddenly changed his mind. "You know what, Georgi, let's take
a walk around the town, all right?"

"You aren't afraid that people will recognize you? I mean,
you're on the television practically every day."

"There's so many leaders now, you think anybody can remember them all? And if they do recognize me, so what?
We're all democrats now, am I right? Anyway, if some fool
takes it into his head to take a swing at me, I've got my
bodyguard with me. Plus, my driver isn't exactly in a wheel-
chair. More like something out of the ape house, if you want
to be honest."

"Where do you want to go?"

"How about down to the Arbat? Not that the place isn't
just about run to dogshit now, filled with all those guys who
call themselves artists, and all those black marketers, and the
foreigners, and the whores . . . But you know, the place isn't
boring at least."

"You go to the Arbat?"

"Not a lot, but I've been. Incognito. And I've seen it on
television, too. Come on, Georgi, get dressed and let's go!"

"Why not? Get a breath of air, anyway. They say that the
cosmonauts always take a walk on Red Square before they
get sent up. And we're sort of like that, about to take off."

"Georgi, I'm not getting ready to blast off into space. I'm
getting set to jump into a whirlpool. Either we can swim to
the other shore, or—"

"I don't like this kind of talk, Boris Fedorovich."

"All right, Georgi, enough about that. Let's go down to the
Arbat, take a look at the girls."

It was only about five minutes' drive to the Arbat, one of
Moscow's three pedestrian malls. They left Kulik's car and
strolled out onto the narrow street that began alongside the
Prague Restaurant and emptied at the other end into the ca-
cophonous, exhaust-choked Garden Ring not far from the
Foreign Ministry Building.

Kulik's apeman driver and his bodyguard, who was of no

less impressive dimensions, strolled along behind at a discreet distance.

Georgi Alekseevich grew irritated immediately because he couldn't set his normal pace on this brightly painted street clogged with people of every description and stripe. The street echoed with an endless hum of voices, pierced now and again by a raucous female laugh. The Arbat goaded him, excited him.

Georgi Alekseevich glanced at his companion. Kulik's face grimaced with distaste for this motley crowd, who were absolutely indifferent to whoever might be sharing the street with them. He clearly loathed these people, who were capable of shoving, even abusing, a man who, as recently as two years ago, would have had them all in speechless shock if he had appeared on the street. But then again, two years ago that sort of shock would have been impossible, because the visit would have been arranged ahead of time with the approval and coordination of all the appropriate committees and organs.

Now there was nobody in charge of the Arbat; that was entirely too clear. The two patrolling militiamen looked absolutely inoffensive, simply another element of the surging Arbat Saturday carnival with their new and obviously unfamiliar, clumsy, imported rubber batons.

The artists were set up along the walls. A lot of them were women, young, not very pretty, and ratty enough to make you cry. The women smoked, making eyes with the loutish boys who slouched around them, braying now and again with laughter.

Georgi Alekseevich was always ashamed to admit that he liked some of the paintings on the Arbat. The newspapers told him that this "artistic flea market" was the very model of bad taste and cheap art, and he would have been happy to agree, except that he kind of liked the tiny little landscapes, the ones that looked like pages from a calendar. He also liked all the ones of church cupolas against sunsets, and the birch tree ones, and the ones with vivid blue streams babbling through stands of young trees. A couple of years before he had just about bought one, but then at the last minute he had been stopped by the thought of what his educated and high-brow son would say.

"Just look at this shit," Kulik growled out the side of his mouth like a ventriloquist. "Won't be long before we clean all this up, will it?" He was speaking softly, but his voice had a steely ring loud enough to make a couple of the local Arbat beauties turn around and stare.

"High time," Georgi Alekseevich agreed, reluctantly tearing his glance from another birch tree picture.

"You know what? Farther along, I'll show you the place, there's one guy selling naked women. Children walk this street, and old women, and there he is with his treasures. Not to mention that the way he paints the women is strange, all foggy, so all you see is tits, nothing but tits."

"Disgusting," Georgi Alekseevich managed to say half-heartedly.

"And what about this? Can you believe we've lived to see this?" They were passing tables full of stacking dolls: Gorbachev-Brezhnev-Khrushchev-Stalin-Lenin. "Black marketers selling dolls of the general secretary! And what happens to them? Nothing! Nobody gives a shit!" Then, unexpectedly, he giggled. "You know, that one really looks like him, doesn't it? They got that spot on his head right and everything."

"Disgusting," Georgi Alekseevich agreed again, but this time absolutely sincerely. "Disrespectful, too. Good or bad, the man is the president, after all."

"He's a stinking piece of shit, not president, Georgi."

"Hey, look at this!" Georgi Alekseevich had stopped in front of another table of stacking dolls, bigger ones, that not only had all the Soviet leaders but the last five tsars as well. "Hey, that's all right! What's one cost?"

A young man in fringed jeans named an incredible sum. At first neither Georgi Alekseevich nor Kulik had any idea what the fellow meant.

"Okay then, you can have it for a hundred bucks, if you'd rather," the dealer said.

"A hundred what?" Kulik asked, revealing his complete lack of information about the life of the country he lived in.

"Dollars, dollars," Georgi Alekseevich explained. "They call them 'bucks' now, or so Andrei tells me."

"My God, the man is a currency speculator!" Kulik almost shouted, which brought about the immediate appearance of a couple of very healthy-looking men behind the doll dealer, who with arrogant indifference studied his two middle-aged customers.

"Let's get out of here," Georgi Alekseevich said under his breath.

"All right, all right. We'll put up with this one more day, and then I personally am going to grind all this into dust," Kulik growled, white-faced and thin-lipped.

Georgi Alekseevich noticed that "I." Not "we." "I." Then he realized that, in fact, the man he was walking beside was about a whisker away from becoming lord and master of this street, of Moscow, and—who knew?—maybe everything that went by the name Soviet Union.

They strolled a bit more in silence. Kulik is right, Georgi Alekseevich mused. Order has to be established again. But how? How he wants to? And what order? Was what we had before order? A fuck-all mess was what we had before. His job had taught Georgi Alekseevich as well as anyone about the wholly fictional Five-Year Plan quotas that were never actually met. And the millions of abandoned, stolen, and gutted cars and trucks, the pilfered auto parts, the scrap metal that was such junk it might better have been buried than put in even for scrap. The wooden hovels where workers lived for decades and for which they were supposed to thank the Party. The monstrous alcoholism, which on payday could lay an entire shop crew on the floor as if scythed. He knew all of that, but he had never mentioned it to anyone. Worse, he would have gotten furiously angry if anyone had mentioned it to him.

"Kulik's right, we've got to put an end to this whorehouse," he whispered to himself.

"What's that, Georgi? You talking to yourself or listening to me?"

"Listening to you," Georgi Alekseevich lied, becoming alert again. "Every word."

"What I was saying is, the whole thing is very simple. We weren't the ones who invented the system, so we aren't the ones to have to change it. People are used to being told what to do. They should know their places. You have your place, I have mine, they have theirs. People have to do what the system asks, work together with the system's laws. The system proved that it works. Well, at least in the war, say. And there's always going to be wars, right? People have to be fighting for something, right? The only time the people really apply themselves, buckle down and work, is when there's a war on. Otherwise they just waste that energy on themselves, looking after their own affairs. War is kind of like a conditioning course for a people."

"So our life is preparation for a war?"

"See, what I'm saying is, the process of preparing for a war is the most natural thing in the world for a people. Without that the people lose their vital strength and disintegrate into just individuals. And individuals don't need a state—or order, either. An individual lives just doing what he needs to for himself. Just for himself. And then instead of a *people*, all you have is a population. A certain number of individuals. But that only turns into a people when the individuals are bound together by an idea."

"And what happens if this people doesn't want the kind of order that you propose to give them? What if the people want something else instead?"

"Hey, you're a dissident now, too, Georgi?"

"I'm just asking. Or maybe no, I'm not just asking. What happens if they boot our ass out of there? Tell us to go stuff our 'order,' tell us that they'll figure out what they want, instead of having us tell them? What then?"

"Never happen. They can't do it," Kulik said, panting from the unfamiliar walk. "They have to have somebody explain things to them. Right now it's these democrats explaining things, the Jews and Yeltsin and that bunch. But we've got the truth on our side. We are the bearers of a historical truth that has lasted for decades, a truth that has allowed us to build, to fight, to struggle—"

"Boris Fedorovich, this isn't a May Day parade that you're making a speech at! Keep it simpler, please."

"Simpler? If you insist. I can make it as simple as you like. We have a duty, don't you see, to put the people back on the right path. For their own good."

"What exactly is their own good?"

"What do you mean?"

"This good of theirs. What is it? And how is it different from our good?" Georgi Alekseevich knew that his tongue was taking him into places he ought not go. If he didn't shut up soon, Kulik was going to be furious. So he shut up.

Too late. Kulik was already furious.

"Maybe what I'm about to say is going to sound too grand, but we have a duty, an obligation. A mission, if you want. And we have to carry this mission forward. We are the sustainers of the government, of its foundation. Of state property, and power, and morality. Yes, that's right, morality."

Kulik stumbled over the word *morality*, but then managed to go on. "I mean that. Morality, even if sometimes we are weak ourselves or don't show enough character. And we don't behave like we ought to behave. That's something we should be ashamed of, no doubt about it. But if we are trying to preserve the moral fiber of society, then we can't go around weakening it with confessions of our own weakness! Peter the Great was a number-one fucker, right? But look at the country he built! Anyway, I don't know, if Peter had been missing any of the qualities that everybody would call negative now, I wonder whether he would have been able to . . ."

The more Georgi Alekseevich listened to Kulik, the more astonished he became. What he was saying sounded like the sort of confession a drunk would mutter into a sticky tabletop, but it also was like a speech at some smoky proletarian meeting two days after the revolution. Kulik spoke like a primitive, but he got your attention. He was babbling absolutely unguardedly now, and if tomorrow worked out, and they seized power, then he would be saying the same thing on the television to millions. He had it down smoothly, even prettily.

I wonder what Andrei's pal Oleg would say to this, Georgi Alekseevich thought. Bukin built the whole thing the other way about, starting from the individual man, whom the state had the responsibility to serve. Bukin stuck the pyramid in the ground the other end down.

Kulik was finishing. "But anybody who doesn't agree with us, the hell with him. Like they say in the army, right? 'If you don't know how, we'll show you; if you don't want to, we'll make you!'" Kulik laughed heartily.

"Well, if we have to make them, we'll make them." Georgi Alekseevich nodded.

Just then Kulik stopped dead in his tracks, even throwing his arms up in astonishment. "Wait a minute, what's this?" Then he ran over to a bearded artist who was tacking portraits, or humorous caricatures, really, to a big sheet of plywood. The pictures had been done hurriedly, with a deliberate crudeness. "Just what is this?" he asked, staring at the caricatures.

"Like 'em, pal?" the scrawny artist asked. "Thirty apiece, you pick the mug that moves your heart most. You won't find better on this whole street."

Georgi Alekseevich followed Kulik to glance over the plywood board. The picture in the middle was of the Leader of the World Proletariat, except that the artist had sketched him with enormous ears and two leathery wings, turning Lenin into a bat. To the right was a picture of Stalin, the Leader of All Peoples, his mustache like a boot brush, and above was Gorbachev, beaming like a light bulb. The rest of the board was covered with drawings of other "opponents and supporters," from Cement-Block Yeltsin to Prime Minister Pavlov, whom Muscovites had dubbed "Porcupine," and whose portrait looked it. Right underneath Pavlov was Boris Fedorovich Kulik.

"Thirty apiece, you say?" Georgi Alekseevich asked. "For that one, too?" He pointed at the drawing of Kulik.

"Three tens per asshole, just like I said, and if you want me to do your face, give me fifteen minutes and you'll think I took a snapshot. That'll set you back another twenty, though."

"So, what do you think, shall we get it?" Georgi Alekseevich said, turning to his friend. He almost bit his tongue, he shut up so fast.

Kulik was vermilion to the tips of his pulsating ears, and his lips were flapping soundlessly. Hands rigid, Kulik was rocking heel and toe. He might have been a member of the Politburo of the CPSU, but at the moment he looked like nothing so much as a child's pull-toy devil whose tail was being yanked back and forth.

Slowly, very slowly, his left hand rose, then his index finger unfolded.

"Who gave you permission for this scandalous hooliganism?"

"What?" the caricaturist asked, puzzled.

"I asked who gave you the permission for this."

The artist's face lost its look of good humor.

"Look, pops, you don't like the picture, then just scoot along, quit ruining my view, okay?"

Instead Kulik lunged forward and tried to snatch his caricature from the board. Strange that it wasn't the Lenin that made him mad, Georgi Alekseevich thought distractedly. The picture was fastened with four thumbtacks, so instead of coming free from the board it ripped in half.

"Asshole! That's the best fucker I've got!" the artist shrieked, then punched Kulik in the chest. "Old fool!"

The first to hit him was the gorillalike driver, who leaped from behind Kulik. The artist clutched his belly, sagging forward. The driver hurried him the rest of the way to the pavement with a punch to the back of the head. Two of the artist's competitors tried to come to his assistance, but one was snatched by the bodyguard and the other one dropped to the cobblestones after the driver's nimble karate kick.

A militiaman sprinted toward the fight, but then froze in midstep when the bodyguard, with a dexterity that would have done a magician proud, snatched out his ID. The apeman-driver knelt next to the artist, flipped the pain-huddled body over, and looked the man in the face. Then he bent close and said something.

The artist answered, very softly; the only words Georgi Alekseevich caught clearly were "fucking assholes."

Apparently the driver had been expecting some other reaction, because he swung again, hitting the artist hard in the face.

Kulik stood motionless during the brief battle. The militiaman joined the bodyguard, frozen in stiff respect at Kulik's back; no doubt he was waiting for an order to cart the artist off to the station as soon as the man unbent enough to walk. Kulik wadded up the portrait he had ripped from the board, thought a moment longer, and then stuck the picture in his pocket and stormed off.

"Let's get out of here." He nodded to Georgi Alekseevich, who was dumbfounded by the scene that had just played out in front of him, with no idea what he should have done. The fight had been disgusting, and it made him ashamed that he was a member of this mighty clan that could do whatever it wanted. He followed a pace behind Kulik, trying to decide what to say to the man if he should ask Georgi's opinion of what had just happened.

When they turned the corner into a side street, Georgi Alekseevich glanced back. The artist was sitting on the ground, glaring at the two of them.

19

A Stroll on
the Arbat Ends

Just as they reached the alley, the apelike driver loomed up behind them to say in a worried and surprisingly human voice, "Boris Fedorovich, better let me bring the car up. You wait here, you and Georgi Alekseevich just take it easy, and I won't be ten minutes. Just wait."

The bodyguard stood a little way off, waiting for the bosses to decide. He was like a spring, ready to expand instantaneously, flinging himself to the defense of his charge. However, his charge was no longer in need of any defending.

"He's right," Georgi Alekseevich said after Kulik had remained silent a long time. "He can go get the car, and we'll stroll toward him."

"All right, you run off and we'll take a walk," Kulik finally decided.

The driver vanished.

The bodyguard followed along behind like a ghost.

"You see, Georgi, that's the kind of crap you're always sticking up for."

"God no, I wouldn't even dream of it."

"Come on, don't lie to me. I could tell by the look on your face that you were taking his side. Don't lie to me."

"Number one, nobody can ever tell anything from my face.

That's what everybody says. But I would have to say that some of us are a little short on humor."

"What humor? What is it that we are supposed to laugh at?"

"It wouldn't hurt to laugh at ourselves occasionally."

"At ourselves, all right, maybe. I'd even do it myself. But look, it wasn't that those nasty pictures were of me, or Gorby, or Yeltsin. It wasn't even the one of Lenin. It was that he was drawing the whole government with bat ears and a blue nose. The *government*, the *state*! You understand what I mean? And what kind of fool is going to respect a state that has a hideous face like that?"

"Come on, the *state*?"

"That's right, Georgi, the state, because that's what we stand for. The state. We are that state. That's why we can't permit this."

Georgi Alekseevich remained silent. He didn't feel like arguing. In fact, he couldn't, because in principle he agreed with Kulik. But to defend the state in the way Kulik just had out there on the Arbat, that he couldn't do.

"Look, Georgi, excuse me for saying this, but as long as I'm talking, I have to tell you that you've messed up with that son of yours, too. There's a kid who could have a beautiful career. All of us would have helped you set him up, move him along. But he took up with the sociology nonsense instead. Come on, think about it. What do those people study? Who needs all that muck? The important thing is to get the people organized properly, tell them what they have to do and what they can't do. What they should spend their time doing. What I'm trying to say is, that Andrei of yours, he's no dummy. He could have gone far, except you didn't put a good word or two in his ear when you should have, did you? You let him down—and us, too."

Georgi Alekseevich didn't even feel like responding to that. What he wanted more than anything right now was to get away from Kulik, lock himself in his apartment, and turn off the telephone. Even better would be to find Andrei at home when he got there, back safe and sound. Unfortunately, that was already impossible.

"You have to release Andrei immediately."

"Of course, of course. Just wait until things start, and then you can take care of him. The fellows out at that place already know about it."

"You think things will end that quickly?"

"Well, I'm no prophet, but I think inside of a day we'll be all right. Incidentally, tomorrow I'm sending you a draft of a new law on criminal liability. You look it over, see what it's about."

"Why me?"

"So things are done right. And besides, the law is just a pleasant thing to read, actually, after all this . . . well, you know. Everybody's going to understand immediately what we want, what we're after, you might say. Ah, look, our chariot approaches. . . ."

The huge Chaika pulled up slowly. The driver braked slightly, and the bodyguard opened the limousine's door nimbly and elegantly.

"We'll drop you off at home, Georgi, and then I'm going on. I've got a lot to do today, as you can imagine. Enough to keep me and two others like me busy, really."

When he got out of the car, Georgi Alekseevich dashed into the vestibule, impatiently rode the elevator up to his floor, and burst through his door, bolting it behind him, even setting the security chain. Outside he couldn't get away; the building and even the vestibule were watched around the clock. But this thin little chain on the door, at least, was a lock that he could use to shut out the rest of the world, the world of Kulik and Khokhriakov and everything they and the others were trying to do. God, what he wouldn't give to know where his Andrei was!

He scuttled into the bath and stood under the pleasant stream of a tepid shower. Then, eyes clenched tight, he washed his hair, turning his face upright into the shower. He dried himself briskly with a rough towel. Then, the towel wrapped about him, he went out to the kitchen, where he gulped down iced tea.

The telephone rang.

Damn, I forgot to unplug it, he thought. Probably Tanya. The sense of heaviness, which the shower had washed away for a moment, returned; he pondered for a moment, then decided that when all was said and done the girl was going to be his daughter-in-law. He picked up the receiver.

Except that it wasn't Tanya.

Georgi Alekseevich knew the voice exceedingly well but couldn't comprehend why this voice—the voice of Russia's number-one democrat!—was coming out of his telephone.

The caller was confident that he would be recognized, but he said his name anyway. He apologized for calling about business on a Saturday (apologizing was not something the old bosses ever did), then asked Georgi Alekseevich to come see him that day, if it wouldn't be too much to ask. As agreeable as an old family servant, Georgi Alekseevich immediately replied, "Just name the time!"

"Right now, if you can."

"I'll call for a car."

"Actually there's one on the way," the voice said softly.

"Then I'll go down and wait."

Remembering that the man he was going to see frequently went out in public with his collar open, tieless, in just his shirtsleeves, Georgi Alekseevich put on his turtleneck, which he persisted in calling by the old-fashioned name of "tunic," then put on his rumpled old pants and a pair of old walking boots that were still covered with country dust.

The car pulled up precisely ten minutes after Georgi Alekseevich had gone downstairs; that meant the car had actually been sent after their conversation, not before. That was something new, too; in the old days everything was done first, then you were told.

Russia's number-one democrat lived nearby in a dacha. His office, neither large nor imposing, was fitted with bookshelves on which the books were arranged in no particular order. Newspapers were scattered about the green carpet, and a tape recorder had been dumped in one corner of the couch. None of this inclined a visitor to Democrat Number One to brace himself military-style for a "serious and frank discussion," as the old order-issuing sessions had been called. The democrat himself, dressed in sweatpants, looked like a soccer coach who had suddenly been put in charge of some ministry, the function of which he was not yet entirely sure he understood.

The man came to meet Georgi Alekseevich rather than waiting, as bosses normally did. He extended his huge hand, which out of earshot some of his underlings called a "steam shovel."

"Take a chair for a second, will you, please, Georgi Alekseevich? I've got a couple of questions of what you might call a strategical nature."

The questions were quite simple, so that Georgi Alekseevich was able to answer them confidently, without stumbling. He was being asked about how matters stood in his department, and especially what the perspectives were for conversion of military production to consumer uses. Georgi Alekseevich didn't even realize that he had become interested in what he was saying, even animated, so that he found himself offering some ideas and opinions he had never meant to give to Democrat Number One because he didn't want to help the man.

The man listened closely, his small, clever eyes watching Georgi Alekseevich's face every second; the visitor found this attention flattering. There was just one thing he didn't like, that Democrat Number One was so insistent about trying to get every last nuance of this improvised report; whenever there was a point that he didn't understand, he would keep asking questions until he finally got it. That wasn't any way for important political bosses to behave.

A half hour passed unnoticed, then more.

Occasionally the democrat's eyes seemed to spark, and he would peer even more intently at Georgi Alekseevich's face.

Eventually both of them grew a little weary, and Georgi Alekseevich found himself regretting that he was going to have to leave this comfortable office.

Finally the democrat stood up.

"Thank you, thank you enormously. And I'll apologize again that we had to call you out on a Saturday. You were resting, right?"

"That's right."

"Well, that's how things are, I guess. Business."

He held out his "steam shovel" again.

Georgi Alekseevich was already on his way out the door when the democrat coughed, cleared his throat, and then said, "Just one more question, if I may. A little more random, I suppose, but it's a question that affects *all* of us, really. . . ." He seemed particularly to stress the "all." "Do you think there's going to be a coup?"

"I beg your pardon, I don't quite get—"

"Don't you think that we're headed for some kind of explosion? A revolution of some kind?"

Georgi Alekseevich felt as though he could not breathe.

"Do you ask that of all your visitors?" he managed to say.

"No. I am especially curious to hear your opinion, though."

There was no time for thinking. The faces of the men who had gathered in Kulik's office the day before ran through his mind.

"I'm not the man to ask that question."

"Why not? We know you're a trustworthy man."

The two men studied each other in silence, and then Georgi Alekseevich left the office.

He was a grown man, almost an old man, and here he was trembling like the brattiest of little liars, almost dumping in his trousers at the question, even though he still had had the guts (or maybe the brass) to lie right in the fellow's face. Of course, he couldn't have told the man the truth. But to tell a bald lie like that, looking the man right in the eyes, that was repugnant.

When he got back to his apartment, Georgi Alekseevich

ripped the phone out of the wall. That was it, he was done. No more of this nonstop, twenty-four-hour bullshit. He wasn't a politician, he was a working man, damn it! A shop foreman, a factory director. All right, maybe even a minister. Let all those political types gnaw one another to the bone if they wanted to, the hell with them! What he ought to do was get Andrei out of their clutches and then get the hell out of Moscow. Go to Yalta maybe, or Sochi. He had already survived two minor heart attacks, for God's sake! He had the right to rest, to heal. At least he had to get Andrei out of trouble, marry him off to Tanya. Let them make him a grandfather.

He caught his reflection in the mirror; he saw a tough, angry face, fit for a man in a position of authority. It seemed to ask him, All right, so what happened, really? What's got you almost pissing on your shoes? You've never been around when a couple of heavyweights square off? Feeling sorry about your baby boy, are you? You've maybe forgotten that this is the same baby boy who tried to sell you out to the Americans? And this is why you got butterflies? Because you had to tell one lie to Comrade Democrat there?

The person in the mirror looked so much like he knew what he was doing that Georgi Alekseevich actually felt better. He shook his head; the mirror man did the same. Then he laughed and stuck out his tongue at his reflection. The mirror man laughed back.

"Order, that's the thing," Georgi Alekseevich said.

Total order, the mirror agreed.

The doorbell rang.

Had he not been feeling better, Georgi Alekseevich wouldn't have answered. But he did. It was Khokhriakov.

"Viktor?" Georgi Alekseevich asked, surprised and puzzled.

"You don't recognize me or something?"

"Of course. Come on in, come in. . . ."

"Georgi, why did you go to *his* dacha?"

That question cut the knees out from under the totally unsuspecting Georgi Alekseevich, particularly since Khokhriakov asked it in the crude, insinuating manner of some hick KGB officer out in some cowshit country office. Khokhriakov fixed Georgi Alekseevich with an unblinking, gimlet eye, as if wanting to make very clear to the apartment's owner that this was an interrogation, not just idle questions.

Fighting back an urge to throw his visitor down the stairwell, Georgi Alekseevich tried to keep his answer light, jokey. "When the bosses give orders, the proletariat says, 'Yes, *Sir*!'"

"This is a serious question. Why did you drag your butt over there?"

"Open your ears and pay attention, General. I didn't drag my butt, I went in a car. A car that they sent for me, because I was summoned on short notice to give a report about the committee that I am in charge of."

"On a Saturday evening?"

"You may have read about how when Mustache was in charge people got pulled out of bed in the middle of the night, and then were forbidden to tell anybody where they had been, or why."

"Don't get clever with me! We've got reports that you skipped down that staircase and waltzed into that car! Reports, you understand what I'm telling you?"

"Meaning I'm being followed now, too?"

That confused Khokhriakov.

"Not exactly followed . . ."

"Just sort of followed, right?"

"I didn't say you were followed. I said there were reports."

Jesus, what a moron you are, Georgi Alekseevich thought wearily, then said, "All right, enough shouting. Why don't you tell me instead what's happened?"

General Khokhriakov wasn't able to say anything very coherent, and, in fact, there wasn't much *to* say. It was nonsense, the whole thing. Kulik's people in the KGB had seen Democrat Number One's car deliver Georgi Alekseevich to the dacha, news they had passed along to Kulik immediately. Still feeling angry after his stroll along the Arbat, Kulik had phoned almost-Marshal Vitya, ordering him to "check into this." Khokhriakov had no idea what "this" was, nor how to check into it, but instead had come over immediately to the apartment of his old friend to demand an explanation. As soon as he heard Georgi Alekseevich's answer he was completely reassured, but had no idea how to behave. The suddenness with which he had just appeared, and the accusing way he had begun the conversation, all that now looked ridiculous in the light of the simple answers he had just gotten from this unruffled and unrepentant "turncoat."

Georgi Alekseevich studied his visitor, who had fallen into confused silence. He was interested to learn that he was now being watched. That meant they didn't trust him, obviously. Apparently they had stopped trusting him recently. Maybe because of the business with his son. Yesterday, maybe; maybe even today, this afternoon. Maybe Kulik hadn't liked how he had behaved on the Arbat during their walk. Not that they would do anything to him, of course. Not now, anyway. Later, after they had succeeded, they would remember all this vacillation.

Khokhriakov was still shifting from foot to foot in the doorway.

"Well, I guess I'll be going, then," he said.

"What's the hurry? You come flying in here, all bent out of shape, and now you're flapping off again. Why don't you have a seat instead, let us chat a little?"

"About what?"

"Hey, Viktor, my friend," Georgi Alekseevich suddenly said, "and if the whole thing falls through, what are we going to do then, eh? Maybe we should talk about that!"

"What do you mean? If what falls through? Bite your tongue, man. What we're doing is the right thing."

"All right, it's the right thing, but even so . . ."

Khokhriakov scowled. "Fuck the lot of you, that's what. You're throwing sand in your own gearbox, bunch of pussies. We've made up our minds, so all that's left to do is act on it. Like in the army."

"Yeah, you're right, like in the army. We have to act intelligently, do everything precisely. And not go into hysterics about it."

"Why do you say that?"

"Because our good friend Boris Fedorovich is acting like an old woman, that's why. I mean, I'm correct in guessing that he's the one who sent you over here, right?"

Khokhriakov remained stubbornly, but tellingly, silent.

"You're doing the right thing, keeping your tongue to yourself. But that means I guessed right, doesn't it? You can tell Kulik if he wants to find cowards and traitors, this isn't the place to look. And starting something like this without complete and absolute trust in one another, that's as good as being whipped before we start."

Khokhriakov nodded.

"See, you think so, too. So tell him that, from the both of us. He has to trust us, and us him, when we start something like this."

"All right, Georgi, I guess you're probably right. Being suspicious of each other could get us to make mistakes. So, just between us"—he stressed the "us"—"has he gotten suspicious? You know who I mean."

If I say that our Kremlin friend suspects something, they'll just delay the event. And anyway, then I'd have to admit that we talked about something other than work, Georgi Alekseevich mused, not quick to answer.

Khokhriakov sensed that. "Why aren't you saying anything? You're saying that there was something, then, aren't you?"

"No, I'm not. Nothing happened. He didn't ask me about anything other than work, and he doesn't suspect anything. At least, that's how it seemed to me."

"Thank God for that."

Well, that's another lie, Georgi Alekseevich thought. Now I've lied to both sides. Why did I do that? I have no idea. If my Andrei were here now, I'd ask him what to do for sure. I'd just tell him, straight out. Although, come to think of it, that's what I did do. And look how that worked out; he's wherever he is . . . and I sent him there, too. And here I am. Under suspicion myself.

"Viktor," he asked Khokhriakov, "tell me the truth. Am I being followed now?"

Khokhriakov had to think about it, which meant he didn't know himself.

"Don't tax your brain," Georgi Alekseevich interrupted, to put a stop to the general's obvious torment. "They can do whatever they want to."

Khokhriakov studied his friend gloomily, then said, "I'd better go. I've got a lot to do. I'm sorry if I did something wrong. I tried to think how to do it best. Best for you, I mean."

"Sure, sure. You go have a rest. We've got an awful lot ahead of us. Keep your strength up, you know?"

They parted as friends.

After the general left, Georgi Alekseevich went out onto his balcony and looked about. The first thing to catch his eye was a bright red Zhiguli parked precisely where the car in which they had carried away his son had been this morning.

"Fucking parasites," he muttered angrily, then went back into his apartment, wondering what exactly Democrat Number One had meant by asking him about the likelihood of an uprising or coup of some sort. Why *him*, of all people?

20
Information Received

Democrat Number One was wily, but not omniscient. He had found Georgi Alekseevich out entirely by chance.

Dale Cooper had no idea how much more his body—that of a correspondent, after all—would be able to endure. The narcotic he had been given in spite of the nice nurse's advice was still working on him when he came to. As he had the last times he came to, he saw the long crack in the ceiling over his head, and he inhaled the same starchy-linen pillowcase smell, wrapped around a rock-hard hospital pillow.

The reporter realized that his hospital room had been turned into a cell in which he was now locked. He could continue to lie there as long as he wanted to, not trying to do anything, studying that same stupid ceiling. Or he could try to do something again, like the last time, for which he would get another jab of drugs, or some hospital toughs would just happen to attack him. Or maybe something heavy and hard would accidentally fall on his head. Either way, Dale Cooper would once again find himself completely defenseless and powerless in the hands of all these bastards.

He was also thinking that a story about all that had happened to him could be just as big a sensation as an account of a coup, especially since everybody would know about a coup a day or so after it happened.

After thinking like that for a while, though, Dale remembered the guy Andrei who had promised to tell him more details about the coup conspiracy. The Russian guy really was counting on Dale to help, as if the article would somehow halt the conspirators—force them to put off their plans or at least to change them—some time between when Dale sent out the information and when it was set into newspaper type.

That seemed pretty funny, especially when you considered how unfunny his present situation was. Dale Cooper, Savior of Mother Russia.

Even so, though, it seemed worth trying. One last time, anyway. Not because of the Russian, whom he scarcely knew. And not because of Russia, either.

Because of Dale. Because he wanted to feel he had done the right thing. And also to let these damn KGB types know that it would take more than a beating and some drugs to stop Dale Cooper.

That thought made Dale furious. He wanted to beat them now, simply on principle. He wanted to get back at them for all the humiliations he had suffered at their hands over the last few hours.

The only way he could do that, he knew, was to get out the news that Andrei and Oleg had given him.

His last remaining link to the outside world was the big-eyed, kindly nurse who had tried to chat with him. But where was she now? Big soft eyes like that, she'd never do a man false. Or her voice, either. Almost that of a startled child.

But the time was rushing on without stopping. Dale heard no noise of any sort, not in the hall, not around his door.

He wanted to try to get up again, then force his trembly limbs to move, to do what he instructed them. Unfortunately, though, the drug that seemed to do nothing to his brain had absolutely paralyzed his body.

At last he heard a squeak; someone was opening the door. Carefully, as if whoever was opening it was afraid some rule was being broken. Then he heard quick, light steps across the room, then the nurse's familiar breathing. He saw her eyes.

You feeling better? the eyes inquired silently.

Dale fluttered his eyelids: yes.

"Can you talk?" she asked softly.

"Yes," Dale said, surprised that, in fact, he could, although he was also appalled at how weak his voice sounded.

"You're a foreigner, aren't you?"

"American."

"Why don't they want you to talk?"

"They're still here?"

"Yes, but your guard is asleep. Everyone's sure you're still out cold."

"What's your name?"

"Marina."

"Marina, I swear, I'm not a spy, and I'm not a drug addict. . . ."

"I know that."

"How?"

"They're afraid of you. I can see by their faces that they're afraid of you."

"Marina, I need your help."

He didn't hear her say anything. She was thinking. Obviously she sympathized with him, but would she take risks for him?

"Marina, are they KGB?"

"Yes."

"What do they want?"

"They want you to sleep."

"For how long?"

"Until Monday. That's what one of them said. 'Let him lie here until Monday, and then he can go to hell for all it matters.' "

"You're sure you heard that? 'Until Monday'?"

"I'm sure."

"Will you help me? This is something terribly important. You have to believe me. I'm not a spy."

"I believe you."

Someone came into the room. Marina leaped back.

"What are you doing here?" Dale heard someone bark.

"What you told me to. I'm doing what I can to help. I was coming by the room and heard him choking, so I came in to turn him over. You know, he could die, choking on his own saliva."

"You should have checked with me first."

"You were sound asleep."

"Like hell I was! I was just resting a little."

"Well, I didn't want . . ."

"What?"

"To wake you, I didn't want to wake you."

"All right, all right." Dale heard the man chuckle, then slap the nurse's behind.

"Hey, what are you doing? You should be ashamed of yourself!"

"Whoo, prickly as a porcupine! All right, all right, I apologize. Just a joke. So how's our boy?"

"Your boy is asleep."

"Just what the doctor ordered, isn't it? Sleep, sleep, and more sleep."

Suddenly Dale felt somebody shaking him. He kept his eyes clamped tight, held his breath.

"Sleeping, sure enough," the man said again. "Well, we'll let him have a good rest, won't we? And if anything else comes up, you tell me first, got it?"

"Of course. I'll even wake you if I have to."

"How many times do I have to tell you that when I'm on duty I never sleep?"

"Ah, you mean you're on duty now? I was—"

"What did you think I was doing? There's a song about us, you know? 'Our duty's hard and dangerous . . .' "

"Sure, I know the song."

"So, you keep an eye on him, all right?"

"Can I straighten his pillow for him?"

"Sure, go ahead. And listen, drop by if you get bored."

"We don't have time to get bored at work."

Then the two spoke quickly, very softly, but in such short phrases that Dale had no trouble getting the drift.

Then the guard left with a warning to the nurse. "Do what you have to do here, and don't be long about it. You've got no business here, really."

Marina waited until he left, then a moment longer. At last she leaned over Dale to straighten his pillow.

"He's gone," she whispered.

Dale opened his eyes.

"Marina, I'm a correspondent." He told her which paper he worked for. "I've discovered just by chance that tomorrow or the day after the Communists are going to try a coup here in Moscow. That's a fact. The man who told me has been killed. There's one more fellow who knows, and he was going to say more, except that I was attacked and beaten. You understand what I'm telling you, Marina? I'm having trouble talking, it hurts. I'm weak. You're not saying anything."

"I'm thinking. Why are you telling me this?"

Now Dale was silent.

"Did you hear me? Did you hear what I said?" she asked.

Still Dale said nothing.

"Did you hear me?" she repeated.

"I did," he said.

"So what do you want from me?"

"The people who brought this information to me wanted to warn people, but they were afraid that no one would believe them."

"Yes, everybody is saying things like that now."

"Except what they were saying is true. All of it."

Marina was beginning to guess what the American wanted her to do. He was beginning to slip back into a coma.

"I guess I could give you a phone number for our embassy. Or another journalist. But it's real late now. Nobody would believe you."

"But they would come here, wouldn't they?"

"To be told that I was unconscious and nobody knew who I was. And you'll never be able to prove otherwise. You're afraid of them, too, aren't you? And tomorrow they're going to seize power. Or the day after."

"That's right, I'm afraid of them."

"See what I mean?"

She took the American's hand. It was cold, his pulse weak.

"Tell me everything you know." She had decided.

"What do you plan to do?"

"We don't have time for this. You're about to black out again."

"What? Speak up, I can't hear you."

Marina pressed close to his ear. Dale saw her as if through a fog.

"I said . . ." Dale squeezed out his story as if with his last strength.

Marina's large eyes never wavered.

"That's it?" she said when he finished.

"Yes," he said, already lapsing into English, and then there was silence.

Marina sat a minute longer on the patient's bed. Then, slamming down her heels deliberately hard, she crossed to the door and went out into the corridor. The guard was drowsing at the far end of the hall. When he saw her, he perked up.

"Hey, it's my friend Nurse Marina! See, I found out your name, didn't I? So what took you so long in there, eh? Come on, sit down, take a load off your feet."

Fighting back an angry answer, Marina smiled. "All right, lover boy, I will. Just let me run back to the front desk, and then I'll be right back."

"What do you have to do there?"

"Comrade Boss, that's no affair of yours," she said tartly, and then walked briskly into the next hall.

There was no one at the main desk. A low-watt lamp hooded in black plastic cast a dull light. There was a Japanese calendar on the wall from which a bikini-clad beauty gazed down on the scarred desk. A big, square, old-fashioned clock ticked loudly and evenly. At the far end of the desk was a little cabinet on top of which, instead of the usual withered bouquet, there was a yellowish telephone, the receiver clumsily repaired with tape.

Marina dialed.

"Yes, hello!" a pleasant female voice answered.

"Good evening. Please, may I have Vikenty Illarionich?"

"He's not in the office right now. Please call back tomorrow. May I ask who's calling, please?"

"Thank you," Marina said, her plan in ruins. And it had been such a simple plan. Foolproof, it had seemed.

Four years before, she had taken a refresher course, the opening lecture for which had been given by a real star, Academician Vikenty Illarionich Udaltsov. Udaltsov was a pleasant fellow, far from old, who wore an old-fashioned goatee; he had made an enormous impression on the nurses. Sometime after that the academician had stood for a deputy's seat in the Congress, and Marina had headed up a big drive in the hospital to support him. During one of Udaltsov's speeches Marina got to know one of his assistants, a young surgeon. For no reason that Marina could understand, this man had given her one of Udaltsov's business cards. On the card were both his work telephone and his home number.

Udaltsov had won his seat, and now his portly face was well-known on the television. He was quick to give interviews, and his confident academician's voice came over the radio about once a week. He had become a solid palace guard for the new elite that was coming to power, and perhaps was even preparing to move out of the guard, to play a leading role himself.

Marina had written both of Udaltsov's numbers in her phone directory, taking secret pride in her tangential access to one of the world's powerful figures. Tonight she had decided to put this "acquaintance" to use, but the academician wasn't at his office. She was afraid to call him at home. And anyway, what would she say to him?

Marina clutched the broken receiver to her chest indecisively, biting her lip.

Then she opened her book again and dialed the first three digits of the forbidden number. Then she paused, thought, and hung up.

There was very little time left. Somebody might walk into the main office any moment. Marina took a pencil from the desk and began to take notes on what she had to tell the academician. Who she was, what was going to occur, when, how she had found out, and . . . well, it would be enough to start with that. She dialed.

"Vikenty Illarionich, please."

"Speaking."

"Eeek!" Marina squealed, and then forgot everything she had planned, instead babbling it all out in one long breath, giving the man no time to think.

"Who is this talking? I mean, what kind of nonsense is this?"

"It's the truth, you have to believe it's the truth. Please."

"What's the truth? Why do I have to believe it?"

"Just believe me, tell them there . . ."

The man said nothing.

"Well, good-bye then," Marina finally said in a weak voice.

She left the main desk and wandered out into the hall, shaking. She had completely forgotten that she had promised the vigilant KGB agent to lighten his duty hours with her presence.

The guard had been waiting impatiently. He leaped up when she came in.

"What took you so long? I was waiting, worrying . . ."

"Work. I had . . . things to do."

She sat next to her new admirer, but apparently he was already having second thoughts about his amorous intentions. He seemed to want to talk more than anything. Marina didn't mind one bit; she settled herself to listen to him.

The KGB man began his complaints in a roundabout way, talking of how hard it was to have the sort of job he did. Saying that even the people who were closest to him didn't understand him, that he couldn't even tell his own mother what it was he did. He kept glancing at Marina out of the corners of his yellowish eyes, either hoping to see some sympathy or perhaps simply afraid that he was boring her.

He was now utterly unlike the forward, presumptive ass he had seemed when he first came to her in the ward. She was even beginning to feel a bit sorry for him. She could sympathize; her work wasn't so pleasant, either. She also wondered from time to time why it was she had made the decision, ten years ago, to go into nursing, especially since now she just didn't have the energy to switch professions.

When the man finally got tired of talking, she began telling him about some of the patients who had been in her ward. How sorry she felt for some of them, and how mad others made her. How depressed she got sometimes when she walked onto the ward with its ugly beds filled with helpless sick people.

The tired, fortyish man with a melancholy face listened attentively, with sympathy. He even began to stare, not taking his eyes from her face, her hands. She recalled after a while that she hadn't even bothered to find out his name. Now it would be embarrassing; it was too late. She liked the man; he seemed to be someone you could count on. Marina almost forgot why it was that the man was sitting there.

"Are you going to be here . . ."

"You want to ask how long I'll be here?"

"Well, yes."

"As long as your patient is here."

Then she remembered that she had deceived him with that stuff she had said on the telephone. . . . Brr, she thought, relieved that he wouldn't find out about it. She was actually ashamed of herself, first whispering the way she had with the patient, then sitting here having a heart-to-heart with this man.

Now and again nurses scuttled past on their various errands, glancing curiously at the pair of them. Suddenly one of them stopped and asked, eyes averted, "Are you Kolomiitsev? "

"That's me," the man said.

There's that much anyway, Marina thought. Now to find out his first name.

"You're wanted on the telephone, out at the main desk."

"I'll be right back," he said to Marina. "Just stay where you are, please."

He came back three minutes later, his face grim.

Marina was still on the little bench where they had been talking.

He bent close over her and gave a quiet order. "Come with me, please."

Marina stood and, still not completely understanding what was happening, she moved toward Dale Cooper's room.

"No, not that way. You've already done everything you could do there."

He pointed in the other direction, and she followed him silently. At one of the intersections of the corridors he told her to stop. Then he got a key from his pocket and opened a wardroom that had been empty for as long as Marina had worked there. Ages ago, Lenin had been brought to this room after he was wounded by a would-be assassin, and ever since the ward had been a kind of holy relic, and so was kept locked and empty.

Kolomiitsev gestured the nurse into "Lenin's ward" and, in a neutral voice, told her to sit down on the ward's sole bed.

Marina did as she was ordered.

"You're a piece of shit, girl, a real piece of shit," he said, grabbing her shoulders. "You know what you did? You know what's going to happen to you because of what you did?"

She said nothing, her head hanging down.

"You had to wag your tongue, didn't you? How much did they pay you for that? You can thank God that it was me on duty and not somebody else. You're an idiot, girl, a fool." He looked over at the door. "I'm going to leave you locked in here until they come to take you away." Then, leaning right against her ear, he whispered, "What did you want to do all that for, anyway?"

Then he left.

Academic Vikenty Udaltsov didn't believe the telephone message, but he felt he had no right to ignore it completely, either. As it happened, just after the call he was supposed to attend a session of the Ecology Committee, which was chaired by one of the newly baked Russian ministers who was rumored to have good access to the "throne." The academician made a good story of his mysterious phone call, with suitable irony. The minister laughed heartily.

However, it wasn't more than a half hour after that session that Georgi Alekseevich was invited around for his "chat" with Democrat Number One.

21
End of the Summer Vacation Season

"Well, well," the gray-haired one said. "You won't find a better guard for you than her, Andrei Georgievich."

"Why would he want to go anywhere?" Maksim agreed. "Now he's got a lady friend, and what to eat, and besides, who knows what might happen outside? A fellow could get beat up or something. Come on, you can kiss the bridegroom." He pushed Tanya in Andrei's direction.

"Don't you dare." Andrei stepped toward Maksim, who did not even flinch.

"He does dare, Andrei Georgievich, he does. And I'd advise you to be a little more careful. Not to mention polite. This man is performing the duty he has been ordered to perform, which means that he has the right—"

"To shove a woman?"

"The right to act as the situation warrants."

Andrei looked from Tanya to the gray-haired man, then to Maksim. He had no idea of what he ought to do, how he should act so as to avoid getting himself and Tanya killed, or at least to avoid making Tanya's already dreadful position even worse. Obviously something had happened in Moscow that had ended his father's ability to protect him, or, the best that could be said, made that protection eggshell thin.

The gray-haired man also looked at Maksim, then nodded. Maksim shrugged, scowled.

"You two should probably chat alone," the gray-haired man said to Andrei. "See you soon."

Both guards left, and Tanya hugged Andrei. She sketched quickly how she had been picked up right at the entrance to her building. The whole thing had been elegantly and politely done. She had not had time even to blink before she was in the car and racing out here. All she had been told was that Andrei desperately needed her help. She had almost believed the men, and so had been almost calm. The calm had lasted until they arrived, when some tough-looking type had come out to the car, looked her over from head to foot, and then growled, "So that's the last of our chickens rounded up." It was then that she understood that something horrible had happened.

Andrei listened, silent. The nightmare of the anonymous photographs suddenly seemed real, close.

Her story told, Tatyana sat down, sighed heavily.

"So, what do you make of all this?"

"I think that we'll be leaving here pretty soon, but for right now we should just sit."

"What do you mean, sit? You don't want to fight these guys? You giving up already? I mean, this is all illegal, you know. God knows what's going on. Have you tried to get in touch with your father?"

"What for?"

"What do you mean, what for? So these thugs would find out who it is they're—"

"Tanya, try to be a little more polite, please. No need to call people names. After all, they are listening to all this."

"So, we're not alone? They're listening?"

"Or taping."

"Even better, then, that they should know what I think of them! Especially since"—she leaned closer to him and, almost silently, whispered—"we're going to escape."

Andrei shook his head, then crossed his arms to indicate that flight would be pointless.

She got up from her chair, came right up to him and whispered into his ear, "You're sure there's no point?"

He whispered back, "I already tried."

"Assholes! The whole bunch of them are assholes, and I don't care if they hear me say so!"

"Stop it, that doesn't help anything."

Tanya kicked off her shoes and stretched out on the bed, closed her eyes. It was very quiet. The only noise was the woman's deep, steady breathing. Andrei studied Tanya's face, which was just beginning to show some freckles he had never noticed before. Her toes twitched as if she were trying to stretch fully to the end of the bed. Eventually even that stopped.

Andrei was utterly helpless now. They had taken her as hostage, and he was completely in their hands. There was no possibility whatever of flight. Now they would begin to interrogate him, asking whom he had passed his father's indiscretions along to. Andrei had no idea how he would behave when they did.

So much had happened over the past forty-eight hours that he couldn't even arrange events into some kind of logical order. He kept mixing up what had come first, what later. Certainly if he couldn't even make a chronology there was no possibility that he would be able to analyze any of the events independent of the others. The only thing that seemed wholly clear was that the father's name had somehow ceased to guarantee the son's relative inviolability. Unfortunately, that meant that they were now wholly defenseless. Andrei could not drive the memory of Maksim's ugly face from his imagination.

Eventually Maksim came in.

He opened the door silently, walked to the middle of the room, glanced at Tanya stretched out on the bed, and then said in a loud, flat, and lifeless voice, "We have to talk, Andrei

Georgievich. As you know, there are a number of questions we'd like to ask you."

"I have already told you everything that I have to say."

"Taking account of certain changes in circumstances"—he nodded at Tanya on the bed, who had instinctively tugged her skirt lower down her pink legs—"there is some point in continuing our conversation further. As for you, my dear young lady, I should warn you that your irresponsible chatter not only does not put you in the best of lights, but even might create certain definite ideas about the state of your morality. Or, more exactly, about your moral profile, shall we say?"

"You can go and stuff it," Tanya said indifferently.

"Lady, if I feel like it, I can go and stuff *you*," Maksim growled, taking a slow step in her direction.

Tanya slid away, toward the wall.

"See, I scared you," he said.

"All right, all right," Andrei interrupted. "If you want to talk, probably this isn't the best place."

"You're right there. We'll leave the lady to her rest. For the time being, anyway."

They left, and Tanya remained behind. She gathered what little strength remained after the events of the day. Actually, it seemed as though perhaps she had more left than she had thought. She was able to suppress even her terror for Andrei. The main thing is to work out some general idea of how to behave. I can't let them see that I'm afraid. They're like strange dogs; you don't want to let them think you're afraid. Dogs are dogs, but these might even come to respect you, even if they don't want to. You'll never get through to them any other way. On the other hand, she realized as she thought about it, she was superfluous here. They had brought her because of Andrei. They were going to use her to get him to tell them something. Did they want her to talk him into telling them whatever it was? If that was the case, what they had heard her say over their microphones or through their bugs would tell them that that would never work, and that they would have to find some other approach.

It was that which terrified her, that "other approach."

The year before she had seen some Swedish film in which terrorists, or maybe gangsters, had tortured a wife in front of her husband—or maybe it was a fiancée in front of her beloved, she couldn't remember. The torture scene, sadistic as it was—and they had shown the rape of the unlucky girl in great detail, at considerable length—had kind of excited her. Now she looked at the thing in a much different light. After all, the KGB men were not some terrorists in a movie, and there was nothing that they were trying to squeeze out of her and Andrei. But still . . .

Tanya swung her legs down off the bed and stood on the small, flowery bedside rug. She went to the window.

There wasn't a soul about, nobody moving on the open space in front of the building. It was like Sleeping Beauty's castle, waiting for a prince on a white horse, carrying his spear. Or maybe a fairy-tale witch's hut on chicken legs. And from over there a bear walking like a man would come out of the forest and go into the hut, just like in the fairy tales.

And then the witch Baba Yaga would come out of the hut.

However, instead of Baba Yaga or a fairy-tale bear, it was a gray Moskvich that drove up the road and stopped in front of the building. The driver hauled himself out and went inside. About three minutes later she heard a ruckus in the hall. Tanya tried to peek out but discovered that the door was locked. That was a nasty surprise. She went back to her observation point at the window and settled down to watch.

Three men came out of the front door. Two of them were not quite pulling, not quite carrying, the third, who seemed scarcely able to lift his feet. When they got to the car, one of the men opened the back door. The man who was between them, with a huge and shaven head, began to list to one side. His two companions straightened him back up with a couple of healthy kicks to his butt, then forced him down onto the backseat. Just before he vanished into the back of the car, the one with the shaved head looked back at the house, directly at Tanya's window. He nodded. Tanya thought that his face seemed multicolored, somehow.

After the Moskvich pulled away, she understood what the colors were—bleeding cuts from a beating.

This was not a place for jokes, she understood.

When Andrei finally came back, she knew better than to bother him with questions. Especially since a woman in a lilac uniform brought them both lunch as soon as he came in. Actually, it was so late that the chicken soup, fried potatoes, and not-bad steak might almost have been supper.

They ate at a coffee table, speaking only of the food. They praised both the soup and the main course. Unable to restrain herself, Tanya looked up at the ceiling and said loudly, clearly, "Many thanks, comrades!"

"Now somebody will come in and wish you bon appetit," Andrei muttered, trying to pick out the vein he had found in his steak.

"No they won't. They only listen for negative comments. And right now our dear native security men have earned themselves nothing but praise."

They began to laugh, now in earnest. Maybe there was some point in laughing, after all? They were together again, even if they were here. Both were in one piece, and the food wasn't bad at all. It was quiet, and the air was clean. And as for the security men . . . Well, if they had meant them any harm, they would have done it long ago. If you thought about it calmly, nothing had really happened yet, had it? They agreed, it hadn't.

Andrei hadn't been interrogated, really; they had just had another heart-to-heart with him, even hinting that he might be released soon.

And Tanya had seen the mysterious passenger in the Moskvich, naturally fearing that Andrei might be brought back in the same condition, badly beaten, scarcely able to walk. That hadn't happened, either.

"You know what I'd like more than anything right now?"

Andrei was surprised by the question, so she repeated it.

"Come on, guess. What do you think I'd like more than anything right now?"

"No, they're listening to us, they're bugging the room!"

"But they aren't *watching* it!"

"Tanya!"

"What 'Tanya'?"

"We're not alone here."

"The hell with them. The hell with the whole lot of them."
She walked to the middle of the room, stared up at the ceiling.
"Hey, you! If you're bugging the room, have some shame and turn the stuff off for a bit. If you've got a tape going, edit this part out, starting right now! Behave like gentlemen, will you?"

Andrei had long known and admired his companion's extravagant gestures, but this shocked even him.

"Tanya, I . . . I don't want to, not here. I can't . . ."

"You can't or you don't want to?"

"I don't want to."

"Do you want me?"

"I . . ."

"You what?"

"I don't want to!"

"Or 'I don't want you'?" She got up off her chair. "You think you don't want me, eh?" She pulled her shirt off over her head. "If you don't want to, nobody's forcing you." She reached behind her back, undid her bra. Her small, almost childish breasts leaped free, the pale pointed nipples bouncing with every movement. "You think you don't want me?" She stepped out of her skirt. "Come on, come and get me!" she said, trying to shed the last of her clothing, but instead she stepped on her own foot, tripped on the edge of the rug, and almost fell.

Andrei caught her. He hugged her, pulled her to his lips.

"They're watching everything we do."

"So, let them watch."

Tanya pulled them both backward, toward the bed. She flopped down on her back, Andrei half on top of her. His hands remained where they had fallen, on her chest. Cool to the touch, firm. She threw her head back, waiting for him to respond, finally, to her desires. It was a longish wait, but finally his fingers began to knead, squeezing her nipples, causing a light and wonderful pain. The pain flashed to her stomach, then along her thighs to her knees, which grew so weak that it was as if she had drunk vodka with the meal. Her legs slid apart, and then could do no more, for Andrei finally took charge, having forgotten about the KGB, the coming coup, the way he had betrayed his father, the way he had betrayed himself, the mess that he and Tanya were in.

She threw her arms above her head, presenting herself fully to his desire. She closed her eyes, so as to concentrate more fully on her body, which was so intent on pleasure, without regard for troubles or interference.

Her body got its pleasure, but once it had, then it grew grouchy. Her breasts sagged, her toes began to twitch in irritation, and somewhere beneath her belly she felt a strange and unpleasant emptiness.

Andrei pulled away from her, turned his back, wondering whether their room, in fact, was only bugged or if there were cameras, too.

Tanya guessed what he was thinking. "What, you're shy in front of them?"

"Goddamn right I am," he said sharply, even nastily.

"Didn't seem that way to me."

"What are you talking about?"

"You were especially good today. When you're upset about something, usually I can feel it right away."

"Is that true?"

"Yeah, it's like you don't even know what to expect from you."

"Tanya, enough of this conversation."

"You know best, but what are we going to talk about instead?"

"Nothing would be best of all."

"If that's what you want, silence it is."

Andrei stared at the naked Tanya, who had not even shifted her position on the bed. He couldn't make out whether she was ridiculing him or if, in fact, she had caught fire, right here and right now.

It began to grow darker. The silence grew so heavy as to be oppressive. They had been sitting alone together for ages, not even speaking, when Tanya, at last, got up, washed, and dressed. No one entered their room, no one disturbed them. Andrei began to get the odd feeling that Tanya had asked to come here, to be with him in his captivity. Come to think of it, even he had ended up in this summer resort almost voluntarily. So it probably was true that his father really had saved him by hiding him here. Maybe it was even better that things had turned out like this. As for the insulting behavior of the KGB guy Maksim, that was probably just one of those things. The man was a thug, and he had stepped out of line.

Night began to draw in.

Finally there was a noise out in the hall. Andrei took Tanya's hand; she pressed closer to him.

Maksim came in. He studied the pair of them with open irony.

"Having a good time? Or did you wear yourselves out? What, cat got your tongues? I had a good little rest myself, listening to the two of you. . . . Well, you keep right on if you want. Except, Andrei Georgievich, you kind of got carried away with the love stuff and forgot that we want something else from you right now, didn't you?"

Tanya inhaled sharply, angrily, ready to say something, but Andrei dug his nails into the palm of her hand.

Maksim noticed even that.

"Good boy, Andrei, good boy. We don't want any emotions or carrying on here. Save that for your bedtime. That's more the place for that sort of stuff, at which, I must say, you two are very good. Especially you, Tanya, you sweet thing."

Andrei couldn't hold his tongue at that. "I have no idea what your authority is for all this, but I will not permit you to be coarse and offensive!"

"Is that how things are? You talk like that to me, your benefactor? Do you know that I've got orders to be a little more *energetic* with you? You know what that means? That means that if you don't tell me what I want to know, right now, then she'll pay for it. Immediately." He nodded in Tanya's direction.

"Pay how?" Tanya spat out.

"Oh, we've got a whole system worked out. Let's just call it 'what's yours is mine' for right now, all right?"

"What do you mean, 'mine'?"

"Let me show you!" he said, stepping quickly to Tanya; first he yanked her to him, then kneed her onto the bed. She fell back, waving her arms.

A split second later, surprising even himself, Andrei leaped onto Maksim, making both of them crash to the floor. It was only the KGB man who got back up, though. Andrei lay curled on the ground, vast pains in his gut and head, trying to make the room stop spinning about him.

When Andrei finally got control of himself, he saw Maksim sitting on the bed, watching him with interest, one arm holding Tanya tightly. Tanya's eyes were round with horror; she tried to throw herself toward Andrei, but she couldn't break free of Maksim's grip.

"You don't like sitting next to me?" Maksim asked her. "We don't need the boy here anymore. He's chucked you over, hasn't he? He prefers business to you, I guess."

Tanya went into a frenzy, thrashing to get away from him, but he simply crushed her tighter against him. The hand he had had about her neck began to slip lower.

"I'm not kidding, you know. He really did double-deal you. Look, even now he doesn't want to help us." Maksim's fingers were fumbling through her shirt toward her breast.

Tanya turned sharply toward the wall, breaking free of his grip for a second. But Maksim, like an experienced lover, accepted her upper parts as lost and began his assault on her lower half. He flipped up her skirt and began to run his hand along her garter straps. Tanya pushed her knees together and tried to butt him in the face, but he moved smartly aside, so that she seemed almost to fall into his embrace. She shrieked and bit him on the cheek.

"You piece of trash," Maksim swore, then he hit Tanya in the throat. She wilted, looking dazed.

Then Andrei rose from the floor, wavering. He grabbed Maksim by the leg and tried to pull him down to the floor. For a second Maksim lost control because Andrei's appearance was too much of a surprise; he had already written the man off, and the pain-racked, pale face looked like that of a real ghost. With unreal, incomprehensible strength, Andrei pulled Maksim down onto himself. Startled, Maksim relaxed his grip, letting go of Tanya.

Tanya, too, was frozen in horror. Andrei was a terrifying sight. His otherworldly, rage-distorted face seemed to look through her, through Maksim. His round, glittering eyes blackened, as if staring deep within himself. He seemed not even to recognize her, or her tormentor, either. For a second Andrei looked even more terrifying than Maksim.

However, this distraction lasted only a couple of seconds. Then Maksim easily snatched back his foot to kick Andrei in the face. Maksim's foppish yellow shoe slashed Andrei's masklike white face with a thin, bloody stripe from brow to cheek. Tanya wondered for a second whether Andrei's head was going to split open or burst. Instead, just as slowly as he had risen, Andrei sank back. Tanya watched as if bewitched how he fell back down; it seemed that his head was disappearing between his shoulders. There followed a soft thunk.

Tanya began to shriek. "What did you do to him, you asshole? I'm going to get you!" Then she flung herself at Maksim, punching furiously.

Maksim ignored several of the girl's blows, which were really more like taps. He didn't resist her, instead just watched her with his calm, confident face. Her hands stopped of their own accord, falling away from her last blow. Andrei was breathing heavily on the floor.

Just then she was seized by the neck. Tanya didn't even try to break free because the slightest movement caused her agony. As if outside herself, as if looking at photos, Tanya watched Maksim throw her down on the hard iron bed, splay her, and then rip up her skirt. She kicked at the air, but that only made it easier for the man to settle on top of her. Tanya thrashed and jerked with all her strength, but every move only seemed to put her more into the power of this dreadful man. She was far from exhausted, but she understood how useless it was to fight against her torturer, who no doubt had considerable experience in such torments.

Suddenly Maksim's grip loosened. Tanya had just enough time to draw a deep breath, and then she saw that an elderly woman in a blue uniform had come in carrying a tray.

"Anybody want tea?" she asked.

It was if she was asking someone other than Tanya, or collapsed, immobile Andrei. She had no reaction to the bloody face of the man lying motionless on the floor, nor to the shameless nakedness of the woman clutching helplessly at the bedsheets.

"They'll have tea, won't they?" the woman said, now to Maksim.

"Sure, they'll have tea. We'll just finish up, and they'll have a cup." He pawed Tanya unambiguously. "What do you think, wouldn't make a bad bedspread, would she?"

"Everything's a bedspread to you, you horny fool."

"Well, not everything. I mean, take you, for example."

"What do you mean, me?" The woman was offended. "Twenty years ago . . . Except I was never a scrawny little thing like that one." She nodded at Tanya.

"What scrawny? Look at this." He snapped Tanya's garters, then snatched down her panties and patted her between the legs. "Not bad, eh?"

The woman waved her hand in familiar dismissal and then went back to the door.

"You see that?" Maksim said to Tanya. "She didn't like you. And she knows these things. Maybe she's right, you know? There's not much on you that's round." He ripped her shirt open and exposed Tanya's chest in a businesslike way. "Yeah, not much there. Still, not every diamond's a big one."

Tanya sat with her eyes squeezed tight, expecting him to rape her and then go, so that she could be alone, to wash all this filth from her. . . .

But what would become of Andrei then? Helpless and defiled herself, she had forgotten about him, lying there half under the bed.

"All right, let's get on with it," Maksim said, grabbing her by the shoulders and pressing her into the bed. He rasped his hands all over her bared body, now without opposition. "What's this, you're a stick of wood now? What do you want? I'll give you what you want," he said, his voice now clearly threatening. He got up from the bed, studying his victim fastidiously. He was silent a long time, and then shoved her clenched fingers between her legs. "If you don't feel like it, nobody's going to make you. Just lie there. Nobody's done anything to you. I'm leaving." He chuckled, stepped over Andrei, and left the room.

22

It Begins

Sunday dragged on. The telephone was silent. An open-faced sandwich, not eaten for breakfast, curled and dried on the table. Georgi Alekseevich paced about his apartment, turning the TV on and off, playing with the radio, picking up old newspapers, which he immediately threw down again. He had eaten an indifferent supper of warmed-over cabbage soup and boiled sausages, then tried to sleep, in vain; he had not had so much as a wink.

He was worried about his son, about Tanya, and even about his wife, out in Tomsk. The only thing he wasn't worried about was what was about to happen. He was absolutely confident of their success, but that confidence didn't make his solitude any sweeter.

If Khokhriakov would just call and say something. A human voice, that's all I want. When you don't want the man, he's right there at your elbow. And now? It's like he sank in a pond or something, Georgi Alekseevich mused.

General Khokhriakov, though, was not the sort to just sink out of sight. The doorbell rang soon afterward, and the opened door revealed the general, glowing and triumphant.

"We're starting. We've started already. That's why I'm here, to tell you that."

"And what am I supposed to be doing?"

"You? For right now, just sit and wait."

"But people are already acting!"

"They said that the fewer people in motion at once, the better. I'll just sit here a bit with you, all right?"

"Please, it's a pleasure." Georgi Alekseevich was silent for a moment, then asked, "How're things with my Andrei?"

"Fine." Khokhriakov waved the question away. "He's not bored, they're having a good time."

"What do you mean 'they'?" Georgi Alekseevich suddenly asked. "There's someone else with him?"

"Of course." Khokhriakov was suddenly uncomfortable. "There's people there, of course. It's a summer house, after all. You know, a resort, like."

"Ah-ha," Georgi Alekseevich drawled. "I see." He was positive now that Tanya had been sent there, too. Just to be on the safe side. "Well, let's sit, have some tea, have a chat, all right? You know, I still feel a bit badly that this is starting on Sunday. It would be nice to let the people have their rest."

"Don't worry yourself about the people. They'll be told everything they need to know tomorrow."

"Well then, how are things? In general?" Georgi Alekseevich asked.

"Things, eh?" Khokhriakov replied vaguely, by which Georgi Alekseevich understood that the general had no idea of how the major points of their conspiracy were progressing. Just as before, the men at the top thought it wisest not to trust Vitya, the almost-marshal, with too much responsibility or information.

They sat over tea, two elderly, hard-worn men at the end of their lives, planning and discussing their respective futures. They knew those futures were limited by time and fate, knew that fate had always governed them. However, they had always assumed, too, that fate would ever bend to their will.

This time, though, fate stood aside, and the men were deceiving themselves. The life of which they were so proud was about to end in stupid farce because they understood it so little. In just a few hours these men, and their fellows, would be cursing fate, sorry that they had let themselves be enticed

by these luxurious apartments (luxurious by Moscow stan-
dards, anyway), angry that life had lifted them up to power
only to dash them low again.

For the moment, though, they sat and drank fresh-brewed
Indian tea.

The phone rang.

"That's probably for me," the general said, puffing himself up.

"That's how things are, eh?" Georgi Alekseevich said, displeased that a call would come to his apartment for someone
else.

Khokhriakov lifted the receiver. "Why am I here? I'm drinking tea with Georgi. . . . All right. I'll get him to the phone.
It's Kulik," he explained, for some reason whispering, as he
waved the phone in Georgi Alekseevich's direction.

"Georgi Alekseevich." Kulik's voice sounded nervous. "The
situation has changed, so we are forced to move to special
measures. You understand what that means?"

Georgi Alekseevich said nothing. He understood that
Democrat Number One had not backed them, which meant
that now everything would be decided by force. Simple brute
force—tanks, soldiers, and so on. They had discussed that
likelihood once, but no one thought seriously that it would
come to a battle.

"You hear me, Georgi?" Kulik said.

"Yes."

"All right, then, we have to be ready for any eventuality.
Pass that along to your people. In the office and down along
the line. I know that you've got good people in your shop.
The Party will help us, too."

"Who's going to help us?" Georgi Alekseevich said, unable
to stop himself from asking because he had heard the empty,
ritualistic phrases of Party meetings in Kulik's voice.

"We will. We'll help. I will help."

"Wait a minute. Are we helping them or are they going to
help us?" Georgi Alekseevich wasn't trying to goad Kulik, but
right now, just as this all began, he couldn't bear to let the

man get away with these empty, bombastic, backwoods slogans.

"We help them, they help us," Kulik said, not at all sure of himself. "Well, anyway, we've started. So what I mean to say is, hang on, hands on the tiller. You wait at home. Tomorrow, crack of dawn, you be at work."

"Yes, sir," Georgi Alekseevich said, then hung up first.

"What did he say?" the general asked. "Is something wrong? Somebody shit things up already?"

Georgi Alekseevich studied his visitor carefully. Khokhriakov's face was equal parts fright and interest. Perhaps there was also a sense of insult that he was not telling others the first news of the unfolding coup, but instead was simply being informed of them. That meant that Georgi was held in higher regard than he was.

"Seems that things could be going smoother than they are," Georgi Alekseevich answered. "There was a hitch with Number One, but they're setting it right."

"We'll set it right." Khokhriakov nodded in agreement, as if intimating that he would be taking a personal part in that setting to rights. Then for some reason he went out onto the balcony and stood there for some time, looking like an opera tenor mooning against his hefty railing. He came back into the room and announced, "I have to go. I have to rest, because tomorrow's the deciding day. So, see you soon."

"See you soon, Marshal."

"Don't go making fun, you. Just don't go making fun. Why shouldn't I be a marshal?"

"Take it easy, take it easy. Go have your rest."

The door had barely shut behind Khokhriakov before Kulik phoned again.

"Georgi, stay right where you are, all right? Just wait there!" Kulik's voice was imperious and alarmed, as if he was both ordering and begging. "Oh yes, and one more thing. All that stuff after our little walk yesterday, forget it. You know what I'm talking about, and how we always like to make double sure of things. Nobody trusts anybody, everybody is suspicious, right? And anyway . . . that boy of yours, well, he wobbled, didn't he? So what I mean is, I'm sorry. I've fixed matters, the boys just overstepped. We'll sort it all out later." Then, abruptly, the phone was hung up.

No joke, everyone is under suspicion, Georgi Alekseevich thought, recalling his conversation with the Number One Democrat. The thought had crossed his mind then that maybe this sly, smiling muzhik might be right, and not Georgi Alekseevich and his friends. He wouldn't have turned his friends in, of course, but in the circumstances a simple significant silence would have been enough. But he hadn't, so like it or not he had lied to the Number One Democrat.

The apartment lights were beginning to come on around Moscow. Georgi Alekseevich loved to peer into the windows of strangers, though he didn't like other people to know that. Today, though, he was alone and could indulge. He turned out his light, settled down near the door to the balcony, and began to study the view. It was like a gallery of still-life studies, because there wasn't a sign of life anywhere. Just quadrants of standard interiors with books and large televisions. In two or three of the apartments he could see paintings. One was especially large; if the color was any guide, it had something to do with a forest. In the various kitchens he could see the modest but bright kitchen lamps. The kitchens were the only places to show any signs of life at all. Every now and again a plump housewife would pass by a kitchen window, or a man's head would suddenly appear. By degrees the ceremonies of supper in Moscow began.

They had asked him not to leave the apartment, to be prepared. They had started, or perhaps they had not yet started. Maybe they would never start. Maybe Kulik was just trying to confuse everybody. He loved to do that, and did it well.

Musing, Georgi Alekseevich wandered to his television, punched the On button with his thick forefinger. Immediately the box sprang to life, roaring and howling. That's the first thing we should put an end to, Georgi Alekseevich thought. Rock and roll on television. Especially at night. Let them do their hopping at the discotheques if they want. And the farther out toward the suburbs the discos are, the better.

He checked the other channels, making sure that so far nothing out of the ordinary was going on in the country, and then he jabbed the Off button. The announcer with the boring voice flickered gratefully and disappeared along with the light of the screen.

23

Accelerating

Someone shook Dale Cooper's shoulder.

"Mr. Cooper? They've come from the embassy for you. Mr. Cooper? Wake up."

Dale opened his eyes. Astonishingly enough, he felt no pain. He was able to turn his head toward the person who had woken him and half raise himself.

"Mr. Cooper, at last! You had us worried. I guess that means everything is all right."

Dale stared at this doctor he had never seen before, astonished. Somewhere behind the doctor he could see the embassy undersecretary, Martin Maffei, fidgeting. He stepped forward.

"Dale, thank God. We've been looking for you for two days now. What made you decide to take a vacation here, of all places? Can you walk? Can you ride in a car? Can I take him with me, Doctor? You ask me, he looks great."

Dale rose carefully to sit on the bed. He tested his body; something deep inside was turgid and thrumming, and his head spun a bit, but he was basically all right. Even felt good, somehow.

"Oh, look at your bump!" Martin shouted with idiotic excitement as he bent over Cooper. "That'll make you a nice souvenir of the joys of being a journalist in the U.S.S.R. The hardboys here aren't any worse than the ones back in New York, are they? I remember one time, I was changing trains on Fulton Street, downtown, and after dark already, and up come these three—"

"Martin, I have to get out of here immediately. I have work I have to do. It's almost three days since I filed; the newspaper's going to fire me."

"Okay, if the doctor doesn't object. There's a car waiting."

"What time is it?"

"Ten, exactly."

"Did you watch the news? Vremya?"

"No, just the beginning. Then I came to get you."

"What were the lead stories?"

"Nothing special. Gorby's out of town, so it's just fluff and feathers."

"No news, eh? That's good. You know what . . ."

They spoke in English, but it was obvious that the doctor understood them perfectly. He didn't make any effort even to hide the fact, listening openly to the two Americans chatter here in the Botkin Hospital. Dale looked him over and decided that, even so, this doctor wasn't one of the KGB men. He was just eavesdropping to practice his English.

"They'll get your clothes, and we're out of here. They have to change the dressing on your head wound one more time, so we'll drop 'round here tomorrow. At the end of the day."

"Doctor," Dale said, "could I ask that the new dressing be put on by the nurse who was with me in the beginning? She's already so used to my head that she doesn't hurt me at all. And anyway, I'd like to thank her."

The request brought no obvious response from the doctor, which meant he really wasn't one of the KGB men.

"I'll ask that she be called while you get dressed."

Dale pulled on his trousers, which an elderly nurse had brought into the room along with the rest of his clothes. Then the door opened and a sharp-chinned nurse stuck her head in to announce, "Marina has left. Her duty ended, so she went home."

"That's too bad," Dale said. "Tell her thanks for me, will you?"

He got up and, assisted by the puppylike Martin, walked out through the maze of hallways, passing other patients in their dark green robes. The doctor followed along behind with a proprietorial air.

They left through a side door. Martin unlocked his car, got behind the wheel, and then opened the passenger door for Dale.

"Thanks, Doctor. You've got a nice place here. At least you got me back on my feet very quickly."

"No trouble at all, Mr. Cooper." The doctor seemed in a hurry. "All the best, and we'll see you tomorrow for the new dressing."

Their car pulled away from the hospital. When they had pulled out of the narrow side street and onto the broad Begovaya Street, Martin asked, "What happened, Dale? You have a fight with somebody, and they won? So big that you disappear for two days? And why didn't anybody in the hospital try to find out who you were? We could have gotten you out of there yesterday if they had."

Dale said nothing.

"What, did you lose your tongue back there in the hospital?"

"Martin, you're sure that there's no news?"

"I just told you that. You want me to say it again?"

"Martin, I didn't put myself in the hospital. I got put there."

"By whom?"

"How should I say? I got some information that I wasn't supposed to know."

"So they decided to isolate you for a while? Let their punks do the job? Little pop upside the head, then sling you in the hospital? But then they let you right out again, so why pick you up in the first place?"

"It has to mean that they don't worry about me anymore."

"What you mean to say is that the news you got hold of isn't news anymore?"

"Something like that."

"Well, what was it you stumbled on, then?"

Now they were driving along Krasnaya Presnya Street, which was monstrously wide, with grandiose buildings on either side, the ground floors of which boasted big glass show windows, empty and impoverished. Their car rattled and hopped over the many potholes, which Martin tried in vain to steer around.

Dale took a deep breath and did his best to tell Martin coherently about his adventures of the last three days.

"Well, well," Martin said when the journalist ended. "Impossible but pretty likely. And not hard to draw the bottom line, is it?"

"If they don't have to keep me locked up anymore, then my scoop isn't a scoop anymore."

"That's why you were wondering about Vremya then! Why not wire your paper immediately?"

"There's no point. I wouldn't make the morning papers, and by night it isn't going to be news anymore."

"Looks like they have everything planned, then, doesn't it? Besides, if your stuff had come out day before yesterday, somebody in Moscow would have put a halt to it, or maybe they might have been scared off."

"You're always exaggerating what journalists can do."

"Maybe so, but your two Russian boys, your informants, also overestimated the press. I do think, though, that maybe your article could take the element of surprise away from 'Stalin's falcons.'"

"What element of surprise? Even the kids in the sandboxes are talking about a coup!"

"That's why this Andrei's daddy and his pals maybe could jump in and actually do it, because everybody's talking about it, so much so that everybody is already used to the idea."

"So what should we do now?" Dale asked.

"Who?"

"Us. Them. Everybody."

"Wait for news," Martin said.

"You know what, Martin? I was almost three days in that bed, and even so I feel whipped. Take me home, and if you can, stay the night. These kinds of jokes sound funnier in company."

"What the hell, sure! Otherwise, who knows? Maybe there'll be some more thugs in your hall, jump out and pop you again."

24

Faster

Marina was allowed out of the room only to go to the toilet, and even then Kolomiitsev waited outside the door for her. Twice he brought her something to eat and a glass of tea.

Marina shucked her slippers and climbed up on the Lenin memorial bed. That kind of sacrilege would have been worse than unthinkable earlier. Now she did it, in deep misery.

Last night and today fluttered over her like a variegated, fine-webbed nightmare. It was a dream. It was real life. She understood nothing of what was happening to her or her role in it. She had just gotten swept up in this. But she didn't regret what she had done, either. She was convinced that she had done the right thing, a good thing, but she had no idea for whom what she had done was good.

She remembered that when she was in school she had loved to help her girlfriends with their lessons, whispering to them. Once she had been severely punished for doing so, forced to stay two hours after school. She had sat in the empty classroom, humiliated, her feathers ruffled, but all the same feeling that she had done the right thing by helping.

Maybe her sense of having done the right thing was aided by the sympathy with which Kolomiitsev looked at her. Respect even, perhaps.

She found herself wondering if the academician had passed her news on immediately to the proper place—what *was* the proper place now? When government people were plotting against the government, then what was the government? Or who was the government? Who was in power? It was the government that had locked her in here. But maybe this Kolomiitsev from the KGB wasn't from the government anymore? The whole question was beginning to get her mixed up, and she decided it would be better to sleep.

Just then, though, Kolomiitsev came to the door and studied her closely. The man's stare sent shivers down her back.

"Come," he finally said.

She hastily got into her slippers and followed the man out into the hall.

"Do you have any things here?"

"What things?"

"Your coat, or clothes of some kind? Things like that?"

"Just my purse." She held up her little brown sack of plastic alligator.

"Nothing else?"

"No."

"All right, then, let's go."

His face wooden and inexpressive after two sleepless nights on duty, Kolomiitsev took her along the corridor. Marina felt like a partisan heroine being lead to her death by some movie SS man. She even was a little sorry that there was no one there to admire her proud, indifferent bearing.

Her "SS man" played his part with punctilious correctness, even pointing out which direction she should take when they came to intersections of the corridors. Each time she nodded her head, even though she knew every nook and cranny of the hospital without his directions. When they passed doctors and nurses she knew, they greeted her, then looked questioningly at the man behind her. She had no idea of what awaited her once they left the hospital.

When they reached the little underground hall near the emergency ward entrance, the cleaning woman looked up from the floor she was scrubbing to ask, "Marina, love, when are you on duty again?"

"Why, Pasha?"

"What, you forgot already? You lent me three rubles, remember? Old fool that I am, I clean forgot about it. I'm real
sorry, I promise I'll give it back. That's why I'm wondering,
when are you coming back?"

"The same as always, Pasha," Marina said, though, in fact,
God alone knew when she would be coming in again. That
thought terrified her.

She had not been terrified, not ever, and then . . . Now she
was terrified. And extremely sad.

She wondered whether to ask Kolomiitsev. But he wouldn't
say anything. And what if it was all a secret? A state secret,
even?

If she had heard the orders Kolomiitsev had been given a
half hour earlier, she would have been less worried.

He had been called to the telephone, where he was told
that the guard on the American was being pulled off and he
was free to go.

"Who's free to go?" Kolomiitsev asked. "The American?"

"The American was always free to go," he was told.
"America is a free country, remember?" The caller laughed.

"So who's free, then?" Kolomiitsev asked, insistent.

"You are! You're free to go!" the caller said. "And now get
the hell out, quit cluttering up the place."

"And what should I do with—" Kolomiitsev started to ask,
wondering whether there were any orders about the nurse.
The phone was already dead, though; the other party had
hung up. Kolomiitsev decided against phoning back.

Which left Marina entirely in his hands. He could let her
go or take her with him, figure out her future back in the
office.

All his doubts disappeared, though, when he saw the poor
nurse curled into a ball of misery on her bed.

Now, coming out into the thick, warm night air, Kolomiitsev looked away, but asked, "So tell me, you worked here
long?"

"Four years."

"Where'd you work before that?"

"I lived in Peremyshl. It's a town near Kaluga."

"That right? That makes us almost neighbors. I went to school not far from there."

"So, what . . ."

"What 'what'?"

"What are you going to do with me?"

Kolomiitsev inhaled deeply, held it, released.

"Go home. To Peremyshl, I mean. Not a word to anybody. Take some vacation, sit quietly out in the boondocks, and forget all of this." Then he bent closer. "And when you come back . . . when you come back, give me a call." He gave her his number. "Ask for Kolya. You got that? Kolya. I'd like it a lot if you would."

He kissed her on the forehead and then walked briskly back into the yellow-lit hospital doors.

25
Faster Still

When Maksim left, Tanya stared a long time at the door he closed behind him, her clothes and mind in equal disarray. The stare was the same one people have when they watch a train pull away from a station with a kind of blank melancholy. That's all he wanted of me, all he did. Paw me a bit, humiliate me, and then leave, for even greater effect, she mused, her thoughts jumbled.

It was some time before she realized she was still sobbing, clenching a piece of her badly torn skirt tightly in her fist. She could not believe, did not dare to believe, that the worst—for now, anyway—was behind her. She looked at the rumpled, nearly shattered bed, the place where she had been so professionally and completely humiliated. Tanya felt like vomiting.

From beneath the bed, on the floor, she heard a groan.

Andrei came to and raised himself as far as his elbows, trying to stand. Tanya squatted down beside him, took him by the armpits, and helped him to the chair. Andrei held his head straight, peering forward. She smiled at him, and he did his best to smile back.

"You're all right, then, you're all right," she muttered, studying his face. "Sweetheart, you're all right."

It was almost as if he were dead and she were praying over him, terrified to touch the cut on his face, terrified that his eyes would close again. She dashed into the bathroom, damp-

ened a towel, and brought it back to daub Andrei's swollen
face with cool water.

It turned out that the cut wasn't as bad as it looked. In
fact, it wasn't even a proper cut, but just a broad scratch
running from Andrei's eye down to his lip. The blood had
stopped, but the bruise flowering around the wound told how
hard he had been hit. Even so, it wouldn't be crippling.

"You're all right, everything's all right," she continued to
mutter, mopping at him.

Andrei licked his lips carefully, took a deep breath, released
it. He was trying to gather his forces, his body laboring to
overcome the effect of the beating. By degrees his breathing
became more settled. Andrei jerked his head upright and demanded, in a very businesslike voice, "All right, what did he
do to you?"

"Nothing, nothing."

"What do you mean, 'nothing'? He was . . ." He eyed her
ripped clothes. "What did he do to you? I demand you tell
me!"

"Nothing, like I said. He tried, but I fought him off. He
didn't dare. He left instead. Back to his asshole friends, after
he smashed you."

"Is he coming back?"

The question reminded Tanya of one a child might ask his
mother after a nightmare full of monsters.

So she replied as any mother would in that situation, "No.
There's nothing to worry about, sweetheart, he won't be
back."

"That's good."

Just that second, though, Andrei's gaze shifted, and Tanya
whipped around. The cursed door had opened soundlessly
again. It was the same old woman as before.

Just as before, she paid no attention whatever to what was
going on in the room. Her expression was even friendly.

"I brought you some cotton pads and iodine. You should
put a compress on the bad spots. It's nothing terrible, he'll
live till his wedding. Who doesn't take a bang now and

again, eh? But listen, if he does need a painkiller or some other kind of injection, just tell me—because I can get you whatever he needs. So tell me. I'm right outside, just by the door."

She set her tray full of medicines down on the coffee table and went back out the way she had come in. When she went past Tanya, she shook her head and said, "Love, you got some sewing to do. Tidy yourself up a bit." She dug around in her uniform pocket and brought out a spool of white thread and a needle. She set them down on the desk.

"Here, you can use these. You can give them back later."

Then she left.

Andrei, of course, could not grasp the full import of what had happened, but the woman's appearance had even more devastating an effect on Tanya than the return of Maksim would have. She understood fully now that she had fallen into some sort of machine that regarded her, Tanya, as no more than a piece to be processed. Raw material of some sort. This machine wasn't designed for people but for unfeeling, unspeaking bits of matter. And the woman was no more than a part of the machine. Maksim was part of the machine, too. The machine wasn't programmed to rape Tanya; it was programmed to "process" her. Who could even tell about this Maksim? Maybe he didn't even feel anything as a man when he was on top of her. Tanya felt some of the shame ebbing away; it hadn't been a man trying to get between her legs but a machine, a robot of some kind. On the other hand, though, five minutes from now the machine could get orders to destroy her and Andrei both.

"What's she want?" Tanya heard Andrei ask.

"She brought cotton and iodine."

"Why?"

"That's how they do things here, I guess. See, they probably felt guilty, like they had wronged us, so they—"

"What is this, some kind of joke? Are they making fun of us?"

"Who are you talking about?"

"Them, all of them. They're going to answer for this, all of them."

"Of course, of course." Tanya reverted back to her motherly voice.

"We have to talk to the gray-haired one. It's time to get out of this stupid situation." He tried to stand.

Tanya stopped him. "Let's wait a little longer. You rest. We can think things through, figure out what to do."

Andrei drummed his fingers on the armrest.

Tanya stood and slowly washed out his cuts, this time with the cotton instead of the towel. Andrei scowled with pain.

Next she tried to put her skirt right, sewed her blouse, fixed her hair. Inside of an hour they looked like young marrieds at a summer resort, putting their few charms into good order. The only obvious remnants of the day's events were on Andrei's chin and cheek, but even they looked better.

Just then the door swung open again.

The gray-haired man bowed with elegant politeness to Tanya, then said sincerely to Andrei, "I am most sorry that the end of your stay with us was so sadly colored by that unhappy incident—"

"By what?" Tanya couldn't stop herself from asking because she remembered too clearly that a stranger's fingers had run wherever they wished to over her body.

"I have come to offer my apologies. Although I must say in all honesty that you bear a certain responsibility for—"

"What do you mean, 'the end of our visit'?" Andrei interrupted. "We can go?"

"But of course."

"Right this minute?"

"Yes. In fact, we will take you and your lady friend back home in one of our cars."

"I won't ride with them," Tanya said flatly.

"But we don't have any other drivers."

"All right, then, we'll go by train, or bus, or anything we can find."

"As you wish," the gray-haired man said. "But taking into consideration certain circumstances,"—here he nodded at the wounded Andrei—"that sort of a journey will probably be very trying for your companion."

Andrei looked piteously at Tanya.

"All right," Tanya said, addressing Andrei, not the gray-haired man. "They can take us back—"

"From where they got us," Andrei concluded in a feeble joke.

"Did you hear what he said?" Tanya asked the gray-haired man severely.

Then Snegirev came into the room to announce apologetically, "Something's wrong with the car. An electrical short or something."

"So fix it."

"But it's dark now, Comrade Lieutenant Colonel."

"We don't have another car?"

"Not until morning we don't."

"But we can't keep them here any longer." He nodded in Andrei's direction.

Snegirev glanced at Tanya, which she noticed. The guard was clearly interested, wondering whether his pal had gotten a chance to work this bit of gash over. Tanya turned her back to him.

"The car won't start," Snegirev repeated, and then, as if trying to convince them all it was true, he went to the window and pointed down at the silent car.

When he went past Tanya, she thought she smelled vodka. Maybe he just doesn't want to risk driving drunk? That's what he's afraid of? she wondered.

Andrei waved his hand dismissively. "We can wait until the morning. If that's all right with you?" he asked Tanya.

Tanya wanted to get away as fast and as far as she could, but one look at Andrei was enough to convince her that he would never be able to get back to Moscow on his own.

"All right, if we have to wait, we'll wait."

"That's all set, then." The gray-haired man seemed almost to rejoice that this couple would be in his care another night.

In fact, though, he wanted to get rid of them as quickly as possible. Events had begun, and he itched to get into the center of things. However, he had promised Kulik's men on his own life that he would watch out for the young man and his girl, and so he was stuck here.

Snegirev and the lieutenant colonel left.

"Well then," Tanya said with fierce mocking affection when they were alone. "Now listen, sweetie pie, why don't you just tell me everything your little heart wanted to explain to me before? Like how you came to be out here, and how I ended up here, too? And what they want from the two of us?"

She was tired of feeling sorry for Andrei. Suddenly she disliked this man, because of whom she very nearly had been raped, right in front of his eyes. This man who hadn't been able even to slow the fellow who had attacked her, pawing her with his big, knowing hands. Andrei had not even noticed the salacious way the driver had looked her up and down just now.

Andrei sensed the change in Tanya's attitude. He began a slow, careful explanation of everything that had happened. Now his secret wasn't a danger to anyone; he had kept it from everyone, and he had lost. Now all that remained was to write his memoirs.

Tanya listened to him attentively, not interrupting. She felt no sympathy for Andrei, but she didn't blame him, either. When he was done, she asked, "Why do you think he stopped the way he did, with me?"

"Probably his orders were to wear you down. I mean, if he had really wanted to . . . to . . . Well, you know . . ."

"To rape me," she said firmly.

"That's right."

"He would have done so, you mean?"

"But then the need for all this passed," Andrei said, thinking about it. "They don't need us anymore now. Worse than that, they have to take care of us."

"They're afraid of your father?"

"Maybe, or at least I've got the feeling that he's back up in the saddle again."

"What do you mean, 'again'? There was some sort of danger?"

"Certainly, there was a moment there when his name suddenly ceased to give the two of us any protection. But now they are all friendly and polite again. You saw that yourself."

"Even so, we ought to get out of here as quickly as we can."

"I won't argue with that."

He stretched out on the bed, while Tanya sat in the armchair, her feet up on the coffee table. Within seconds she was sound asleep. Andrei, though, could not sleep, straining instead to catch noises in the big building, especially because there were almost none to hear. The silence was so profound as to be unnatural. It made him suspect that the people who lived or worked in the building were all tensed, waiting for something.

He also had no idea how long he would continue feeling more or less in control, confident. He began to wonder whether he was awake or dozing, thoughts swimming and melting. Finally, unable to help it, he drifted off, too.

Then a radio began to play on the other side of the wall, deliberately loud, as if the owner wanted to wake up everybody. Andrei strained to catch the words as a stern-voiced announcer reported that Gorbachev's ill health had forced the creation of a State Committee for the State of Emergency and then said that there would soon be an announcement by the new Soviet leadership.

Tanya slept on, sprawled in the armchair. Andrei loathed the thought of waking her, especially since the news he had just heard really wasn't such news, at least for them. The only thing that might have counted as news was the clinky clumsiness of the name the coup leaders had chosen for their committee.

Finally the noise woke Tanya. She listened to the radio for a moment, then suddenly cursed as foully as a sailor. It was the first time Andrei had heard such words come from her mouth.

This was followed by a knock at the door. The gray-haired

man entered, still politeness itself, to announce that tea was ready and the car was fixed.

Tanya nodded at him with a gravity that would have suited the last living princess of some middling European dynasty.

Stiff and creaking all over his painful body, Andrei managed somehow to wash up. The tea was brought in. Andrei looked out the window to see Maksim lounging against the car. The other man, his partner, was nowhere in sight.

After tea, Tanya, still imperial, announced that she wanted a shower. Andrei couldn't tell whether she wanted to make a show of her independence, when everyone was trying to hurry her out the door, or whether she really thought the cold water would freshen her up.

Andrei asked, "First could you help me get downstairs? I want to sit on the bench outside, breathe some fresh air." He was worried that the endless hallways and staircases of the place would make him giddy again.

They pushed on the door, which opened easily. The building was as deserted as it had been when they came in. The only sign of life was two women watching a television in one of the connecting halls; the program was a ballet. One of them said hello to Tanya as she and Andrei walked past.

Maksim met them outside.

Tanya helped Andrei to the nearest bench, which was already warm with early-morning sun. Andrei leaned back against the seat's back, raised his face, and closed his eyes to the sun.

Tanya went back up to their room, undressed quickly, and got into the shower. The cold immediately covered her body with little purplish gooseflesh bumps. She showered quickly, then stood on the bathmat to dry herself with a small but fluffy towel, rubbing her skin warm. Refreshed, she wanted a cigarette, so she went out into the main room to look through her bag. She found her pack, got a cigarette, lit it.

Just then heavy, sweaty hands grabbed her by the shoulders.

Tanya leaped around, saw it was Snegirev.

The man was deeply, seriously drunk.

His face was mottled liver and rose, his eyes bulged, and his lips hung loose beneath his fat fleshy nose. He tried to say something, but it emerged as nothing but gurgles deep in his throat. He was holding on to Tanya so tightly that it was almost as if he would fall if he didn't. It seemed as if he didn't even realize that the woman he was holding on to was naked.

Tanya shoved his hands off her and ran out of the room. Snegirev, though, wasn't to be denied.

"Hey, come on, one for old time's sake! It's not like you'll be able to leave here!"

He grabbed her by the shoulders again, then thrust his knee between her legs. That exhausted his strength, though; Tanya was able to push the drunk away. Then she grabbed a huge ashtray and hit him on the head with it as hard as she could.

She jumped back into the bathroom, throwing her clothes on as quickly as she could move, while still keeping one eye on the guard stretched out on the floor. The guard didn't move. Once she had her clothes on Tanya went back out to her uninvited visitor. She stifled a scream. The man was lying on his back, staring sightlessly at the ceiling, a thin trickle of blood running from the right corner of his mouth. Nearly numb with shock, Tanya fumbled for a pulse.

Outside she heard the car honk.

"Hang on, I'm coming," she mumbled, preoccupied with the man. Then, realizing she couldn't be heard, she shouted, "Coming!" in the direction of the window.

Tanya grabbed Snegirev by the armpits and dragged him over to the big three-door wardrobe, one door of which had an ornate brass key protruding from the lock. Working with desperate haste, Tanya stuffed her victim into the wardrobe, trying to push him against the back wall. On the third try she managed to get his head propped against the left wall of the wardrobe. Hangers rained down on her, then a boot brush. Old newspapers tumbled from the upper shelves, and even some old socks, forgotten by a stranger. She would never have figured there would be so much junk in what she had assumed was an empty closet.

At last, though, the man was stuffed inside.

"You ought to be ashamed, drinking so much!" she said very loudly, trying to convince herself that this last attempt on her feminine charms had been made by a simple drunk. She studied him for another second, then turned away decisively.

She went over to the window, where she saw Andrei hobbling toward the Zhiguli. "I'm coming right down, Andrei!" she shouted with a wave.

26
It Starts

The three of them got into the Zhiguli, Maksim driving and the other two in the backseat. Tanya was careful to sit behind the driver. Andrei looked indifferently about him, thinking of nothing except how much he cursed that moment when he had chanced to hear his father's careless words, a few simple phrases that had caused so many subsequent nightmares, and even deaths. The world looked empty and senseless now.

"Your partner trusts you to take us back alone?" Andrei asked indifferently, slightly surprised that they had pulled away from the front steps.

"He was celebrating," the driver explained irritably.

Tanya held her breath, said nothing.

Andrei only remembered that the coup was under way once they had passed inside the city limits and were on the Ring Road, entering the huge city, dull gray from its restless sleep of the night before.

They raced along the straight highways for ages, passing buses, slithering around trucks, picking their way through the throngs of private cars.

The city was quiet and as indifferent as ever. Andrei studied the scowling faces of the pedestrians at the crosswalks; they would have heard of the coup already, but they clearly did not want to know anything about it or to take any part in it.

The passengers didn't speak; they were wondering what

role was going to be assigned them in whatever the aftermath of these events would be.

"Nothing, absolutely nothing," Andrei muttered softly to himself.

Neither of the others said a thing.

Then, as if she had just woken up, Tanya said, "Let me out, please. I have to go back home. I'll phone you soon, but you don't need me right now, correct?"

"Do what you want," Andrei said.

"Pull up over there," she said, addressing Andrei, not the driver.

However, the car obediently pulled to the sidewalk. Tanya opened the door and got out.

"I'll call you from my place as soon as I get there," she said, then slammed the door and disappeared up the street.

Andrei watched after her, trying, in vain, to track her through the bustling crowd.

The car resumed its trip through Moscow, which seemed very ordinary in the bright sun of morning.

There was nobody in sight around his father's building. Andrei looked up to see that the blinds in all the apartments were still shut. He wondered what the inhabitants of this "privileged building" were thinking; were they happy, or were they frightened of the possible outcomes of the risk they had taken on themselves?

Andrei had no desire to run into his father. He didn't want to hear the old man's explanations and justifications, didn't want his father to see the bruises and wounds of his battered face. He was relieved enough to sigh when he found that his father's apartment was empty. When Andrei was halfway across the living room, the telephone rang. Automatically his hand reached for the receiver, but then he thought better of it.

Instead of answering he switched on the television.

The "Official Announcement by the Soviet Leadership" was being read in a numbing but threatening monotone, the speech thundering with the sorts of phrases from the past that he had all but forgotten. The words seemed to come from some primitive, dead language, or even to be just flatulent, thundery noises rattling around in the bottom of a deep and gloomy abyss, from the lip of which Andrei had long ago walked away. The speech brought to mind one of those dreadful movies from the late 1940s where all the generals and political advisers were as wise as gods, weightily pronouncing truths so simple they could have been illustrated with pictures from a child's ABC.

Andrei watched the television as if hypnotized, believing yet not believing that the coup had, in fact, taken place.

The phone rang again, and this time—after a slight hesitation—Andrei answered.

"Yes?"

"Hey, you're home already!" Khokhriakov's voice came tinnily through the lines. "That's great. Now I can tell your father not to worry."

Andrei hung up, saying nothing. He didn't want to remain in his father's house a moment longer. As he was shutting the door behind him, the phone rang again—long, insistent buzzes.

27
It Ends

What happened after that was something no one had really thought possible.

Responding hastily to Yeltsin's widely broadcast appeals, people converged on the high, white, and tastelessly designed building on the banks of the Moscow River that only recently had become the home of the Parliament of the Russian Soviet Federated Socialist Republic. They clustered around, refusing to let soldiers and KGB troops get near the parliament. Before long the five long words of the republic's unwieldy name were shortened simply to "Russia," and the clumsy building just across the river from the high-Stalinist tower of the Ukraine Hotel began to be called "the White House."

Tanya spent thirty-six hours of those August days on the steps of the White House, not worrying about troops coming, because they wouldn't have fought anyway, but rather worrying about her Andrei, who was also there, in front of the same building. His battered, swollen face bought him an edgy respect from the other people gathered around parliament, even though Andrei naturally didn't tell people where and how he had picked up his "decorations."

Once it was clear that his father's comrades in arms had completely failed, he went over to Tanya's place to lick his wounds. He had no real desire to participate in the victory celebrations.

On the same day that the tanks the ever-more-incompetent coup plotters sent failed to reach the White House, Oleg Bukin was buried in a grave at the Nikolsky Cemetery, far from the center of the city. It was raining. A couple dozen of Bukin's relatives had gathered, many of them people Oleg had seen only a couple of times in his life. There were also three co-workers, who slipped away from the funeral as soon as they decently could to hurry to the "heroic, epochal deeds of courage" that were unfolding on the Krasnopresnenskaya riverside drive near the White House. There was also some strange fellow with a short beard who kept trying to make a funeral oration near the bus that was carrying the body. However, he was asked to stop, and he did.

When the coffin was nailed shut and lowered into the ground a middle-aged woman began to shriek, but she was immediately supported by Oleg's cousins, or second cousins.

Oleg Bukin's relatives never knew that the next funeral bus to arrive contained the body of unlucky little Nadya, whose coffin was kept closed.

Boris Fedorovich Kulik didn't give up until the very end. Even when the men who had held the pathetic and stupid press conference at which the State Committee for the State of Emergency attempted to justify itself were already racing to the summer home of the Most Important to explain their actions and to whine for forgiveness, even when the democratic volunteers were already defacing and chopping down the Feliks Dzerzhinsky statue that had stood so long in front of KGB headquarters, Kulik was still bawling orders into the telephone, telling the army that it had to act, that all was not yet lost.

When he was arrested, Kulik glanced contemptuously at the two fair-faced men in civilian clothes and the long-necked major who had been given the job, and then for some reason showed them all his Party membership card.

After five months of incarceration in a clean and pleasant cell, Kulik discovered that he really only missed two things:

his favorite cold tongue sandwiches, and a woman. He even knew which woman—the cute little number he had sacrificed to necessity just before "the events."

The most interesting events, though, came at the summer house where Andrei and Tanya had been involuntary "guests."

The woman who came to clean their room the next day— the elderly lady in the blue uniform who had offered Tanya thread and whose name was Anna Nikitichna—decided to sort out the closet. Unable to find the key, she finally went to the next room and took the one from the closet there; all the closets at the "resort" used the same key.

She was horrified when a corpse tumbled out onto her feet.

Despite all that she had been a witness to in the resort, Anna Nikitichna shrieked, then studied the stray-dog face of the dead man before going off to report.

It didn't take the gray-haired man even three seconds to know who the sickly-sweet-smelling body belonged to.

"Snegirev." He scowled, then added, "Can't even keep the vodka in, now."

"So what should I do?" the woman asked, dull with all that she had seen and survived.

"Nothing," the boss said. He was right, too; twenty-four hours later he was no longer boss. The young man who came to relieve the gray-haired lieutenant colonel told him that he would sort out the Snegirev business later because there were far more important things to do at the moment. Before sundown the body of the clumsy rapist was cremated.

Maksim went on his regular vacation, in the beginning of September, to Moldova. From there he managed to work his way out to Romania, and from there disappeared. Croatia is one likely destination, Serbia another.

Dale Cooper, the American journalist, spent two nights outside the White House talking to people and passing out cartons of cigarettes. He filed two fairly indifferent reports, for which his editor chewed him out by phone. After a press conference with the victorious democrats he found a bar and got monstrously drunk, after which he wasted an hour trying to convince the other customers that he had held the fate of Russia in his own two hands.

When he was making his way back home, he was stopped by a militiaman. Dale tried to salute the sergeant with a two-fingered victory sign, but the man replied that Dale would either have to pay a fine on the spot or else be walked to the nearest militia station, where he would be booked.

It turned out that the militia sergeant disliked Yeltsin, so it cost the American journalist twenty dollars to get himself off the spot.

Marina, the nurse, followed the advice of her unexpected guardian angel and spent ten days in safety out in remote Peremyshl. When she got back she did telephone Kolomiitsev. Two months later they married, and a month after that Kolomiitsev got a promotion and a transfer to Leningrad, already called Saint Petersburg again. Somewhere in the course of the move she misplaced the telephone book that had the number of the famous scientist and politician.

General Khokhriakov was so frightened he almost shat himself, but he was spared any trouble for the simple reason that people forgot about him. No one had ever taken him seriously, neither the coup leaders nor the democrats. He sat in anxious terror at his summer house for nothing. Equally for nothing, he burned all the monstrously stupid reports he had prepared for the Committee on Patriotic Education of Youth; he had forgotten that these were carbons, the originals long ago submitted and probably gathering dust in a file someplace. He finally begged a meeting with the head of one of the main divisions of the General Corps, a fat indifferent general before whom Khokhriakov made a botched and incomprehensible attempt to explain his political beliefs. The only thing the fat general could make of all of it was that Khokhriakov was asking for a promotion, and so he told Khokhriakov the truth, that no new full generalships were anticipated in the near future.

Equally baffled, Khokhriakov understood this to mean that he was being threatened with expulsion from the army, demotion, and very likely even a court-martial.

Instead, though, Khokhriakov got a generous pension and an excellent summer home, which was registered in the name of his long-dead mother-in-law. He was only reminded of the coup attempt once, when a reporter called from the newspaper *Salvation* requesting an interview. Khokhriakov knew that this newspaper was in almost open support of his former comrades in arms, and he was terribly flattered to be asked, but after much consideration the general decided that he would refuse the interview, just to be on the safe side.

On the other hand, he was extremely pleased to participate in the All-Union Officers' Convention later in the fall, at which he was able to dress up as of old in the fine parade uniform with the three big gold-embroidered stars.

28
Father and Son

Georgi Alekseevich learned nothing of all this.

The morning of the coup he phoned his home every half hour, but there was never an answer. Georgi Alekseevich was sure by the last call, though, that his son had gotten back. He could picture the boy all too easily, standing by the phone, watching it.

Georgi Alekseevich was also certain that his son would never phone him.

Around eleven Khokhriakov confirmed that Andrei had been returned. That's even how the general put it: "They've brought him back."

That whole day Georgi Alekseevich conducted negotiations, gave orders, offered advice. Some people congratulated him, some said that even sterner measures should be taken. Somebody told him that a huge crowd of drunken rabble and hideous hags had gathered on Krasnepresnenskaya, screaming at the top of their lungs that they were going to "shut the road to communism" with their own bodies.

Georgi Alekseevich couldn't find Kulik; the man was off somewhere, also giving orders.

There were three dark green tanks outside Georgi Alekseevich's windows. At first they had seemed to be unmanned, rather like some sort of marine monsters that had crawled up onto the shore. In the afternoon the tanks were surrounded by little boys, and silver-haired grandmothers came out to offer the tank soldiers sandwiches and milk. Some papa parked a baby carriage next to the huge tank treads and held his little girl up to show her something and tell her and his wife a story of some sort. "It's like Sunday in the goddamn park," Georgi Alekseevich muttered to himself.

It wasn't an ordinary thing to have tanks outside your window, of course, but letting the whole thing turn into some sort of carnival—that was no way to do business.

Georgi Alekseevich even was going to point this out to Khokhriakov, but then changed his mind—the only place the general ever saw tanks was during military parades.

Watching the tanks be swarmed over by little boys slowly destroyed Georgi Alekseevich's mood. It wasn't businesslike, wasn't solid.

Kulik finally called in the afternoon.

"Are congratulations in order?" Georgi Alekseevich asked him.

"More or less, yes," Kulik replied.

That "more or less" immediately killed Georgi Alekseevich's final hope that the coup could turn out well.

Neither of the men said anything for a long time.

"Why are you not speaking?" Kulik finally asked.

"What am I supposed to talk about? Things are clear enough."

"What's clear?"

"Who's to be congratulated."

Now Kulik was the one not talking.

"Oh, well. Boris Fedorovich, what are your orders?"

"You need orders?" Kulik asked, then said, "Do what you think best. Try to get your people to be decisive. Have them be ready for sharp changes. And tell them . . . well, to keep calm."

"Maintain order, too?" Georgi Alekseevich laughed into the phone.

"Well sure, order, too. Goddamn you," Kulik suddenly barked.

Georgi Alekseevich was surprised. "What's that you said?"

"They're idiots, all of them. Cowards, too. Georgi, at least you hang in there, all right? For now things are going well. Watch the TV tonight."

Georgi Alekseevich did, alone in his apartment. After the moronic press conference at which the six confused and fumbling coup leaders attempted to brazen through their transparent explanations, Georgi Alekseevich poured himself an entire glassful of cognac, downed it, and then stared gloomily at the floor.

The men on the television weren't warriors, weren't politicians. They weren't even gamblers. The new Soviet leaders looked like nothing more than a bunch of kids chasing out-of-bounds soccer balls for a professional team.

"So why didn't Kulik go on the television? Or they might have asked me! You wouldn't have had *me* sitting there like some sort of grave old moron! They're as stupid as goddamn *bricks!*" God, just yesterday he had been standing at attention in front of these idiots. . . . He should take better account of himself.

Georgi Alekseevich watched the press conference to the end. The journalists were openly disbelieving. Female reporters asked ironic and ambiguous questions right in front of the cameras, for all the world to see. A well-known Moscow television commentator of famous girth lectured the newly declared Soviet president as if the president were some sort of C-minus student handing in late homework.

The screen wasn't even turned off before Khokhriakov was on the phone.

"Did you see it?"

"See what?"

"The press conference. How those damn pen squeezers dared to act. Our boys, though, they did all right. They acquitted themselves nicely, don't you think? They didn't fall for any of that political provocation. Those damn foreigners, what can you do with people like that? But who'd have thought our journalists would turn into such shits? We'll have to teach them some manners later on."

"You're an idiot," Georgi Alekseevich said.

"What's that?"

"I said you're an idiot. Do you understand anything at all about what's happening?"

"What do you mean? I understand everything!" Khokhriakov protested, offended. "And I'd have to say that I don't understand precisely what political position it is you're taking."

Here's the man they should have had up on that stage, Georgi Alekseevich thought. Khokhriakov and his stupidities would have been like some sort of grand finale.

All he said, though, was, "Forget it, Viktor, don't get pissed off. We're all bushed, we ought to get some rest."

"Well, of course." Khokhriakov understood this in his own way. "We'll crush those types, and then we can rest easy."

"Oh sure, we'll crush them, no problem," Georgi Alekseevich said, then hung up.

The next morning he went to see Kulik.

He found Boris Fedorovich digging through papers in a big red folder; the date on the cover said it came from the mid-1970s.

"We've stirred up some business this time, Georgi," Kulik said by way of a greeting. "We've really done it, you and me."

"What's this about, Boris Fedorovich?"

"It's what it's always been about," Kulik replied ambiguously.

"Did you see yesterday's show?"

"I saw it, Georgi, I saw it. That's why I'm trying to sort a few things out now." He nodded down at the folder.

"You're doing a little housecleaning, you mean?"

"You're against that?"

"Well, it just looks a little, you know . . . gloomy."

"Good God, you saw the press conference! Those limp-dick idiots! Speaking politically, of course."

Georgi Alekseevich went behind Kulik to look at the documents in the folder.

The first paper to catch his eye was a report he had prepared himself, about using prisoners as labor on construction projects that fell under his committee's control. The report spoke of the high fatality rate in these "special brigades" and asked for more prisoners. However, he had requested that the replacements "have the physical conditioning appropriate to completing the tasks for which the committee has been given responsibility." The report was signed at the bottom with the big scrawl of Kulik's predecessor: "Approved."

"Pretty little paper, eh?" Kulik winked. "What say we pass it along to the archive as outdated and no longer of interest, eh?"

"Give it to me," Georgi Alekseevich said, reaching for the paper.

"How come? You want to liquidate it yourself? All right, take it. A souvenir."

Georgi Alekseevich wadded up the yellowing paper and stuffed it into the jacket of his sport coat.

"I take it this means you figure they're going to be raking us over?"

"Georgi, I don't think anything. I'm just getting ready. To be on the safe side. And I'd advise you to do the same. But you're going to have it easier. That son of yours is the next best thing to a hero. He's probably out there on the barricades right now, right?"

"That's none of your business, Boris Fedorovich. Probably none of mine, either."

"Hey, why so sour, Georgi?" Kulik suddenly became buoyant. "We're still in great shape! You see the tanks?"

"What tanks? Playground equipment, that's all they are. You tell me something instead. Those boys on the television last night—are they going to do anything, or what? They put the squeeze on Spotted Dome yet? Have they rounded up Yeltsin and his band? And where are they now? You got nothing to say? You don't know the answer or you don't want to tell me?"

"They're consulting. Consulting . . ."

"So why aren't you consulting with them?"

"I've just come from there, Georgi," Kulik said. Then, as if it had been ripped out of him, he added, "Anyway, I never drink in the morning."

"Ah-ha! So that's how things stand! They're all celebrating, you mean!"

"No, they're not celebrating."

"So what then?"

"Nothing. Arguing. They're all arguing . . . and pissing all over themselves, they're so scared."

"That's what you should have started by telling me. Well, see you later, Boris Fedorovich. We'll see each other this evening, I imagine."

"You want me to 'annul' your papers? There's a lot of yours in here."

"Do what you want."

"Thanks for the trust."

Georgi Alekseevich stayed at his desk only until midday. Nobody was working properly anywhere, and Georgi Alekseevich had no desire to "mobilize" his people in support of the new Soviet leadership. He felt as if he was going to be sick, to vomit as he did when he was young and was facing a complicated, important test. In the past, though, he had gotten A's on all his tests.

When he left the office he asked his driver to go by the Supreme Soviet of the R.S.F.S.R., which proved easier said than done. The streets were blockaded so that he could get no closer than Kutuzov Bridge, across the river from the parliament building.

Entrance to the bridge was blocked by two tanks loyal to Yeltsin. The Russian tricolor fluttered above one of them. The other flew the yellow-and-blue flag of the Ukraine. There were also several buses and a couple of heavy trucks. Nearby a young man in a white raincoat was pouring gasoline into bottles. A line of people stood patiently waiting for the bottles.

A militiaman went over.

"Hey, kid, you crazy?"

"What do you think?" the young man answered, not even looking up. "They send tanks against us, what are we supposed to do, turn around and show them our butts?"

"Right," the militiaman said, then waved his hand indifferently. "Just be careful you don't get any on yourself." Then he turned and left.

Young men and women—and even whole families with children—strolled along the bridge. The whole scene exuded confidence and calm, a certainty that nothing was going to happen. The fellow with the gasoline bombs seemed out of place at this picnic, which for some inexplicable reason was also being guarded by tanks.

The tank soldiers were drinking tea from thermoses while a scrawny lieutenant was excitedly discussing something with a civilian who wore a Russian tricolor badge in his lapel.

In that setting Georgi Alekseevich's black chauffeured Volga was like a flag in front of a bull. Even so, Georgi Alekseevich got out of his car and circled the tanks carefully, listening to the way the soldiers laughed, flirting with the girls, then listened to the impassioned speech some wormy type in a too-tight coat was giving about the danger that communism represented for Russia.

Then Georgi Alekseevich leaned against the railing of the bridge and lit a cigarette.

Gray clouds floated and coalesced above the bridge. The pale sun poked out now and again. When it emerged, the Moscow River turned a greenish blue sea color. Two small barges made their way slowly up the river, apparently playing the part of navy for the besieged parliament. Across the river he could see the barricades made of pipes and iron fences and unidentifiable trash, of which there was never any shortage in the huge capital.

Georgi Alekseevich tossed his cigarette butt onto the sidewalk, spat into the river, and then went back to his car. Before he reached it, though, he noticed a tall, lame man whom an equally thin woman was helping along the bridge, near the far end.

Now looking closer at the two, Georgi Alekseevich exclaimed, "Andrei!"

It was his son making his slow way along the bridge. He was not quite holding Tanya by the shoulder, not quite leaning on her. They didn't see Georgi Alekseevich, and he was frightened to call out again. What if they should turn away? What if his son just kept walking?

Georgi Alekseevich shivered, and then hobbled toward his car, suddenly old. Already leaving, he turned around to see Andrei staring back at him. The son understood that he had been found out, and he turned away, leaving as quickly as he could move.

At home, Georgi Alekseevich's mailbox held a letter without a stamp. It was in Tanya's handwriting:

"Georgi Alekseevich, Andrei forbade me to telephone you. I was with him *there*. He was beaten. He doesn't consider you at fault, but he doesn't wish to see you. I was almost beaten myself. Now Andrei is all right. If anything more happens to him, he is carrying a letter for his mother out in Tomsk. There is nothing bad about you in that letter. I apologize for the curtness of this letter. When we see each other we can talk more. Tanya."

He had been beaten. They had beaten Andrei. Tanya, too; they had beaten little Tanya. So what excuse did that asshole Vitya have? Georgi Alekseevich was furious.

He tried to call the general, but there was no answer.

Kulik's phone, too, went unanswered. The work number and home number both. No doubt, though, Kulik had known nothing about what they did to Andrei anyway.

Georgi Alekseevich looked at himself in the hall mirror, made a fist, shook it at himself. How *could* he have cast his own son onto the whims of fate like that? And to give them little Tanya besides! Except he really hadn't said anything about Tanya. So which one of them had had the idea to send the girl out there too? He recalled the way Andrei, clutching Tanya, had left the bridge, heading for the heaps of bent pipes that people had dignified with the term *barricades*. If anything were to happen to him . . .

If what Kulik was dreaming about were to happen, then they would all be squashed like so many squirrels on the highway. Andrei and Tanya both.

And the important question was—for what? For order?

Georgi Alekseevich felt powerless to stop or change anything.

Late in the evening he was brought an envelope that contained a request that he appear later in the evening at some meeting to "coordinate unfolding developments."

He didn't go.

He spent the whole of the next day sitting alone in his office, watching the tanks, on which somebody had now painted "The People and Army Are One." His loyal longtime secretary, Vera Petrovna, brought him tea at regular intervals. She also was taking tea out to the men in the tanks, and the guards at the front door of the committee building began to let the soldiers come in to use the toilets.

The television broadcast for a third time the same idiot, who now announced that it was hoped that the new Soviet leadership would permit the purchase of cheap socks again. Moscow radio was playing songs from the civil war.

Vera Petrovna came in without knocking. "Georgi Alekseevich, they're saying that the White House is going to be stormed tonight. Have you heard anything about it? My niece is there."

"I haven't heard anything, not a thing. I don't imagine, though, that they will actually go to that extreme."

"I hope to God you're right!"

He was lying to his favorite secretary. He already knew about the attack and the preparations for it. Even so, he didn't believe that such a thing was possible.

Georgi Alekseevich didn't believe in much at all anymore.

Still, that evening he nevertheless went to the "coordination meeting," to which he had been invited once again.

When he arrived, everyone was sitting around coordinating. Each spoke to the limit of his small ration of wit, trying to hide the huge fear that lurked in each of them. When it was

Georgi Alekseevich's turn to speak, he said, perfectly calmly, "You know, I don't think anything is going to come of all this."

"Damn you!" Khokhriakov shrieked. "It's people like you who are making us lose this while the whole world watches! Guys like you, always talking talking, but when it comes to doing something, nothing, right?"

"Sit down and shut up, Viktor," Kulik ordered sharply. "And I guess you are tired, Georgi Alekseevich. We're all tired. You especially, though."

"That means I can leave?"

"You can."

Georgi Alekseevich left, knowing that he would never be back in that room again. If the others won, this office would hold a new boss, and if these men won, they would never forgive him for what he had just said.

Outside, he sent his driver home and set off to walk about the city. He was in no hurry. It was an odd feeling for Georgi Alekseevich not to be in a hurry. Frightening, too, because that meant he wasn't needed anywhere. Some girl on the corner gave him a leaflet. The headline read: "CITIZENS OF RUSSIA! ALL DEPENDS ON YOU!"

Georgi Alekseevich would have been happy to talk with the girl at some length. No doubt she had a better idea than he did of how matters stood and what was about to happen in Moscow, and to him, and to his son. To Kulik, too, and to the rest of the people among whom he was used to living and working. The girl with the leaflets, though, had already vanished back into the crowd from which she had emerged.

Can this be all there is of the "events" everyone has talked about for so long and that we all put such hopes on? he wondered.

Georgi Alekseevich passed one more dead evening without visitors or phone calls. Not even Vitya the general came by to discuss events in the city.

During the night he heard shots, and got up and dressed.

Then for some reason he took his umbrella and went outside. After a bit he came back inside.

He fiddled with his radio for a long time. A muddle of a dozen signals let him gather the essentials of what had happened, that there had been or was going to yet be a storming of the parliament, and that the "defenders of the White House"—a phrase that now was not even said with irony—were "firm in their determination."

Georgi Alekseevich was far from firm in his own determination.

Nor did he go back to sleep.

The next morning he telephoned Vera Petrovna to say that he would be late for work.

"All right," she asked briskly. "What shall I say if someone is looking for you?"

"No one is going to be looking for me anymore," he said.

Kulik telephoned after lunch.

"Georgi, you were right yesterday," he said. "Everyone's running away. You know where they're running? To Misha Spotty Top. You got it right, what you said yesterday. And you did the right thing, too, when you told . . . well, you know who you told . . . about all this. Us, we're a bunch of idiots. Cretins, the lot of us."

Georgi Alekseevich had no idea how to react to what he had just heard, whether he should be upset or rejoice. He basically said nothing. "God love 'em, Boris Fedorovich, things will turn out as they are meant to."

"Farewell, Georgi," Kulik said, then hung up.

Georgi Alekseevich stood a bit longer, thinking, recalling the noise of the shooting in the night, the excited, tense announcers. He threw on his coat and went outside. Today he was in luck; the first Volga he saw stopped for him. He realized then that he had left his money home, but the driver didn't take so much as a kopek. "A day like this, it's the least I can do!" the driver said radiantly, brushing away Georgi Alekseevich's confused and embarrassed explanations.

Barely able to wait for the elevator, Georgi Alekseevich

kept pushing on the button, then hammered on the door. Tanya opened up at once, then put her fingers to her lips.

"Shh! He's sleeping."

Georgi Alekseevich sighed with relief. He felt returned to life. He wanted to ask his son's pardon, and that of this young woman, too. He wanted to be with them, in their company. On their side.

"Shh, don't wake him," she whispered.

"I won't, I won't . . ."

"Let's go out into the kitchen. I'll make coffee."

While Andrei slept, the two of them sat in Tanya's little kitchen drinking her hot and tasty coffee. Later Tanya poured Georgi Alekseevich a big glass of sticky-sweet cognac.

They talked for more than an hour. More exactly, Tanya talked and he listened. She told him about the barricades and the tank soldiers, about some comical infantry captain who kept swearing to all and sundry that he was with the defenders and not the others, that he had been ordered to come. She talked about the way young men had tipped trucks over.

Georgi Alekseevich listened, not daring to ask about what he really wondered, what life had been like for them in that prison where they had spent two days.

Tanya guessed that that was what he wanted, but she wouldn't let him ask.

Then, unexpectedly, Andrei came in.

"You're here then," he said, unsurprised. "Tanya, is there still coffee?"

"Georgi Alekseevich and I were just—"

"I see what you were just."

He drank his coffee in silence, then left.

She ran after him.

"Andrei, you can't do this, it isn't right."

They closed the door behind them, but Georgi Alekseevich could still hear every word.

"Why is he here?"

"Don't do this, Andrei, don't."

"I asked you, why is he here?"

"Andrei!"

"Keep your nose out of my business and what me and my—"
He paused, not even wanting to say the word *father*.

Georgi Alekseevich got up and left the apartment. He
jumped into the elevator, forgetting his coat in Tanya's
apartment.

He left Tanya's building, walked to the Garden Ring Road,
got into a trolley. He rode to the Gorky Park metro station,
where he got out and went down into the subway.

A few years before, once when he and his wife were coming
back from seeing friends, he had taken the metro and been
astonished at how fast the trains were traveling when they
came out of their tunnels. It was a thrilling sight, one he had
not forgotten.

Georgi Alekseevich let two trains go past, but it was too
cold to stand in the underground air with no coat on. When
the third train roared into the station, its lights blinding him,
Georgi Alekseevich stepped off the platform onto the rails.